～～～ EXPERIMENTS
with LIFE and DEAF

Also by Chuck Rosenthal
LOOP'S PROGRESS

EXPERIMENTS
with LIFE
and DEAF

Chuck Rosenthal

PERENNIAL LIBRARY

Harper & Row, Publishers, New York
Cambridge, Philadelphia, San Francisco
London, Mexico City, São Paulo, Singapore, Sydney

LIBRARY OF CONGRESS CATALOG CARD NUMBER: 88-45053

ISBN: 0-06-097180-0 (pbk.)
88 89 90 91 92 FG 10 9 8 7 6 5 4 3 2 1

For Gail and Marlena

ACKNOWLEDGMENTS

The author wishes to thank Marta Peluso for her continued support and inspiration, and for all the furious seasons; Dr. William P. Garvey, Mercyhurst College, and the Mercyhurst College Writers' Institute for the time and money given to support this project; the Utah Arts Council for its awards to *Loop's Progress* and *Experiments With Life and Deaf*; *Quarterly West*, in which portions of this novel, as well as *Loop's Progress*, have appeared; and Gail Wronsky, without whom there would be no Loop, no experiments, no progress.

The more blatantly irrational the society becomes,
the greater the rationality of the artistic universe.
—*Herbert Marcuse*

Those who will learn from history
are doomed to make new mistakes.
—*Neda*

~~~~~ EXPERIMENTS
with LIFE and DEAF

Bobby Hansen
Experiments with Deaf

I DON'T KNOW how I missed him from two inches away, but I did. Still, that gunshot scared the hell out of him and he jumped back, then lost his balance and fell backwards, cracking the back of his head on the corner of the hi-fi console. I found out the next day that he was in the hospital for being a vegetable.

I guess he never got to tell anything to anybody. Bobby Hansen wasn't even feeding himself let alone talking. They brought him onstage in a wheelchair at school assembly a few months later and he was the closest thing you ever saw to a human potato except he drooled. Got himself a standing ovation. I gave him a hand myself. It sure was brave of him to come out onstage, or brave of whoever made that decision for him.

Bobby Hansen, the principal said, was of tremendous stock. Already the doctors reported he was wriggling his toes, and if she knew Bobby Hansen, why he might even be back on his feet for next football season because, well, because we sure needed him. We all gave Bobby Hansen another big standing ovation.

I had a lot of mixed feelings about Bobby Hansen and this

Bobby Hansen situation, but I needed Bobby Hansen around like I needed a hole in the head. Some people might say I was wrong to burglarize his house, but there's more sociology to it than that, and once I was in there he didn't give me a chance. He tried to hurt me, not me him, and he ended up the vegetable. It was a big accident. A coin flip. If it was up to me I would have Bobby Hansen intermittently be a vegetable.

My mother Helen understood, circuitously, because lucky for her she didn't know.

"Good thing Red's starting to sell toilet paper," she said to me. "The Infant hasn't coughed up for weeks."

Well Red, our patriarch, wasn't exactly nuts about that toilet paper job, but it looked like it came around just in time. This Bobby Hansen business certainly put a crimp in my enterprising tendencies, and coterminously the generosity of Helen's Infant of Prague. I just couldn't be sticking money under that little rascal that I needed for myself.

"The Hansens had everything," said Helen.

It was a nice day. April sun came through the kitchen window for almost ten minutes before being blocked out by our neighbors', the Jinxes', roof. I hadn't gone to school. There was going to be a sports award assembly. I had a headache. I made Helen some toast. Poured her some coffee.

"Some people have everything all their lives," I said to her.

"I'm not simpleminded, Jarvis," she said to me. She put strawberry jam on her toast, jam she made last summer after she and Red spent a Sunday out picking strawberries and Red came back with a bad sunburn on his arms and forehead. Man, Red was mad, and Helen kept saying he looked like a strawberry, needed to dye his hair green. "I'm a Catholic," she said. "I'm talking ontologically. People think they live in a world of causality and that's what they think choice and sin is about."

"But it aint?"

"No," said Helen.

"Well?"

"Well go back to church," said Helen.

• • •

Our other next door neighbor was Karl Marxman who'd taught me everything I knew about burglaring and who'd told me in the first place not to go back and re-rob Bobby Hansen's. He was in his basement with his circus cannon and his howitzer, the pig that he claimed he'd eat on every next coming holiday, and his talking crow.

"You don't got to tell me a thing," said Karl. He had more hair than ever on his head and face but he hadn't grown any new fingers or teeth. "Our burglar careers are over. But if that kid starts wriggling his lips instead of his toes you're going to have to be thinking about a new life."

Crow walked over to the pigpen and lay down on top of the sleeping pig, feet up.

"Franky Gorky," said Crow.

"There's something wrong with that bird," said Karl. "He's preoccupied."

Well if he was preoccupied with Franky Gorky he wasn't the first. Franky Gorky was about as famous and dead as you could be in that neighborhood. Though Karl looked a little preoccupied himself. Since Cuba went Communist they'd been cutting back at Bucyrus Erie where he worked, especially since the U.S. government made a big documentary film just before Castro turned worm, praising all his wonderful reforms, and everywhere there were big cranes and graters with BUCYRUS ERIE plastered all over them, and now the Commies had them, so people started associating Bucyrus Erie with the Communists which of course made perfect sense. Now I'd shut down our gold mine in Glenwood and Karl was about to lose his job.

"Don't worry," Karl said to me. "We'll eat the pig for Easter." He walked over to Crow and picked him up by the tail.

"What a card," said Crow, rather unemphatically.

"There's something wrong with this bird," said Karl.

•   •   •

That very next day my old friend that hood Tony Blanion was waiting for me outside school. He must have bought my patterns because I was getting out of there about an hour early as usual and he just popped out of the shadows like Doctor Dark. Next thing I knew he was matching me step for step, which he had to do if he wanted to talk to me, that was something I learned from Red, keep moving, make them react to you, besides if there's more of them they either get left behind or have to come out right away, which of course might not do you any good but at least clarifies some of the issues.

"Listen," said Blanion. "You know whose ass they're shakin down over this Bobby Hansen thing, it's my ass."

And I didn't say anything. People got things they didn't earn all the time and sometimes they deserved them and sometimes they didn't.

"Hey, it's not going to fly," said Tony Blanion.

"You worried about something?"

"I got shit to cover."

I'd picked up the pace but he was right there.

"It's not going to fly," said Blanion. "I know what crack was flashin." He grabbed my arm and made me stop so he could light another cigarette and comb his hair. "Bakin bread with all that dough? Have a nice Xmas over there on Celebration Avenue?"

I started walking again. "It's 24th Street."

"Hey," said Blanion. "You shat on my crackers. If the cat bag comes down I'm gonna blow, and you won't last long in the wind, fucker, you and the black smack addicts." He stopped and I just kept going.

"Okay," yelled Blanion. "But that motherfucker's wriggling all his toes. He felt a pin in his thumb yesterday. The rug's comin off the butt!"

It had been a long time ago since Blanion stabbed my friend Willie and Red trained Willie for that fair and square revenge fistfight instead of letting Willie just go hit Blanion with a hammer. Blanion won that fight anyways and Willie kept that hammer with him ever since. But he never did use it. He just kept it in his attic, over behind his pillows with his toolbox where he kept all the tools for our experiments, which, since those days, had become more and more intrapersonal. Us Dialecticians just gathered up there in the attic and Willie gave us our experiment with deaf for the day and that was that. Then we were happy Dialecticians.

Willie, himself, still kept experimenting with deaf in a lot of other forms. He didn't hang himself anymore, and Blanion'd taught him all he needed to know about knife wounds. If he shot himself again he wouldn't have enough working parts to get around. He'd pretty much learned everything there was to learn about deaf from this side of things and he was thinking about what he could learn from the other side. Seemed like an inevitable trend around there.

And he didn't have to say anything to me, but as of recent there'd been a real dearth of critical vocabulary up in that attic and I knew Willie thought the rest of us Dialecticians were in a rut. When I got there those twins, Revis and Revco Danger, were already sacked out on their pillows splitting dualisms, and Raymon was off in the corner with, of all birds, that crow of Karl's, slipping a little of that elusive powder into one of the holes in his beak. "The conception of these effects, Crow, is the whole of your conception of the object," said Raymon. Crow tilted his beak and Raymon hit the other nostril.

"Deaf," said Crow.

"That's right," said Raymon.

As usual it was hot up there and Willie was in his own pillows, a soft filament of residue on his brown skin, that mutilated left hand of his rubbing his chin stubble.

"It would seem our friend Mr. Blanion is holding fis big card," said Willie.

Well it certainly was a wonderment who knew what in that neighborhood, let alone how they knew it.

"Maybe," I said, "I should just hit him on the head with the hammer."

"Fis is not such a big fing," said Willie. "Our friend Mr. Blanion is not such a fish as to make you fill a baftub for him."

"Maybe I should leave town."

"What is the experiment," said Willie, "and what is the tool?"

"Maybe the hammer is the tool."

"Fis hammer is not the tool."

Well sometimes you could talk to Willie and sometimes you couldn't, that was the price of his living on the ethereal razor. I got myself ready and Willie set me up with a hypo.

"I, myself," said Willie, "do not prefer the development of these experiments into the sensual digression. Soon enough I would prefer to change them."

Well that was just the news I needed. The last thing I wanted was to try to work all this out with a clear head.

"I'm worried," I said.

"Do not worry," said Raymon. "It is a pluralistic universe."

"What a card," said Crow.

"Happy Birthday!" said Kara Ruzci.

My life was getting more and more complicated and it seemed like it was time to pick up the most favorite found object I ever stole, my camera, and head down to the Bayfront Culture House to see my photography teacher, Kara Ruzci. Maybe a little artistic distraction would keep my mind off the big questions.

"It's not my birthday," I said.

"No," said Kara, "it's *my* birthday."

She came over and gave me a hug. She tousled my hair. "It's good to see you," she said. It was good to see her too. She looked so little and cute I thought I could put her in my pocket.

Kara Ruzci took off her canvas photographer's darkroom apron. "Kara Ruzci learns from her mistakes," she said. "She is like an elephant. This time she keeps you in her sights."

I don't know how Kara Ruzci is like an elephant, but the last time I saw her was just before Christmas at the Culture House Christmas party after which I promised to see her again and then I never did. This Bobby Hansen business got in the way.

Kara Ruzci took me by the hand and led me out of the Culture House to her green Ford Falcon where she had a bottle of champagne in the backseat and we drove down to the Bay and watched boats and smoked pot and drank champagne. We had a good time. She even got me talking. I told her how Helen believed every Christmas could be my grandmother Bush's Last Christmas, and about Karl's cannons and how last Christmas night one of Karl's cannonballs landed in Grandma Emma and Grandpa Whitey Loop's backyard. She told me about her Italian grandparents in Hoboken, New Jersey, and how on Christmas Eve they had a big supper of spaghetti and rigatoni, and ravioli stuffed with meat, cheese, and spinach, and fried smelt, and fried dough stuffed with anchovies, and when they were all done they left it all on the table so at midnight all the dead relatives would come down and eat it, which of course they never really did, they just came down and ate the essence of the food, and of course you couldn't go in there and commingle with them, you had to stay out in the living room and get all excited and exchange presents and get generally distracted so as to create the right atmosphere in the kitchen as to not intimidate the dead out of coming on down to share the essence of your Christmas Eve dinner.

That was certainly a fine story, I had to admit.

And me and Kara Ruzci were having such a nice time I decided to let her experiment with deaf, no big deal, just a little up the nose. It made her a little sick.

"Well you better enjoy it," I told her, "because pretty soon we're not going to be doing these kinds of experiments anymore."

"No?" said Kara Ruzci.

"No." It made me a bit depressed.

Kara Ruzci started the Falcon and drove and drove, along the Bay, up and down the streets of Erie, out to the zoo and around the golf course and the new fancy family YMCA, we even drove by Bobby Hansen's. "This is certainly a nice birthday," said Kara Ruzci.

Then she put the car on the highway and drove out to her place, a little house in the country, looked like a cross between a farm and a suburb, there was a pine forest across the road and animal shacks in the back but neighbors about a hundred yards on either side. We took a walk and Kara Ruzci showed me where she had her garden during the summer and she showed me her dog graveyard of all her dogs who'd been hit by trucks, four graves. "Brave little dogs," she said. "Scientists from the word go." That Kara Ruzci understood a few things.

It was a cool windy day with clouds getting pushed everywhere, one of those days that everywhere else in the world gets in March, or the equivalent thereof, depending on the hemisphere, but on the Great Lakes comes in April if you're lucky. We stood there in front of the dog graveyard and Kara Ruzci kissed me on the lips. Then we kissed some more and some more and then we went inside her house that was so cluttered with photographs and paintings and just plain stuff that we had to walk through paths like a maze to find the bedroom where me and Kara Ruzci made love, very slowly and clearheadedly as I remember, considering our state.

"How come that doesn't happen more often?" I said to Kara Ruzci as I lay entwined with her in her bed feeling warmer and better than I'd ever felt ever.

"Because it's a special event," said Kara Ruzci.

She was as right as night about that.

But later in the darkness came a sound like the moon and I woke to see Kara Ruzci sitting up in bed. Her eyes closed and her lips parting like wings, she sang some gentle far-off non-English song, slow and fluteful, Kara Ruzci in her sleep, in the darkness her face some dim pond of silk, singing, to something at the foot of the bed, singing, singing.

The World
Experiments with Deaf

I NEEDED SOME open space. So I wandered over to the football practice field, but the track team was there running around and jumping into pits. Then out on the other side of the track I saw Stinky Jinx, scarf afurl, stepping over hurdles like so many wiener buns. I'd never seen anything so fast. He crossed the finish line about forty yards in front of everybody else, then skipped back down to the other end. I went over there and stood at the finish line and when the gun went off all I saw was a blur and then felt a breeze go by, matter of seconds. Stinky was skipping his way back to the starting line when he saw me.

"Oh Jarvis," he said. "How nice of you to drop by."

We shook hands. Stinky had a grip like a tinfoil buffalo.

"You like this better than football?" I said.

"Well," he said, "it's certainly more carefree, but, you know, I miss the comradery."

"But they don't make you take your mom's scarf off."

"Well that's quite true," said Stinky. "You know Mom let me keep it, for luck."

Just then Funly Funster came up behind us. He was a lot taller and a lot skinnier than in his chubby militaristic youth, though he still had that flattop. He carried a big hunting knife in his belt now and walked with his hands in his pockets and his coat open so you could see the handle of the gun in his chest holster.

"*Fun*ly!" said Stinky.

"Knock it off," said Funly Funster. "World War III just started."

"Oh," said Stinky. "It'll probably be on TV and Dad has to work *all* day. He loved World War II so much," Stinky said to me.

"Those bastards got missiles in Cuba."

"Well *we* have them in Europe, Funly," said Stinky. "It's only fair."

"Whose side you on?" said Funly.

"Myself," I said to Funly, "I would prefer to avoid the dualisms."

"Try dodging fifty megatons of TNT," said Funly.

"Does this mean there won't be an Olympics?" said Stinky.

"Listen," said Funly. "We got the Monroe Doctrine. It's as old as the goddamn hills. It says we can help Europe but nobody helps anybody over here but us. It's right in the Constitution. Natural Law." Those weapons sure gave Funly an air of authority.

"The Russians don't care about Erie, Pennsylvania," I said to Funly.

"Yes," said Stinky. "Everyone knows our major industry is tourism."

"We're fifteenth on their hit list," said Funly.

"In the state?" I said.

"In the country!" said Funly, sneering. "Center of the industrial and shipping triangle; Buffalo, Pittsburgh, Cleveland."

Stinky put his arm around Funly. "He's so dramatic," Stinky said to me.

"Listen," said Funly. "If those missiles don't come out, then we're going in, and if we do there's going to be some craters."

Well that Funly Funster sure had lost his sense of humor, must have gone with the weight, or maybe when his Grandma

Funster died and started haunting his house. Still, he and Stinky seemed to have become true blue friends, even with all the changes; usually if I saw one I saw the other.

Nonetheless, it had been a while since I'd thought about the end of the world, not since Sister Mary Ricardo in first grade who seemed to really get a big kick out of The Last Day with all those angels circling around blowing their horns and the graves opening up and everybody coming out looking none the worse for the years and Jesus up there dividing the universe of humanity into good on the right side and bad on the left; I always got worried because I knew he'd be facing us and I might get mixed up between his right and my right, a mistake like that could be disastrous. I had a lot of ambivalence about the end of the world, even back then. In some ways it seemed kind of appropriate and in others kind of abrupt. It sure would solve this Bobby Hansen thing.

Back at the house things were pretty calm. I thought Helen might be planted in front of the Infant but instead she was moving around pretty good, though carrying her rosary from Lourdes that was blessed by the pope. Bush was over, looking as old as gold though none the worse for surviving months after her Last Christmas. Of course Red was at work, you couldn't stop selling toilet paper because of world crisis, in fact toilet paper was probably just the kind of thing you needed plenty of during The End of the World because who knew how long The End of the World would last.

My genius sister Neda was in front of the Zenith, eating a Mars Bar very slowly, studying an electrical engineering text, and watching cartoons. "A semiotics too complex for reasonography," said Neda. Neda was no longer fat. She had eyes like blue dimes, hair like wine, and lips that looked like they'd just kissed James Dean. "I think they're going to preempt the 'Mickey Mouse Club' for this rinky-dink shit down in Cuba," she said to me. She offered me a Mars Bar and I took it.

"Funly says this is it," I told Neda.

"Funly doesn't know dick," said Neda. "The Russians don't

fight foreign wars and when they do, they lose. They've backed down to us in fourteen out of the last seventeen international crises, directly proportional to their distance from the Soviet Union. Their technology is shit, they use locomotives to launch gumballs, and we outnumber them at least five to one in warheads. Besides, Khrushchev is a puppy. All Kennedy's got to do is open the back door and let him out."

The cartoons ended. Neda was right. No "Mickey Mouse Club."

"Well what if we don't," I said.

"What's the matter," said Neda, "you afraid of dying?"

I guess genius has its limits. And it wasn't so simple as just being afraid of dying. To say the least I had the developing feeling that I needed to spend more time with Kara Ruzci, given I had the time even if the world didn't end.

"What do I care," said Bush. She and Helen were having coffee in Helen's holy room, right under the Infant. "I'm eighty."

"Not everybody's eighty," said Helen.

"You think I'm lucky?" said Bush. She motioned to me. "Come over here, Jarvis. Sit down." Bush pulled a box of chocolate out of her purse. "Let's have some wine."

Helen got out the Mogen David but she made me mix mine with 7-Up.

"What are you going to do?" said Helen. She would have looked a lot like Bush except she was still young and her hair was dark and her skin olive, while Bush was pale and blond and as old as you could be. "There's nothing to do. You wait for things to happen, then you live with them."

"Neda says nothing's going to happen," I said.

"Neda should rule the world," said Bush. "But she'd have to grow a mustache." Bush pushed the chocolates at Helen. "Sure you don't want one?"

"No thanks," said Helen. "I got a pact with the Lord."

Bush either never remembered or always forgot about Helen's pact with the Lord, but ever since Helen had that big operation after she almost died having my younger brothers

Joseph and Andrew, she had that pact with the Lord that had something to do with either making Red convert to Catholicism, which hadn't happened, or keeping Red from killing her, which in that case I guess was working as well as anything else.

"Well what's he doing for you," said Bush.

"Never mind," said Helen.

"This could be your last chance."

Helen declined.

"Maybe we had the World's Last Christmas last Christmas," I said.

Bush winked at me but Helen said, "Don't make fun, Jarvis."

Bush and me had another round.

"Jon knew all about this a week ago," said Bush. "His voices told him. That's when his breakdown started."

Old Uncle Jon who lived with Bush could feel a Communist advance seven thousand miles away a week before it started. I guess he felt this one sometime last week just before Bush's cousin Edju and his British wife Elizabeth came in from Cleveland for a visit. We all knew how Jon cried the day we gave the Russians Eastern Europe. And Castro was an ex-Catholic. Now he was threatening to shove Russian wieners down our throats, upset about the Bay of Pigs probably, even though we told him we were sorry. Jon's voices, which he brought back with him from World War II even though he never went, told him that the Cubans had a missile with his name on it. Then they left. Then Edju came. Jon never trusted Edju because he surrendered to the Austrians and the French and the Germans and the British in World War I and then had Bush pay his way to America with her last dollar and now Edju was a wealthy engineer in Cleveland and never paid Bush back. Besides, Edju spoke eight languages poorly and all at once and you never quite knew what he was saying. That was enough to convince Jon that Edju was trying to kill him. Probably with a knife. He spoke to the kitchen knives about it, he said, "Now you wouldn't do anything to hurt Jon, would you?" and the knives said, "no, no," in high voices, but Jon didn't trust them and hid them someplace in the apartment.

Bush had a hard time cooking without knives. "Hmmm so, so very much so," said Edju. He was nobody's fool. He took Jon for a ride in the country and left him off at the insane asylum in North Warren.

"He doesn't belong in an asylum," said Bush.

Just then Red came in with his briefcase and his bowling ball and his toilet paper samples. "Russians and Cubans," said Red. "Jesus Christ, what's next."

"The Chinese," yelled Neda from the front room.

"Red," said Bush. "Where's the whiskey."

Outside the neighborhood was arming to the teeth. Karl's gun club, the Sons of the Pioneers, was garrisoned at Karl's with enough whiskey and guns to make a hole in the sky, which is just about what they planned to do; any Russian missiles got shot at Erie, PA and the Pioneers would shoot them out of the sky before they hit ground. There were Pioneers on the front steps, Pioneers on the back steps, Pioneers under the porch. There were Pioneers hiding in the shrubbery and staked out on their bellies amidst Karl's uncut lawn, Pioneers on the porch roof and Pioneers at the top of the house on either side of the chimney. Karl rolled his circus cannon out of the basement and put it on the back porch then got the baby howitzer and put it on the front. They weren't protecting their own houses because they figured the KGB knew plenty about the Sons of the Pioneers, so rather than get picked off one by one the Russians were going to have to take them en masse. Down in the basement Karl had his headquarters where he set up his shortwave radio to monitor the Russian advance. He had his wife Sophie in the kitchen making sandwiches that his daughters Beema and Maggie brought out in baskets to the men and he had Karl Jr. running the perimeters checking morale. Already some of the Pioneers in the yard had managed to crawl to the back fence without shooting each other and were in pretty hot debate about whether they should fan out and take over the adjoining yard on 23rd Street or consolidate their forces in Karl's yard.

Across the street big Dean Danger came out on the porch with a shotgun every half hour, walked to the steps, then took out a mirror and flashed over to Karl's lawn, then another light beamed over to Funster's roof from there and Funly's dad Jimbo Funster beamed back to Danger. Jimbo Funster didn't like niggers but I guess this was a crisis. He and Funly sat behind the sandbags on their porch roof with their camouflaged helmets and tripod telescope and infrared scoped rifles. Nobody was going to take 24th Street without a fight.

"They're all fuckin nuts," said Red.

I had to give Red that one.

Next thing you know President Jack's on TV deciding to barricade Cuba. The neighborhood lit up with lights and mirrors and Red checked out his toilet paper supply in the basement. He figured he could make a killing on people who had bomb shelters, though I guess somebody had to do it, and if there was anybody in the world who could sell toilet paper door to door to bomb shelters it was Red. He stuffed the Studebaker Rainbow to the gills, looked like a pastel armadillo. Helen just hung on to her rosary with the medallion filled with holy water from Lourdes, you never know when one more rosary's going to put you over the top. Myself, I got the hell out of there. I'd been thinking about where I'd like to be when the big eraser came down and as much as I liked the Dialecticians I figured I'd rather not be experimenting with deaf but with the one thing other than deaf.

I had to wait outside the darkroom for Kara Ruzci who was in the middle of the photosynthetic process and so couldn't open the door and fuck up the cells. There was some kind of bebop flappety crap on the hi-fi and for once I was glad that nobody in that place listened to the radio. Then Kara Ruzci came out of the darkroom and with her was some tall guy, she barely came up to his waist, with a little dark goatee and thin hair on the top of his head. He looked a hundred years old if not thirty.

"Hey, you didn't forget me," said Kara Ruzci.

Kara Ruzci really had a sense of humor.

"This is Igor Kresky," she said. "A friend of mine from New York."

Me and Igor shook hands. He smelled like a Greek after a bath.

"Here to do some work?" said Kara.

"No," I said.

"Oh," said Kara Ruzci. She went back into the darkroom and Igor Kresky smiled at me like I was some kind of gefilte fish.

"Listen," I said to Kara Ruzci when she came out.

"Me and Igor are going to dinner," said Kara.

"Well maybe I'll hang around here," I said.

"Why don't you come by tomorrow?" said Kara Ruzci.

I don't know exactly how it came about, I was looking for some subtle way to explain to Kara Ruzci that maybe it was The End of the World, maybe tomorrow would be bad timing, but I guess it didn't come out so good.

"Don't start that," said Kara Ruzci. "Just don't."

"Sorry," I said.

"What have you been doing? Where's your camera?"

"Don't start that," I said to Kara Ruzci.

"Listen Elephant," said Kara Ruzci. "Come by tomorrow." And she and her camera and Igor Kresky left.

When I reached the Dialecticians Willie wasn't there and Revco wasn't smiling.

"We are having ourselves a little *de*lay," said Revis.

"If I were to put this in terms of boding," said Raymon, "I would say it does not bode."

Willie must have been up to something because it had been a long time since I'd seen him outside the attic and his absence had already reawakened Raymon's ability to avoid the dualisms.

That's when Willie came in. "It would seem," said Willie, "that to regard one's deaf as coterminous wif the apocalypse is no longer a solipsism." He limped over to his pillows and the Dialecticians started settling down.

"So you did not have your experiment wif the other," Willie said. "It would seem fis is not your lucky day."

Willie sure was on top of things. Not that I was in the mood for dialectic. I was trying not to think about our friend Mr. Blanion or Bobby Hansen or The End of the World or most of all Kara Ruzci running around with that cosmonaut Igor Kresky and him placing his smelly self around her or worse in her or even sharing her eyes over din-din. Myself, I was in the mood for a little experiment with deaf, though it looked like Willie, himself, was not in such a mood as this at the time.

"Myself," said Willie, "I would prefer to change the nature of the experiment."

Well that was a big disappointment for all us Dialecticians, though we'd been expecting it for some time, it just seemed like now was a real bad time considering the nature of affairs.

"Myself," said Revco in one of his unusual moments of articulation, "I would prefer to change the nature of the experiment tomorrow." Revco did not look like a happy Dialectician.

"What way have you planned to put the fur on this cat, our Mr. Blanion," Willie said to me.

Well I didn't have any plans. Planning was not one of my specialties. I always figured that to make plans you had to know everything and I hardly knew anything, which all in all usually saved me a lot of worry and disappointment.

"The hammer is not the tool," said Willie. "So what is the tool."

Well that was a good question. You'd think after all that experimenting with deaf I'd have learned something, but I didn't. Then again, Willie'd kept that hammer of his next to his pillows ever since Blanion stabbed him, and that was a million years ago.

Willie sat down on his pillows. "That is why I would prefer to change the nature of fis experiment."

Willie could hold a conversation with you without you ever saying a word and be right on the money every time. He reached behind his pillows where he usually kept his toolbox and hammer and pulled out a transistor radio that he turned on and tuned to an all-news station. "If you do not listen," said Willie, "you will not hear what kills you. But if you listen, you will hear what kills you."

That amounted to cold turkey for us Dialecticians. If we were going to experiment with deaf and not deaf with us we had to re-addict ourselves in other directions, not that that implied permanent abstinence, just a certain kind of control, enough to get us interested in other projects.

So we had ourselves some sweating and cold chills and puking and the Cuban Missile Crisis on the radio which most of us Dialecticians had a hard time taking in the right vein, considering the circumstances, though by sheer repetition a few things sank in about the naval blockade and the U.S. Navy stopping and boarding Russian freighters and some tense moments I guess when everybody was convinced that World War III was about to start. Meanwhile during some of my calmer moments I picked up my camera and recorded the Dialecticians in this new phase of experimentation.

We were not happy Dialecticians in those days but there wasn't much we could do; it was Willie's experiment and he had the tools.

The Webcor
Portable Stereo

R ED MADE OUT like a bandit selling his toilet paper door to door to bomb shelters. Every bomb shelter in town had a year's supply. In fact Red got a bonus from his company, Cleveland Chemicals, who sent him a Webcor Portable Stereo. Red brought that thing in and put it on the floor in the center of the living room. He unhooked the speakers from the side of the turntable and put one at the front of the room near the long silver radiator under the big front window, and one on the other side of the room under the pictures of the two little babies with tiny wings which were allowed to stay in the living room along with the picture of St. Joseph holding young boy Jesus because they'd been there before Helen started her holy object proliferation and got the rest of her stuff banished to the holy room. They had special sentimental value. We all had to gather in the living room and sit on the couch in front of the stereo, which wasn't easy, considering there were five of us, including Helen, and Andrew and Joseph were becoming regular-sized human beings, and though Neda was a lot skinnier she still had a worldview that required a lot of room. Of course we all had to be there but nobody could touch a goddamn thing but Red.

Well we didn't have any stereo records except for the one that came with the machine, *All Your Old Time Favorites,* which were certainly old and now I guess certainly ours in a certain kind of way but certainly nobody's favorites, except Red liked "Old Wooden Cross" a lot, being a Protestant, so we had to listen to that over and over a bunch of times with Red pointing with his bowling ball each time the voices came out on one side and the music on the other. "How about that," said Red. "How about that."

"That's really impressive, Red," said Helen.

"We're really having a good time now," said Andrew.

Of course Joseph, born deaf in one ear and blind in one eye, had a finger in his good ear and Red never could remember what ear was the bad one if he ever remembered that Joseph had a bad ear at all.

And even more of course there was nobody in the whole world who hated Red's little manufactured family get-togethers more than Neda, even in her new period of thinness and benevolence. So when Red pulled out the 45 rpm adapter so we could listen to Gene Autry doing "Back in the Saddle Again" and Roy Rogers and Dale Evans doing "Jesus Loves the Little Children" and had trouble fitting the fat adapter on the little spindle, Neda told him, "You're doing it wrong, Red," which of course got Red mad. The one thing humans had over machines according to Red was the ability to force the issue, for Red it was a pliable universe, and things like record players were no match for Red. In a minute we heard that "red or yellow black or white they are precious in His sight, Jesus loves the little children of the world," through both speakers with Roy Rogers and Dale Evans and a chorus of little children chiming in at the end which made Helen wonder whether those were Roy and Dale's children seeing as they had about a dozen of them, one with water on the brain, that they adopted because either Roy or Dale, everybody always said Dale but Helen suspected it was Roy, one of them couldn't have kids naturally.

"What the hell," said Red.

"What about the starving millions with leprosy," said Neda.

"Jesus Christ," said Red. "It's just a goddamn song. It's a nice song."

"Jesus loves them too," said Helen.

Just then we started to get a noise from the center of the room too that came from the Webcor Portable Stereo turntable and sounded like a crustacean in a food blender.

"Goddammit," said Red. He looked like he was going to stare the noise out of it, but that didn't work.

"You fucked it up, Red," said Neda.

"You watch your goddamn mouth," said Red. He sure did hate filthy language in the house. He shook the Webcor a couple times and when that didn't work he took the adapter and in no time at all had half the Webcor in pieces in his lap. "Goddamn cheap thing," said Red.

"We'll have to send it back," said Helen.

Neda put it back together the next day.

How World War III
Affected the Funsters

THINGS SETTLED down pretty quick in the neighborhood. The Pioneers got out of the Cuban Missile Crisis with a couple self-inflicted wounds; Karl said they had a little skirmish over some ham salad sandwiches, "wasn't even ham," said Karl, "it was baloney." Dean Danger went back to refurbishing the bar on the corner of 24th and Celebration, figured he could have his Grand Opening on the Fourth of July, and down at that end of 24th Street some people who said they were magicians moved in and got an awful lot of short-term visitors, like sometimes they didn't even shut off their cars. In the holy room the Infant of Prague was in his heyday for helping Jack Kennedy kick Khrushchev's butt down in Cuba. Helen had his crown polished and sent his clothes to the dry cleaners.

Rumor had it that Stinky Jinx had cracked the U.S. record in the high hurdles. He'd done a sub-ten-second hundred yard dash and in the big city track meet coming up in the beginning of June he was going to put Lank Ward's twenty-five-year-old high jump mark in the baby books. It looked more and more like Stinky was the greatest athlete in the history of Erie, Pennsylvania if not the world and his dad Big Dick Jinx was talking

Olympics, put five interlocked gold rings across the horns of the buck on his Buckhorn Potato Chip truck.

Crow was back in the air. He only visited us Dialecticians for a few minutes during our wifdrawal and though he took the end of the experiments with a lot of composure he got real bored listening to the Cuban Missile Crisis on All-News Radio. "Suit yourself," said Crow, and walked out. He had a philosophical attitude for sure, but he was too independent, you couldn't really talk to him. Crow spent some of his time across the street on that top porch above Dean Danger's where the Puerto Ricans kept their parrots, but that horn music must have drove him nuts because soon he was back up in the bedroom with Joseph and his old buddy Andrew, copping corn curls.

Now that the Pioneers were gone Karl had his dogs back on the porch roof. It looked like everything was pretty much back to normal except we hadn't seen the Funsters for a few days. Of course it wouldn't be beyond the Funsters to respond to the end of a crisis with a military buildup, no time to relax or have a letdown, right after a big victory, they were probably all in the basement canning tomatoes and making bullets.

For the first time in months and months the Dialecticians were in the street, sometimes even dribbling or talking about basketball, but most the time hanging out at the Variety Store and talking about new experiments. Us Dialecticians were pretty excited about what Willie might cook up, nothing of course he, himself, wouldn't prefer to try first, and then again now that deaf was no longer interested in us we were all pretty interested in getting re-interested in deaf. All the rest of us Dialecticians agreed as we drank quart bottles of orangeade and ate bags of big fat old-fashioned Buckhorn pretzels on the corner in front of the Variety Store that Willie had certainly done us a favor, you can't be one-track Dialecticians. What we needed most now, said Raymon, was black leather jackets, DIALECTICIANS written across the back. That Raymon had a real conventional streak.

Myself, if it wasn't for an occasional concern about our friend

Mr. Blanion and what he would say and what he could say and what would it matter if he did, and the increasing dexterity in Bobby Hansen's pedal extremities, I'd have been feeling pretty good. In fact I still had the two hundred some bucks I got that night at Bobby Hansen's house, which in some ways maybe was bad because if I hadn't found that money then Bobby Hansen's vegetablification might have been seen as the big accident it really was instead of an armed robbery, though I guess the bullet they found didn't help much either. Karl just took that .22 pistol to Bucyrus Erie and ground it into dust, then gave me another one.

The only thing left to do now was to see Kara Ruzci, which I did. I took my Nikon and rolls of film of the Dialecticians' wifdrawal and bused down to the Culture House and hoped I wouldn't have to deal with that fish Igor Kresky, which I didn't. Kara Ruzci came out of the darkroom, which made me realize for the first time that that was what Kara Ruzci basically did, come out of the darkroom. Anything she did was basically some short-term reprieve from that darkroom with its blackness and chemicals and dim peering momentary lights, all for her images, images, images that had nothin to do with nothin, and Kara Ruzci herself was kind of just an image with her white skin of too much darkroom and clothes which were usually black, which I also suddenly noticed, and big big eyes that always looked like everything outside of the darkroom was some kind of surprise. She sure was pretty, but when she came out of the darkroom she cried.

"Hey," I said.

"Hey," said Kara Ruzci.

"Listen."

"Listen what."

That's pretty much how it went. Kara Ruzci was depressed about something. Though that didn't stop her from working in the darkroom, working and crying. She was a sad Kara Ruzci if I ever saw one and she didn't want to talk about it. I developed my film and hung it up to dry and then waited around a little bit, watching Kara Ruzci, which I tended to do anyways although today she really didn't give me much choice about doing anything else because all she was interested in was her images and general weepiness. I liked Kara Ruzci but I got tired of that after a little while.

"Hey," I said to Kara Ruzci.

"What."

"I'll come back in a couple days and print those up."

Kara Ruzci looked at me like she was the saddest person since the beginning of the world.

Back home I found Willie in the holy room with Helen. Their coffee cups were half full and their sweet rolls were half eaten and they were kneeling down together in front of the ugly dish cabinet arabesque under the Infant. Praying. Then they got up. Willie grinned. Helen grinned. The Infant grinned. Everybody was having a good time. I tried to walk into the holy room but it felt like there were a billion invisible rubber bands in the archway. If I wasn't the sensible human being that I was I'd say that things were exploding in there only they were invisible.

Helen and Willie came out of the holy room. "Well," said Helen. "Look who's here."

"Who," I said. I hadn't noticed how much things had changed. When Willie used to come over to see Helen he was just a kid. Now he looked twice her size and it hit me that I was a lot bigger than Helen too.

"Willie and I have been talking about Jon," said Helen.

Willie rubbed his chin with his bad hand. "I am very interested," said Willie, "in his experiments."

I'd been so used to only seeing Willie in his attic, sitting on his big pillows collecting residue and experimenting with deaf, I'd forgotten about the symbiotic spiritualism he had going with Helen. "You should talk to Andrew," I said to him.

"He did," said Helen.

"We are not," said Willie, "in the same ballpark. He is interested in information while I, myself, would prefer the phenomenology."

"I forgot," I said.

Willie gave Helen a big hug and Helen looked at him like sometimes she did at Andrew, like he was the sweetest holiest thing that ever lived.

I followed Willie out the door.

"Praying?" I said to Willie. "You going to have us all praying up in the attic?"

"You and the other Dialecticians," said Willie, "should not drink so much of the orangeade."

"Listen Willie," I said to him. "Don't fuck with the Infant." I looked hard at Willie. I knew he had some powerful stuff, all us Dialecticians respected him for it, but the Infant was a whole other game. Helen had years of experience, generations. She had the One True Church in her pocket from day one. Willie was an innocent when it came to the Infant and the sight of him on his knees in front of that statue was making my skin zip.

Willie put his arm around me. "Jarvis," said Willie. "There is beliefin because of finkin, and finkin because of beliefin, and then there is just beliefin and then just finkin."

"Yeah," I said to Willie, "and what else."

"Everyfing else."

Back inside Helen was celebrating. She had out the Mogen David and 7-Up.

"Remember that receptionist job I was thinking of interviewing for up at Marycrest?" said Helen. "Well it's opened up again and I have an interview."

Apparently nobody could hold on to that receptionist job up at Marycrest which was the little Catholic all-girls college on the edge of Glenwood that me and Karl walked through every day on our way to case houses. Those nuns drove people nuts. But Helen figured if she could handle Red she could handle nuns, in fact if she could handle Neda she could handle nuns, in fact her very existence up to this point was evidence that she could probably handle nuns, and I had to hand it to Helen, she was the most rational nut I ever knew, she could probably handle nuns, made sense like a fence as long as she could get it by Red without getting killed.

Upstairs where I hardly ever went was like a shack. There was only a rough bare wood floor up there that Red created when he tore up the linoleum after some fight with Helen, and only one little radiator outside the bathroom for the whole place, which was the only good thing about having to pee when Neda was dominating the facilities. But up in that front bedroom, where I occasionally tried to sleep, Joseph and Andrew had sequestered themselves for most their lives.

Joseph was a nice looking kid, looked a lot like the boy Jesus, but he was born blind in one eye and deaf in one ear. And Andrew was born blue with a receding hairline and a caved-in chest. He got a little lighter and bigger as he got older but that was about the only change. Of course he almost killed Helen in birth, so to Helen's mind he was God's gift. Andrew took that job seriously.

Helen believed Andrew knew things that other people couldn't know, which you had to grant as confirmed on the basis of what he wasn't telling us. Helen believed that Andrew talked with animals and he did. He talked to any animal whether they talked back or not, so you had to give him that too, especially if you counted Crow. And Helen believed that Andrew completed the spiritual circle of being in that house and he did that too. Helen sent messages to the saints through the Infant, the saints talked to the dead, and the dead talked to Andrew, but only on his own terms. Joseph had to shut down, closing his good eye and good ear, and Andrew wore an antenna that looked like a halo. Pretty stupid. Except way back when Grandma Funster died, then haunted the Funsters, then left, it was Andrew who found her hanging around with Jon's voices and sent her back. You could argue with the logistics but the facts were disconcerting.

Now, there were a lot of dead people in that neighborhood,

depending on how far back you wanted to go, but probably the most famous dead person of them all was Franky Gorky who existed like the dinosaurs before any other kid in that neighborhood ever did. Franky Gorky was the primordial child. He was sweet and good and loving. Birds sang at his window in the morning and wild animals ate out of his hand. But one Christmas day long, long ago, when Franky Gorky's grandma, Grandma Gorky, came visiting from Buffalo and had to park on the other side of the street because she got there a little late and the Gorkys' side was all filled up with Christmas visitors, Franky Gorky did the first wrong thing of his life and darted across the street without looking both ways and slipped on the ice and got rubbed out by a drunk driver. Every Christmas since then the Gorkys came home from mass and then went out to the cemetery and placed gifts at the foot of Franky Gorky's grave, then returned home and lit a candle on the street right where sweet little Franky Gorky bought the farm. They'd wait there till a car drove by and rubbed that candle out too.

Franky Gorky was the lesson to every kid who ever existed on 24th Street that no matter how good you are, if you don't look both ways you're going to get rubbed out by a drunk driver.

"He never existed," said Andrew, handing Crow a corn curl.

Well I knew better. Back when I was a little kid I used to hang out with Georgie Gorky, Franky Gorky's less than legendary and, at the time of Franky himself, nonexistent little brother, who was now just a common hood, and we used to go into Franky Gorky's sacred bedroom which the Gorkys kept just the way it was on the day that Franky Gorky died, and me and Georgie smelled Franky Gorky's pillows and played with his rosary and holy cards.

"He existed," I said to Andrew. "I almost knew him."

"If he existed you almost knew him," said Joseph. He had the most benign look you'd ever seen on anyone. Being partially blind and deaf must have given him a head start.

"Look here," said Andrew. He pulled a stuffed sock doll out from under his mattress. Thing had a horse chestnut for a head,

FG printed on its chest. "This is the beginning of a grand experiment. If Franky Gorky existed, I'll find him." He put the doll back. "But that's not why I called you here."

"You didn't call me here."

"I called you here because I know where those Funsters are."

That evening me and Joseph and Andrew cut Red off after work just as he got out of the Studebaker Rainbow and dragged him over to the Funsters' where we banged on all the windows and doors and finally we even went into the yard where Red bonged away on the big metal door at the front of the bomb shelter. Nothin.

"What the hell," said Red.

"If they think it's The End of the World they're not going to come out to say hello," said Andrew.

"Christ," said Red. "I sold all that toilet paper and I didn't even think of Funster."

That weekend Red organized a little country ride so we could all visit Uncle Jon at the asylum in North Warren and maybe even get him out for a little air and at the same time take a drive over to Funster's hunting cabin, may as well kill two birds with one stone, no offense to Crow.

It was going to be a family Sunday drive, no doubt about that. Over the years in dealing with Red I'd learned that you could get away with a lot, sometimes I stayed out all night and when I came back he couldn't tell if I was high or dry, though he could smell booze, I didn't want him to smell booze on me, but most things just slipped right by Red, and Helen too, they didn't know shit about discipline and just as well. But if Red wanted something, particularly something he wanted the family to do together, then he wasn't taking prisoners, it was volunteer or die, he got that way about eating supper together sometimes and with little events like the Webcor Portable Stereo and whenever he decided to take a drive on Sunday. "It's a family, aint it," said Red. "It's a goddamn family goddammit." And that was that.

So we all packed into the Rainbow, me and Neda and

Andrew and Joseph in the back like rats and Helen and Red up front, and Stinky ran out of the Jinxes' when he saw us leaving and wanted to come too, which normally might have been okay, Red being a real proselytizer of intimate family violence, but we were on our way to pick up Bush so Stinky was out. I knew he was pretty upset about this Funster business, he hadn't seen Funly for days and the City of Erie Championship Track Meet was coming up that weekend with the county and district meets right after that.

"Find him, Jarvis," said Stinky.

"We're trying, Stinky," I said. Good thing I was the biggest and oldest or I wouldn't have got the window.

Like Bush who got the window up front, though not because she was big though she sure was old, Bush had been old for twice as long as I existed, and Helen was never much for the window anyway, she liked sitting close to Red and sometimes she held on to his arm, which she had to do with both of hers to get around it, and Red said, "Hey, c'mon, I can hardly drive," and then Helen let go and then Red said, "Hey, what the hell, I do something wrong?" and Helen said, "What the hell, what the hell, that's all you ever have to say about anything is goddammit or what the hell."

"Goddammit," said Red.

Bush gazed out the window like a moon sergeant. "Take it easy on him," she said to Helen. "He's a big baby."

"Goddammit," said Red.

"Men are big babies," said Bush.

When we got to the hospital Helen and Bush went in and got Jon. Obviously nobody'd been thinking enough about content to volume in the Rainbow and Helen ended up in the back with us and Jon squashed next to Red and everybody pretty damn unhappy except for Bush who just stared out the window and Helen who sat under Joseph and Andrew even though they were big enough to have her sit on them. Helen liked being in the backseat with her kids, you could tell. Of course Jon was lucky enough to have the rearview mirror to talk to.

"The doctors are trying to kill the men and me," said Jon when he got in the car. "You'll have to take us to Quebec."

"We can't go to Quebec," said Red. "They're cleaning Quebec right now." That was a good one for Red. You could see he wasn't too happy about the seating arrangement, in fact you could see he wasn't too happy about the arrangement period, the worst part of it being that it was all his idea; Red always ended up resenting good deeds anyways but when they were his idea it drove him crazy, you could see the emotions banging right out of his ears, though at least in this case he had Jon where he could keep an eye on him.

Neda'd been trying to keep quiet for quite some time, being in her new humane period, but when Helen transferred to the back Neda lost her window seat and now she couldn't estimate cow herd populations, which she really could do at a glance, Neda could look at a bunch of anything and know exactly how many of it there were, if you went out and counted those cows she'd be exactly right every time, and now she couldn't calculate the distances of far-off objects by making instantaneous triangles in her head, and she couldn't even read because it was too crowded. She checked her purse for Mars Bars. If she was going to do battle she'd have to be ready and it would be ten or fifteen minutes after the last Mars Bar before her mood started to sink.

"Red," said Jon. "We can sneak into Quebec. I know some secret ways to get into Quebec."

"I aint drivin the whole goddamn family to Quebec," said Red.

"Leave them here," said Jon. "Just take me and Bush." He turned to the backseat. "He's a good man. Protestant, but he'd come back for you."

Red turned off the highway and onto the dirt road that went to Funster's cabin.

"Men," said Jon. "This is not the way to Quebec."

"A good Quebec is hard to find," said Neda. She had her first Mars Bar out and her eyelids three-quarters down.

"He's going to kill us, Mother," Jon said to Bush.

"Not in front of us," said Neda. "He'll take you into the woods."

"He's got that bowling ball in the trunk," said Jon.

"That's true," said Red. "So watch your goddamn step."

Jon turned to the backseat. "Helen, the men and I are sorry, but Red's nuts. He's a dangerous man, Helen."

"Relax, Jon," said Helen.

"Tell us something new," said Neda.

"Mother," said Jon to Bush. "Your son Jon is very worried."

You knew Jon was serious when he went to third person. Bush talked to the window. "What's the matter, you got plans? Are we going to move to Miami?"

"They'll be waiting for us in Miami," said Jon. His hands floated to just above his shoulders, we could see them from the backseat. "Red, the men and I are going to have to insist that you take us, and Mother too, to Quebec."

"We aint going to Quebec," said Red.

"Come on, Red," said Neda. "Let's go to Quebec."

"Goddammit," said Red.

"Relax, Red," said Helen.

"God-damm-it," said Red.

"Stop the car," said Jon. "He has to make a phone call."

Helen tried to rub Jon's shoulders. "You have to have a phone to make a phone call, Jon."

And there must not have been a phone for thirty miles. Plenty of trees. Some birds. Not too many phones. It sure was good to get Jon out of the hospital for a little fresh air.

"You don't have to tell me about phones, Helen," said Jon. "We've spent a lot of time with phones, right Mother?"

"He's excellent with phones," said Bush. "He can phone with the best of them."

"Yes, he can," said Jon. "So Red, you better let him out."

Red stopped the car. "Okay," said Red. "Get out. Make a phone call."

"Red!" said Helen.

"Make your call. We'll meet you back here in a half hour."

Jon was elated. He pushed Bush out the door and jumped out of the Rainbow. Then Bush didn't get back in.

"What are you doing?" said Red.

"Somebody has to watch him," said Bush.

"She knows what side her bread is buttered on," said Jon.

"Bush, you're eighty years old," said Helen.

"You're telling me," said Bush.

"You and your men be careful now," yelled Neda. "There's a nut out there."

"Thank you, Neda," said Jon. "You know your father should be locked up."

Red hit the gas.

Helen wouldn't crawl into the front seat and join Red because she was too mad at him so we all had to ride down that bumpy dirt road with five of us stuffed into the backseat of the Rainbow and nobody in the front but Red. Helen wasn't going to let anybody up there, it was too dangerous. "You know, there are ways to solve things other than brute force," she said to Red.

"Right," said Red. Red wasn't saying anything but I knew he figured he'd already done one of the most nonviolent altruistic gestures in his career as a human being, which meant things better pan out because he was already taking the family for a ride, looking for Funster, taking Bush out to see Jon, getting Jon some fresh air, I could see it rolling through his head, he practically had an illuminated V for virtue hovering over him. "They'll be all right for a few minutes," said Red. "There aint nothin out there but a lot of trees and bushes."

"And copperheads and bears," said Neda.

"They'll be all right."

"Bush is pretty old," said Neda.

"Goddammit," said Red.

"And Jon's nuts."

Well you weren't going to reason with Red, besides we all knew he did the right thing, if only there'd have been a right thing to do. So when we got to Funster's cabin, pretty much a little two-room shack with a small area cleared around it in the middle of the woods, Helen waited by the car while the rest of us went up and around the cabin to scope things out. But there wasn't much to scope. The place was locked up tight, nobody inside.

"I knew they weren't here," said Andrew. "They're in the bomb shelter."

"We tried the bomb shelter," said Red.

Everybody looked at each other but none of us said anything about Quebec.

We got back in the Rainbow and this time Helen got in the front seat though she kept herself way over by the door. Of course Bush and Jon weren't waiting for us on the road. We got out of the car and looked everywhere, even Helen this time, but we couldn't find Bush and Jon anywhere. So we got back in the car and headed for the hospital.

"Shit," said Red. "What are we going to tell them."

Helen looked out the window now just like Bush. "A lie," she said.

Bush and Jon weren't at the hospital, not that we'd expected them, so the front seat was pretty quiet on the ride home; Red and Helen were like the losing team after a big ball game though in the back we were pretty much like altar boys who'd served too many requiem masses. Joseph shut down and Andrew pulled out a portable halo and tuned in to the celestial spheres, Neda'd given them the window so they could get better reception. She sat next to me and watched the landscape. "Let's get drunk tonight," she said.

Helen was nobody's dummy, you always figured she knew what she was doing even if what she was doing was something that nobody knew; it had been a long day and I guess she didn't want to sleep under a volcano so when we got home she told Red she was interviewing for the receptionist job at Marycrest in the morning.

Good thing it was spring because that did it for the doors. The chairs were next, though Red didn't throw them around much, he just kind of picked them up one by one and crushed them to pieces like a buffalo eating a beer can. The game was all tied up in the backyard, God killed the cherry tree and Red killed the prune tree, so that night Red went for the lead. He got the ax handle and went after the pear tree, he didn't ever want to pick another pear, besides if he killed that tree it would make him sad as hell, maybe sad enough to kill something else. But it was springtime and the pear tree was feeling pretty resilient. Red knocked the shit out of that tree, it shook a few times even though it was taller than our two-and-a-half-story house, but it didn't go down.

Red came back in the house. His clothes were plastered with sweat and his muscles were doing the limbo. There wasn't much left in the house but the windows and walls but it didn't matter, windows were too easy, Red had his standards, though he did level the refrigerator with his haymaker. The door fell open and the light didn't even go on. Then Red staggered to the closet and got his bowling ball, holding it out on his extended arm and then tucking it like a football. He moved out the front doorless way to the porch and eyed the giant maple tree in front of the house, wound up.

Good thing he didn't miss or he would have rubbed out the Rainbow. The air CRACKED. The sky opened up. The earth shook. The maple tree shuddered, then split down the center, a crack about four inches wide and a foot deep. That bowling ball came back at the house like a shot but Red stepped in front of it, took it on the chest. Then he measured out a little place for himself on the fallen vestibule door and lay down.

Red lay there for quite a while, flat on his back, pumping his bowling ball and breathing like a mountain, though in a little while he started pumping more slowly, then slower and slower until when I went out there he was just lifting it a little bit with his index finger. His eyes were just about closed.

"Red," I said to him. "I'm not going on any more of these family excursions."

Red opened his eyes. He said something but it wasn't anything. Then something moved through him, it started at his feet and went to his head, hesitated at his lips and then went down his arm to that bowling ball. He focused on me and I could see that ball shivering under his grip. Then it stopped. Slowly he raised the ball straight into the air. Held it. I took it from him and put it back in the closet.

Neda came downstairs carrying a huge purse and we left the house with Red still on his back on the porch and Helen in the holy room amidst the chair splinters, candles ablaze. The Infant's arms floated in the air like Uncle Jon's. We headed down the street to the Old Maids' Field, took the first path and stopped in the first clearing. From there, even in the dark, I could see the tree where I first found Willie hanging himself, experimenting with deaf, and across the street the dark un-fun house of the missing Funsters and the quiet sandbagged porch roof, gunless and Funsterless.

Neda pulled out a pint of Jim Beam and a six-pack of Koehler Beer. She sure had turned beautiful. She smiled and under those just-kissed-James-Dean lips were the straightest whitest teeth since the invention of straight and white, which ran totally against everything I'd ever learned about teeth seeing as I hardly ever ate any candy at all and had a mouth that looked like the Marines landed in it, luckily only in the back where I merely needed them. We drank whiskey and washed it with beer.

"I couldn't get any heroin," said Neda.

"That's all right," I said. "We're on orangeade now."

We sat there pretty quiet, guzzling and listening to crickets. The stars were out. Neda pointed out the planet Mars Bar.

"There's always that alternative," said Neda. "To put things in those terms."

"Polytheism," I said.

"I could be a nun," said Neda. She pulled out a joint and lit it. "I could write fortune cookies."

"You couldn't write fortune cookies."

Neda passed me the joint. "You think the easy things aren't

easy," she said. "From there you figure it's a reductio ad absur-
dum, no?"

"No. Besides, I don't know what you're talking about."

"Exactly," said Neda.

We were quiet for a while, passing the joint until Neda put
it out. "I'm doing this because today I realized that there's nothing you and I can share," she said. "Not a fucking thing."

There were about a dozen dumb answers to that, all mine,
made me realize how easy it was for Neda to break people in two,
like the only reason there was anything left anywhere was the fact
that Neda chose not to destroy, and still I never felt threatened
by her.

"Sometimes I hate Red," said Neda. She drank whiskey.
"Because if I didn't, nobody would."

Neda sure knew how to cut butter. I figured she had generations of concepts buried in every infinitive. She not only
knew what she knew, which was close to everything, but also knew what you knew even before you knew you knew it, if
not that she sure knew how to turn a phrase, it always sounded
like you'd find the whole world in there if you went looking.

We were both pretty drunk now, though not quite done
with the booze. Neda smiled a little and put her hand on my knee.

"Think Red would teach me to drive the Rainbow?" I said.

"How many lives you got?" Neda pulled out a pack of Pall
Malls. I was seeing a lot of firsts, though she smoked them like
she'd been doing it for years, offered me one and I turned it down.
"Have your girlfriend teach you."

"You going to be an engineer?" I said.

"You going to be a lesbian?" said Neda.

Neda certainly was an advanced mind.

"Listen," she said. "Have your girlfriend teach you. Buy her
a puppy."

"Hey," I said.

"Mister Secret. You got a secret then the secret's on you."

"Fine," I said. "If everybody knows everything then I still
don't got to talk about it."

Neda kissed me on the forehead. "You're not so dumb."

"I'm a Dialectician."

"I know." She got up. "I love you, Jarvis."

"So where'd you get the pot?"

"Andrew."

That night I hitched out to Kara Ruzci's who was happy to see me and who awoke in the middle of the night and spoke to the foot of the bed, silla pa-ella padil.

Red was up early the next morning pounding things back together. He had a big rope around the maple tree encouraging it to grow back into one piece.

"Where you been all night," said Red.

"I fell asleep in the field."

"You smell like decay. I don't want none of my kids smelling like decay."

"I'm sorry."

"You know what my mother would have done if I stayed out all night when I was a kid?"

"Killed you."

"Goddamn right," said Red. He made me help him put the inside vestibule door on. I got to hold the screwdriver.

"Your mother's in church," said Red. "And she can't smell. She woke up and she can't smell. I got neighbors missing, in-laws missing, a kid who stays out all night, my house is falling apart, now your mother wakes up and she can't smell. It's them goddamn candles. You can't spend that much time in front of candles."

Red sure was in a talkative mood.

"I'm going to put this screwdriver down," I said.

"Stay here, I need you."

"You don't need the screwdriver."

"I can't reach it on the floor."

"I'll put it on a chair."

"Goddammit," said Red. "There aren't any chairs."

Well he was right as night about that.

"Your sister didn't go to church," said Red. "She's upstairs in bed smelling like decay." He looked at me. "I don't want my kids turning into boozers. Look at them Stuckas. House full of boozers."

"Don't worry," I said.

"Don't worry," said Red. He was having trouble making the door fit. "Goddamn thing's all bent. What kind of door is all bent."

The Year of Two Hundred Books sure gave Red a feel for the rhetorical question. He got the top hinge pretty close and then clobbered the bolt through. Good thing he hadn't read four hundred books and taken two years. The bottom half of the door was only about a foot off. "You wouldn't think wood would bend like that," said Red. He pointed across the room. "Get that hammer."

I got it. Held it. Red bent the door with his hands, forced the bolt through the hinge.

"Hey," he said. "It's Memorial Day. You don't go to church on Memorial Day."

But nuns still held job interviews.

Stinky Jinx was the first white person to win the hundred yard dash in Erie, Pennsylvania since World War II. He could run like the sun and during the hundred yard dash you heard two bangs, one when the starting gun went off and one when Stinky broke the sound barrier, his hoo-hooing coming down the track a few seconds later; you couldn't even quite see him until his parachute opened and then you could make out his brand-new silver silk scarf, which I had to admit went real nice with his powder blue uniform and crew cut. Big Dick still insisted on that crew cut. Of course his coach let him wear anything he wanted as long as he stayed in the stadium, that not always being the easiest thing to accomplish once Stinky got going. South High football players blocked every exit. It took Stinky a little longer to win the high hurdles because he didn't like to come down between jumps, but you could stand at the middle of the race and study the Doppler effect as he hoo-ed by, it was just too bad Mr. Wizard wasn't there filming it all.

I went to the track meet with the Dialecticians but you really couldn't keep us Dialecticians together long unless you confined us to a room and gave us an experiment. Raymon, Revis and Revco hung around by the starting line drinking quart bottles of orangeade and conducting preliminary experiments not with deaf but the other, though in this case I figured those girls were equally torn between the charm of the Dialecticians and Stinky's makeup. In the silhouette of the Friday night stadium lights you could make out those Dialecticians a mile away, Revco big and square like a hammerhead shark, Revis like a candle wick, and Raymon like an appendaged bowling ball, they looked like the Oz Brothers. I don't know where Willie went.

I was in the stands with Big Dick Jinx when Stinky did the pole vault, an event he didn't really like because the pole gave him calluses that took him hours to file down and it didn't do much for his nails either, besides, Stinky hated sawdust. Already in the long jump, an event that we used to call the broad jump in Erie, until Stinky, he jumped over the whole pit just so he wouldn't have to land in that nasty stuff, and in the high jump where Stinky cleared seven feet without a blink, he came down on one toe and just tippy-toed right the hell on out of there, dusting off his silver slipper track shoes with a towel.

"Kid's got flair," said Big Dick, waving to him.

"Hoo-hooo!" said Stinky.

Stinky must have pole-vaulted forty feet. He flew over the bar and then his parachute opened up and he made a few quick maneuvers so he wouldn't come down in the sawdust pit.

"That must be some kind of record," said Big Dick.

Stinky got ready for the 440, his last event.

"I got to get him to run the mile," said Big Dick. "Then we can start thinking decathlon."

I didn't know about that, I figured Stinky wouldn't be too high on heaving shot puts, but that was between him and Big

Dick. Big Dick looked all around. There was probably more drunks than track fans in the stadium, nobody gave a rat's ass about track, and Big Dick was thinking publicity, he wanted to drive around in that Buckhorn Potato Chip truck and cop accolades. He was thinking autumn and Stinky's first season of varsity football, though myself, I figured Stinky would prefer basketball where he could capitalize on the comradery and wear a lot cuter uniform and where the touching was better and more controlled; I'd watched a college game with him on TV once, though it was hard to get him to pay much attention because he was reading *Vogue,* and he really liked all the hand-slapping and butt-patting. "It really looks like a delightful sport," said Stinky. "Football has all those barbarian accoutrements." I was getting to know Stinky's adult self and sometimes he'd let fly.

Still, I knew what he wanted was for me to introduce him to those Dialecticians. We had the basketball thing pretty cornered on 24th Street, among other things, even if there were intimations that the Magicians down the street were running little experiments in their own banal kind of way, but I wasn't sure Stinky had the temperament. "Oh Jarvis," said Stinky. "You're protecting me. You don't think I'll fit in," which was probably half true and half blue.

The 440 was a little more fun to watch because it was longer and Stinky lost concentration; he'd blitz a hundred yards and then slow down and start skipping and hooting until everybody caught up to him and then zip way out front again, you could see Stinky didn't know a track record from a Nat King Cole record, it was all just some big hootenanny to him. Big Dick just shook his head and said, "What a card."

Big Dick had to hustle right down there at the end of the meet so Stinky wouldn't give away all his trophies. I couldn't believe how tall Stinky was, seemed like everybody'd grown two feet since Bush's Last Christmas.

"Don't give those away," said Big Dick.

"Oh Dad," said Stinky. "You can't even put flowers in them."

"Just don't give them away."

"I'd give away everything to find Funly," said Stinky.

"We'll find him," I said. "Andrew and Joseph are working on it."

"Those *guys,*" said Stinky. "You can't solve everything with a crow and a halo."

You could see he was really depressed about this Funster business.

"Now don't get down," Big Dick said. "We got the Districts next weekend."

"The Districts," sighed Stinky.

"You put on quite a show," I told him.

"Yes," said Stinky. "Quite a show." He gazed sidelong and airward. "Would you believe they wanted me to dedicate this whole business to Bobby Hansen?"

"Well that would have been okay," said Big Dick.

"Who's Bobby Hansen?" said Stinky.

Exactly.

As I headed out of there I figured Stinky'd make everybody forget about Bobby Hansen completely before his sports tenure was up, except for a few die-hard fans and coaches who'd imagine what a backfield South would've had with Bobby Hansen *and* Stinky Jinx back there, though Red always said you couldn't have two stars in the same backfield, one of them always started fucking up or died or something, look what happened when the Browns drafted Ernie Davis from Syracuse and thought they were going to have Ernie Davis and Jim Brown in the same backfield; Ernie Davis died, then Jim Brown quit and Leroy Kelly started running the ball like Captain America, couldn't even walk across the street when he was sharing the backfield with Jim Brown, so more and more it looked like Bobby Hansen was a casualty of universal law.

Those Dialecticians were still inside the stadium experimenting with the other and I started thinking about my own experiment in that regard, Kara Ruzci, who was turning more and more into a complexity every time I ran into her. I have to admit, many of my relatives and acquaintances had their eccentricities, but at least I had an angle on them, even if a bit simpleminded as a matter of self-protection; I may be naive but at least I'm catholic about it. But the only steady thing I had on Kara Ruzci was that she spent a lot of time in the darkroom and had a tendency to sing in her sleep to some invisible somebody at the foot of her bed, other than that she had a lot of different spears and she threw them all over, besides, that singing in bed spooked me out a little bit. Even so, I had a feeling in my cells about Kara Ruzci that had only gone away twice and momentarily in her bed, replaced then by a certain euphoria. So what is the experiment, I was asking myself, and what are the tools, but I got interrupted by our friend Mr. Tony Blanion.

Who I guess didn't want me to spend any time in idle speculation concerning his presence because he shoved me against the stadium wall and put his knife under my chin.

"Okay," said Tony Blanion. "It's time to sit on your cake."

Blanion wasn't alone. He had several of his pundits with him, including Stubie Stucka, and Georgie Gorky who said, "Yeah, too bad we didn't bring the cake," reminded me that Georgie stopped reading comic books because they weren't realistic.

"We're having a little fund drive," said Stubie. Stubie wasn't a kid anymore at all, though now he wasn't taller than me. He had a face like a sycamore tree.

"Well," I said to Stubie. "Red's got a whole pocketful of quarters," referring, obliquely, to that game Red used to play with him where he hid a quarter in one fist and nothing in the other. If Stubie guessed right he got paid and if he guessed wrong he got nailed. Stubie took a beating for years for about a quarter a month.

Stubie put his face right up next to mine. He smelled like he was experimenting with breath. "You like livin?" said Stubie.

"Do I got to answer that?" I said to Blanion.

Blanion pricked my neck. "You're going to lose the zoo."

"How about if you give us some of that Hansen money and we keep quiet," said Georgie Gorky. I never noticed how much he reminded me of an elderberry.

Of course I, myself, was more inclined to keep all the money and let them talk all they wanted. Something told me that giving them money wasn't going to be the answer. "Bobby Hansen's lifting weights with his toes," I told them.

"Yeah?" said Georgie.

"Don't listen to him," said Stubie.

"So it's just a matter of time," I said.

"Don't slice dice," said Tony Blanion. "It's rhyme time."

"We're going to blab," said Georgie.

"Okay."

"We're going to tell."

"Okay."

"Hey," said Stubie. "Get this straight. We're going to the cops."

"It's sinkin in," I said.

"This aint Hollywood," said Tony Blanion. "Wise up or you're going to be a carpet farmer."

But I guess it was my lucky day because a cop car was cruising the stadium and pulled up to the curb. Everybody ran. Including me.

Back home Red was sitting on the porch. "Don't come up here," he said. "Your neck's bleeding."

I hadn't noticed but I guess it was.

"Don't come up here and bleed on the porch, I'll never get it off."

Red made me go around the house to the back where he came out with a rag, looked like one of his old underwear. At the back of the house was the window to the holy room and it looked like Helen had a light show going on.

"How you get cut on the neck?" said Red.

"I had a conversation with our friend Mr. Blanion."

"Don't talk to that kid," said Red. "Just deck him. That's the only thing he understands."

"He had a knife."

"Then take the knife away and deck him."

"You just can't deck everybody," I said.

"You can deck anybody," said Red. "You'd be surprised what it does for people."

I had to give him that one. Where would I have been without Red to flatten me.

"I think I'm going to deck Andrew," said Red.

Andrew'd been leaning on Red pretty heavy about breaking into the Funsters' bomb shelter and Red had just about had it. He was already taking the blame for Bush and Jon being missing, he knew it because nobody'd said a word. One thing you couldn't do was fool Red by being quiet.

"Why don't you stand over the garbage can," said Red. "You're bleeding on the cement. You know how hard it is to get blood off cement?"

Selling toilet paper had really made Red fastidious.

"Your mother's going to work," said Red. "She should never have had that operation."

"She'd have died."

"Maybe I should deck her. Maybe that would do her some good."

Willie and Helen were in the holy room and you couldn't get in that damn holy room when the two of them were in there cooking. You came near that doorway and felt stuff you didn't ever want to talk about. You could hear the angels in there slicing up the air with their wings if you believed in angels, which I didn't.

Willie and Helen must have felt me trying to come in because they broke up their conversation and came into the kitchen. That's when I saw Crow who hopped in and jumped up on Helen's lap.

"Infant of Prague," said Crow.

Helen gave him a corn curl. "He's all right," she said.

"God bless ya," said Crow.

"It would seem you have been talking to our friend Mr. Blanion," Willie said to me.

It would seem he was right once again.

Now Helen noticed my neck. "Jarvis," she said.

"I'm all right."

"All right," said Crow.

"Stay out of this," Helen said to him.

"Suit yourself," said Crow.

Helen grabbed his beak. She sure had a way with animals. "Maybe we should call the police," said Helen.

"It would seem to me," said Willie, "that there are only two kinds of police. Bad."

Helen surveyed the situation. She could see she wasn't going to get anywhere. "Men are crazy," she said. She let go of Crow and he hopped off her lap. He walked through the holy room and towards the stairs. I figured he was headed for Andrew.

"He certainly has a mind of his own," said Helen.

"It is a very small mind," said Willie, "but it is all his own."

Helen turned to me. "I got the job," she said.

"I talked to Red. We better batten down."

"Boy," said Helen. "Sometimes I'd just like to deck him."

Upstairs Andrew was already on his way out. "I can't fool around anymore," he said. He was on his way to get Karl to blow a hole in the front of Funster's bomb shelter.

Karl already had the ramp set on the back porch. "The howitzer's more accurate, but we'll go with the power," said Karl. Joseph and Andrew and Karl Jr. helped him roll the circus cannon down the ramp and onto a cart and they rolled the cannon between the houses. Red was waiting on the front porch.

"Don't say anything," Andrew told him. "We're getting those Funsters."

"They'd come out if they wanted to and they aint in there," said Red.

"Don't worry, Red," said Karl. "I got everything under control."

That was enough to worry Red. He turned to me. "Get the ball," he said.

I went to the closet and got the bowling ball. Suddenly that thing felt like it weighed eighty pounds. I'd have just rolled it onto the porch but I'd have been too embarrassed, so I lugged it to the vestibule in two arms and when I got to the door let it hang down in my right hand, like I was being casual. Red took that ball and threw it behind his back and right up over his shoulder where he caught it in front of him on his index finger, let it spin for a minute, then tossed it into the air and caught it with his fingertips right in the finger holes. He didn't bowl anymore but by now I bet he could hit strikes throwing overhand. We went down the steps and followed the procession down the street and over to the Funsters', along with Crow who took flight out the bedroom window and came down on my shoulder, which was kind of unusual for Crow, not that we didn't get along okay, it was just that there were a lot of other people with a lot more corn curls.

Andrew, Joseph, and Karl Jr. dragged the cannon up Funster's driveway, past the old barn that was now the garage, and into the backyard, Karl following and me and Red and Crow following him. That's when it hit me that not only were the Funsters gone but their hunting dogs too. Either they starved to death in there or the Funsters took them in the bomb shelter. I checked and they weren't dead in the barn so the Funsters must have had them, guess they had enough room for dog food in there along with everything else, including Grandpa Funster, and they must have figured there'd be hunting to do after The End of the World, either that or they could eat the dogs.

Now the yard was filling up a little bit. Big Dick Jinx came over along with his wife Pat and Stinky and his little sister Becca, Neda was there now, and Sophie came into the yard with Beema and Maggie who were a little bigger but still dressed like rag dolls and did the cancan anytime that cannon was out. Karl Jr.'s crossed eyes looked like pollywogs the way he was torn between wanting to help with the cannon and bang Beema's and Maggie's heads. "Urb-brorple-bupbup," said Sophie. You sure couldn't disagree with that.

Dean Danger waited outside the yard by the gate with his hands in his pockets looking like a black silo, though Revis and Revco, and even Raymon, came right on in. They knew the Funsters hadn't been around for weeks and besides, they were Dialecticians, they had their orangeade with them, they were ready for anything. Across the street, on the Gorkys' porch, Stubie and Georgie smoked cigarettes. I guess the Puerto Ricans didn't quite feel at home enough yet in the neighborhood to participate in this kind of fracas, but the parrots were out. Crow ducked his head and looked over his shoulder every time they flew over.

"They should have their wings clipped," I told Crow.

"God bless ya," he said.

Karl went up to the big metal door of the bomb shelter and knocked real polite, he certainly had his delicate side, but nobody answered of course. "I figure," he said when he got back to the cannon, "that they got in there and lost power. All their communication systems are out. Another couple weeks they'd probably be out testing the radioactivity anyway." He pulled the cannon back a few feet so it was lined up with the door.

"The thing we're disregarding," said Neda, "is that the Funsters are acting under their own volition. They aren't letting any of us in there, given that it's The End of the World."

"Now Neda," said Karl, getting a fuse out of his pocket, "we're neighbors. That's not how things work. We got all the volition we need right out here."

Neda looked at Karl like he was a piece of Muenster cheese. To the left of us Beema and Maggie were warming up, they weren't chanting yet but their little legs were swaying this way and that in unison and their fingers were opening and closing, and behind us I could hear Stinky hooting softly like a sleepy train, sounded a little bit like a midnight Kara Ruzci. We must have caught Stinky in the middle of something because all he had on was a bathrobe, not even any makeup, though you couldn't help but notice how uncommonly red Big Dick's cheeks looked.

Karl set the fuse and now Beema and Maggie went into full kick, just as pleased as fleas that once again we were going to *shoot* the cannon and opening their little palms every time they said *shoot*. Meanwhile Red was looking pretty calm, his lips were tight while he abstractly flipped the bowling ball off the tips of his fingers. Karl lit the fuse.

"Bombs away," said Crow.

That was a new one, though I'd never been around him when the cannon went off, which sure as shit it did, shook the whole neighborhood, and the cannonball lodged right in the bomb shelter door, but it didn't budge it.

"Shit," said Karl. "Good thing I brought another one."

"Gibble arp," said Sophie, handing Karl another ball. Who knows where she was carrying the damn thing.

So we had to do it all over again. Karl moved the cannon up closer and put the back end on some bricks so he still had the angle on the door. It looked like it was all his show now because Andrew and Joseph were long out of sight and Karl Jr. was over with Beema and Maggie cracking heads. You could find practically everybody in the neighborhood somewhere in or around that yard except for Willie and Helen and the Puerto Ricans, and of course the Funsters themselves, and it looked like everybody was taking this next shot pretty seriously because this time people were holding their noses and heading for cover, I guess everybody figured that when that door went down the Funsters were going to come out like the Marines hitting a beach and smelling like canned Spam. Of course Red hadn't moved an inch and I stayed near him, if anything happened he was probably the safest thing to be behind. Karl loaded up again. "This better do it," he said. "I wasn't prepared for a full-scale onslaught."

Well those Funsters sure did build a good bomb shelter, because that cannonball hit that door like a meteor hitting cheese-cake, smoke bloomed, shrapnel hit the air, but it didn't give.

That's when Red wound up with the bowling ball and let fly. Cracked the hinge. The door fell open.

"Shit," said Karl.

"You loosened it for me," said Red.

"Right," said Karl.

And everybody hit the dirt. Here come the Funsters! Guns first. But no. No Funsters. They weren't in there. Andrew and Joseph hightailed it over the back fence, heading for 25th Street and infinity.

"Ruple," said Sophie.

Karl just shook his head.

"Goddammit," said Red. "Goddammit."

"J -J-JESUS," SAID Funster when the Funsters got back from Florida the next day. The Funster family looked tan, and fatter than ever, they were certainly a tan chubby bunch, except for Funly who looked like something you'd soap your car down with at a self-serve car wash, he was thinner than ever with a flattop like a sponge cake, and Grandpa Funster who was dead except that nobody told him. Funly was snorfing around in the wreckage and Jimbo was at the back of his station wagon fiddling with a giant blue stuffed fish that looked like a dinosaur. "I g-g-got to tell everybody when I'm g-going on vacation?"

Red didn't say anything. He wasn't happy about having to go over there, especially because it was his bowling ball that cracked the door open and he hadn't even wanted to try to get into Funster's bomb shelter in the first place, he'd gone over there to keep that from happening, but once he got over there it looked just as plain as day that everybody in the neighborhood figured that's where the Funsters were, in the bomb shelter, and he couldn't really decide what to do until everything got going and then he did the most virtuous possible thing and pitched in and helped out, only it turned out he was right in the first place after all, so there he was the only sane person at the event and ending up responsible for the disaster, though he would have been the one who had to tell Funster anyway because everybody pretty much implicitly accepted the fact that if anything happened in the neighborhood Red was the one who dealt with it, or if anybody happened to want something to happen they came to Red, although later on of course if it had to do with something outside the neighborhood then you went to Mr. Dean Danger. Nonetheless, Red was responsible, so by the time he got over to the Funsters with me and for some odd reason Neda on his flanks, I guess the situation was macabre enough to interest Neda, Red had got it worked out that he'd been wrong all along and it made perfect sense to figure the Funsters were trapped in their bomb shelter, considering their record and all, and what the hell were they doing leaving the neighborhood for Florida in the middle of the Cuban Missile Crisis anyways.

You had to think Funster knew all that because he kept pretty busy with that stuffed fish.

"I g-got him in there," said Funster, "but I c-can't get him out."

"It's just the door," said Red.

"It's having that n-nut in my yard with a cannon," said Funster.

"I can fix the door," said Red.

"He's good with doors," said Neda.

"T-Tell me about it," said Funster.

Funly came up with his flattop and trench coat opened just enough so you could see his pistol. "Looks like an inside job to me," said Funly.

"Inside wh-what?" said Jimbo Funster.

"Stinky will be glad to see you," I told Funly.

Funly sneered.

Red and Jimbo struggled with the stuffed fish.

"M-Must have expanded in the heat," said Funster.

Red was getting a look in his eyes like he got with the Webcor Portable Stereo.

"Neda," I said.

Neda moved them out of the way and got the fish.

"I think B-B-Betty has some Mars Bars," said Jimbo.

"That's all right," said Neda.

"Maybe I n-need another vacation," said Jimbo. He gave Red some shark meat and we headed home.

It didn't take long for Jimbo Funster to decide he needed another vacation and it didn't take long for it to end, he left that afternoon for his hunting cabin and was back by evening, knocking on our door. He had his army fatigues on, camouflaged, with matching helmet, and grease painted under his eyes, but he looked like he was going to cry. "We-we-we," said Jimbo.

Helen made him come in and sit down. She gave him a glass of Gukenheimer.

"We've been r-run out," said Jimbo. "Th-there m-m-must be a half dozen men in there. They've g-got the g-guns. Everything."

I guess when Jimbo found his hunting cabin occupied he tried to negotiate but it didn't last long, Funly opened fire from behind the station wagon and the intruders released a barrage. Jimbo was lucky to get back to the car with his life. He and Funly tried a siege but they were beaten back. Funly was in the back of the station wagon now with a flesh wound.

"There's just t-too many of them," said Jimbo.

Well hunters were always breaking into other hunters' hunting cabins, it was like stealing somebody's girl, but usually you got there after they'd already drank your beer and eaten your pork chops, you didn't usually catch them and if you did it didn't usually come down to violence, but Funly got trigger-happy and those guys must have been drunk or nuts or both.

"They can't live out there," said Helen. "You've made your point. Now they have plenty of time to get out."

"R-Right," said Funster. "But n-n-not much time." He looked at Red. "Y-You owe me one."

And Red looked at me because I always owed him one.

"Don't bother us with the facts," I said to Helen.

"God forbid," Helen said. After all she was only right and it was only dark and there were only guns involved.

So me and Red packed over to the Funsters' and helped Jimbo extricate Funly from the back of the station wagon, which was no easy task because Funly was about the same size as that stuffed fish of Jimbo's, though not quite as stiff, but considerably more delirious; he looked like a scarecrow after you took it out of the dryer and said stuff like "bullet bark archipelago!" and "left cookies wheel!" verbs had abandoned him, and those guys who shot at him must have been the best or worst shots in the world because Funly had enough near misses in his camouflage uniform to win him the bad target of the year award, hardly any blood.

"G-Good thing he's s-so skinny now," said Jimbo. "They r-really threw a lot of l-lead at him."

"Burnt hamburgers!" yelled Funly.

It must have struck something deep in Grandpa Funster because he crawled onto the porch, body and all, and looked over the railing and said, "fly boat." Those Funsters must have had it in their genes.

After we got Funly in bed we got in the station wagon and headed out, stopping in front of our house so I could run in and get Red's bowling ball; he must have been putting weight in the damn thing, it weighed a ton, gave me the idea that I'd know just what to get Red next Bush's Last Christmas, that is if Bush didn't already have her last Last Christmas, and if she and Jon ever came back from that phone call, I'd get Red a bowling ball bag, at least there'd be handles. Then we headed for Funster's hunting cabin. Took us forever. Funster was so nervous he got lost twice.

It had been a long time since I'd gone anywhere with Jimbo, not since I was a little kid and before he shot me when sometimes he let Funly bring me out to the cabin, so of course I forgot that we had to stop and eat about three times on the way, which didn't bother Red at all, he got to eat all night instead of sleep all night, Red got to eat lunch all the way to the cabin which was almost enough to compensate for the fact that he wouldn't be able to get out and sell toilet paper in the morning, though you could see that bothered him a little bit, Red was a real go-getter about selling toilet paper and he didn't like to leave any holes for the competition to fill.

By the time we got there it was dawn. Funster parked the car a couple hundred yards down the road from the cabin and made the first approach himself. In a little while we heard shots and soon after Funster came stumbling back to the car. "St-St-St-Still th-there," said Funster. I guess he tried sneaking up from the back side but they weren't going for it. Funster figured there had to be limited ammunition in the cabin, he didn't keep that many rounds there himself, just in case somebody ever did break in, and they couldn't have carried that much in, so he figured we should park out front of the place and draw fire. When they slacked off, that's when we'd know they were low, then we could make a feint at the cabin, maybe two if we had to, and draw out the rest. It might be days, but eventually we'd be in the driver's seat, there just wasn't enough food and ammo in there to keep six or seven guys that long. All we had to do was sit tight and get shot at for a while. Sounded like a wonderful idea. I sure wished Neda was there, if ever we needed a genius it was then.

So we drove Jimbo's station wagon toward the cabin, everybody keeping below the windows, even Funster who had his forehead only high enough to see through the steering wheel and out the front. When we got to the cabin Jimbo cut the ignition and hit the brakes and we piled out the far side of the car. Unfortunately we forgot the rifles and the bowling ball so amidst a barrage of fire Red had to crawl back into the back of the wagon and throw everything out to me and Jimbo. Even from underneath the car and around the back tire I could see there was a rifle sticking out every window. I realized that here we were talking about waiting these guys out and we didn't even bring any food. We were a real smart bunch. Every once in a while Jimbo popped up and snapped a shot out at the cabin that was answered with a volley that shattered glass and shook the whole car. I have to admit, I was starting to get a little scared.

Every time they slowed down one of us fired off and they started cracking again, until by evening, just like Jimbo said, things started to slow down. All I could do was think about hamburgers and it didn't take much to see that Red was thinking about all those lunches he'd eaten last night and kicking his own ass for not packing any of them, besides, Red wasn't much for battles of attrition period. Something had to happen soon, it was getting pretty clear that we wouldn't wait them out without food and Funster's car was quickly turning into something like the piece of tinfoil you cooked your turkey on top of, in not too long our bodies would be keeping bullets from hitting trees, and that was disconcerting.

Just then Jimbo fired off again and it was answered with a shelling like the Japanese would have given Godzilla. The last tire went out and I would have become an open-faced sandwich if Red hadn't put his shoulder out and stopped the car from rolling over. You could see he was starting to get upset. Helping Funster was one thing and experimenting with deaf another.

"Jesus," said Funster. He'd had the stutter knocked right out of him.

"Where's the weakest part of the cabin," said Red.

He just couldn't take it anymore. Even though we were at least thirty yards away, which had to be double his range, he was going to stand up and launch, try to bring down the whole cabin on top of them, it was either that or be dead, besides, if he got the right English on the ball he might even get it to come back to him.

Funster pointed out the right front corner, said Red should hit it low. He couldn't guarantee it would bring the whole cabin down, but if Red knocked out the support pole it would bring down at least one side, that would be enough to confuse them and corner them in what was left of the cabin, and then if Red could get that ball to ricochet back to him, well then he could finish them off.

Well you can't solve everything with a bowling ball, that's what I told the both of them. I'd seen Red do some pretty amazing things with that bowling ball but I didn't have a good feeling about this. Every bit of sense that I had left inside told me you couldn't bring down a house with a bowling ball, even a little house, besides Red would have to hit it just right and it was out of his range, and even if he did knock the house down we still might be stuck with a shoot-out. "Let's just declare victory and get the hell out of here," I said.

"That j-just makes t-too much sense," said Funster.

And I could see Red wanted something tangible out of all this now, even if it was a bullet between the eyes. He'd missed a day of selling toilet paper and a day of meals, especially lunch, and he wasn't going to miss anything else and somebody was going to pay. He picked up the bowling ball, squeezing it gently like a sponge.

"The two of you fire on that side," said Red, pointing left, "then hit the deck. When they're done returning fire I'll jump up and bring down the house."

So me and Funster crawled over to the left side of the car, behind what used to be the engine, and Red crouched behind the back, pumping his bowling ball. Red gave the signal and me and Funster fired and ducked while an explosion of lead hit the front of the car. Then Red stood and stepped from behind the car, winding up, everything quiet and slow like after the ice cream man leaves and everybody's licking their ice cream. The setting sun glinted off the bowling ball, and then, out of nowhere, we heard, "Red!"

Red stopped.

"Red!" yelled the voice from the cabin. "How did you find us here in Quebec?"

"Goddammit," said Red. "This aint Quebec."

"It's Quebec," yelled Bush. "You may as well face it."

"And drop the ball," said Jon. "We've got a bead on you."

"I'll bead you," said Red.

"Bush," I yelled in. "How long have you been in there?"

"You tell me," said Bush. "There's no clock in here. Just guns."

"We've got plenty of guns," said Jon.

"T-Tell me about it," said Funster.

"Who's that?" said Jon.

"Funster. The guy who owns the cabin," said Red.

"The Mayor?"

"Right, the Mayor," I said.

"Goddammit," said Red. He didn't want to give Jon any-thing, even if it meant getting him out, in fact I'm sure Red had a lot of ambivalence about finding Jon at all.

"Tell him we like it here in Quebec," said Jon. "But there are too many French. Tell him it would be better without the French."

"He's working on it," I said.

"The men can't speak French," said Jon.

"I could use some whiskey," yelled Bush.

"Do something about the French!" yelled Jon.

"We aint doing anything till you come out of there," said Red.

"I'm afraid Mother wouldn't allow that, Red. Things haven't gone well for us out there. Besides, the men and I have been kidnapped."

"By who?"

"Mother."

"Bush?" I said.

"In a manner of speaking," said Bush. "Could you bring some chocolate with that whiskey?"

"He's not coming out," said Jon. "The doctors are trying to kill him. The Communists are trying to kill him. Red's trying to kill him. Everyone is trying to kill him."

"Think about Bush," I said.

"He thinks about her all the time," said Jon.

"She's old," I said.

"Tell me something new," said Bush.

"She loves him," said Jon.

"That's true," said Bush. "But she could use some whiskey."

"I've had enough of this," said Red. He cocked the ball.

"I wouldn't if I were you, Red," said Jon. "We've got you covered like a dump truck."

"That's a pretty good turn of phrase, Uncle Jon," I said.

"Thank you, Jarvis," said Jon.

It never hurt to give people their due.

"Your father's a very sick man, Jarvis," said Jon. "You should tell the Mayor."

"The M-Mayor wants his cabin and his g-guns," said Funster.

"I can't really do that just now, Mayor," said Jon. "You can see I'm rather caught up in the middle of things. Maybe if you could do something about the French."

"Half the city's F-French," said Funster.

"That's too bad," said Jon.

Well it looked pretty much like we'd reached a stalemate. Funster had his back to the station wagon counting up his losses, Jon and his men had their guns pinned on Red, and Red had his bowling ball cocked at the cabin. It looked like we could be there forever if somebody didn't have something that somebody else wanted and they were willing to give up, but Red wasn't going to budge and Jon wasn't budging and Funster sure wasn't and I didn't have anything. That left Bush.

"You got any whiskey?" I said to Funster.

"In the glove compartment," said Funster. "B-But it's m-my whiskey." He wasn't in a very giving mood but I still went to work on him, though it didn't do much good, took another day and night and maybe another day and night, it's hard to remember, it was like vacationing in the desert, the only time I ever saw Red so still and quiet was when he was sitting next to the Zenith watching everybody watch TV; I wondered if this was how they solved the Cuban Missile Crisis, though I'm sure the negotiations weren't nearly as interesting and the French Canadians were kept out of it. Every once in a while there'd be a noise in the cabin and Red cocked his bowling ball but then we'd hear Jon yell for him not to try it, though the last time he yelled, *"Ne le jetez pas!"* which we all took to mean the same thing; it was nice to know somebody was learning something from all this.

Funster lay on his back now, his skin festered by the sun, his fatigues like a polyurethane garbage bag. He breathed like the dead bodies after a massacre in the movies. *"Sacre bleu,"* mumbled Funster.

"I could sure use a little whiskey," yelled Bush.

Things hadn't changed a bit except for the influence of the French, though you had to hand it to Red, he'd put an end to the shooting.

"I'm getting the whiskey," I told Funster.

So I crawled into the car and got Funster's flask. Funster was out and Red and Jon and his men had each other pinned down so it was between me and Bush.

"Bush," I yelled in. "I got the whiskey."

It was quiet for a while so I yelled in again. "Bush." I could see I was causing a lot of commotion in there.

Bush put her nose to the window. "Show it."

I put the bottle in the air.

"I'm leaving now," Bush said to Jon.

"Don't believe him, Mother," said Jon.

"It's brown."

"It could be anything."

"Light some on the hood of the car," yelled Bush.

I poured out a little bit and lit it with a match.

"Now you see," said Bush to Jon. "It's that much wasted."

"Mother," said Jon. "This is how we lost Eastern Europe." His voice started to crack.

"For Europe it would take a lot more whiskey." Bush came out the door looking like she'd been alive all her life and none too happy about it.

"What you have to do anymore for a drink," she said to me when she got to the car. We could hear Jon weeping in the cabin. "He takes things so seriously since the war," she said.

Red began to approach the cabin cautiously, though I guess he could have walked right in there, without Bush, Jon was through.

Inside the cabin there was a gun stuck in every window with

a string on the trigger that led to a chair in the center of the room. Jon had manned and loaded the guns and Bush pulled the string. Now Jon was on the floor, crying hard.

"It's okay," said Bush, patting him. She still had the whiskey. "We had a nice stay in Quebec."

"Les hommes et moi, nous détestons les Français," cried Jon.

"Everywhere you go," said Bush, "people shove their beliefs down your throat."

We thought we were miles from the highway, but Bush showed us a path behind the cabin that got us there in five minutes. The hardest part was carrying Funster out.

Polly Doggerel

ANDREW HAD HIS halo out but Joseph wouldn't shut down.

"I'm thinking about puberty," said Joseph. "You can't do this kind of stuff during puberty."

"You see what beauty does," said Andrew. "He thinks the world is going to be paved for him."

"It certainly looks that way," said Joseph.

There was no denying it, Joseph was beautiful, he looked like Jesus before He got His beard and His face got too narrow and His eyes too big, before He started looking Jewish, which was in some ways just the subverse of what they were teaching those two in the schools now, now that Pius XII had bought it without even letting anybody know what was in that letter from Our Lady of Fatima, that rascal, and some new little fat John XXIII was in, the Catholics were saying stuff like Jesus was a Jew before He invented Catholicism, and the Jews didn't kill Jesus, the Romans did, in fact everybody killed Him except His mother, even us; Neda said Jung would have loved it, Uncle Jon sure did, he always said the Communists were responsible for killing Jesus and now that the future was involved it was easy to see.

Of course Andrew and Joseph being mystics none of that affected them. Nonetheless Joseph sure was beautiful and the addition of his hard-ons to the phenomenal world was a scary thing to consider. Red used to tell us a story when he got drunk about a little dog that lived under the beer hall when he was in Hawaii in the Marines and lapped up all the beer that spilled through the floorboards, got to be everybody's friend, and one day a female dog in heat came on base but the little beer hall dog was too little to get to her so they built him a ramp. That's as much as Red ever told us about sex, which was more than Helen ever told, but that's the way Joseph figured it was going to be; they were going to build him ramps, and looking at him it was difficult to argue otherwise.

Andrew slipped on the halo. "I don't need him," he said. "I only included him so he wouldn't feel left out."

"You need something," I said. I sat down by the window and watched Crow across the street sharing a few drinks with the parrots. "You blew it pretty good with the Funsters."

"So much for the myth that dead people don't tell lies," said Andrew. "I got it straight from Grandma Funster."

Joseph stared intelligently at the wall. "Think it all the way through," he said. "It might have been a good deed."

"Pretty circuitous," I said.

"Death can have a big effect on people," said Joseph.

"It didn't affect Grandpa Funster," said Andrew. "It didn't even kill him." He adjusted his halo. "Look at Willie."

"Deaf is not interested in the Dialecticians," I told him. "The Dialecticians are interested in deaf."

"Tell me about it," said Crow. I hadn't noticed he'd landed on the windowsill.

"Hey," said Andrew. "Listen."

Far off, faintly, I heard an all-male choir singing "Anchors Aweigh."

"Looks like the asylum gave Uncle Jon his walking papers," Andrew said. "The cops were over at Blanion's this morning. Twenty years from now somebody in Utah will invent an artificial ear, but by that time Joseph won't want it."

"Music," said Joseph. "I think it's going to have to be music."

Downstairs Neda was listening to military fight songs while reading *The Iliad* in Greek and watching "Combat" on the Zenith.

"Verstehn," said Neda.

"I'm going out," I said.

I dipped into a little of my Bobby Hansen money, it seemed silly to hold on to it, and went down the street where I'd noticed somebody was selling puppies, an old house with an enclosed porch and a dirt yard to the side and back with sixty-four different kinds of mongrel dogs running around in it, a cardboard sign out front written in red crayon that said "Puppies." Inside the enclosed porch was a fat woman and a man with his legs chopped off just above the knees and a big box of puppies, every single one of them sitting on somebody else's head.

"I'm Mrs. B and this is Mr. B," said the woman; she looked like she lived in her clothes like you'd live in a tent and Mr. B had a cane, a self-explained contradiction if you ever saw one. "As you can see," Mrs. B said, "Mr. B aint got no legs."

"Used to have legs," said Mr. B.

"But not anymore," said Mrs. B.

"Go in the hospital with legs," said Mr. B. "Come out without legs."

"Diabetes," said Mrs. B.

"You're the one should have lost your legs," said Mr. B. "Just look at her," he said to me.

"Now he can't even make a living," said Mrs. B. "We have to sell these damn dogs. I don't even like dogs."

"I like dogs," said Mr. B.

"But you don't feed them," said Mrs. B. "You don't clean them. You can't even take a shit without me."

"Depends where you want it," said Mr. B.

"You want a dog?" Mrs. B said to me.

"I don't want a big one."

"These are all tiny dogs," said Mrs. B.

"I don't want it too small."

"These are all medium small."

Mr. B leaned on his cane. He looked like a triangle with only one-and-a-half sides. "All the big ones are out back," he said.

"Where," I said.

"Out back."

"All these here are medium small," said Mrs. B.

"I want a female." Something just told me that Kara Ruzci would want a female.

"Look for two holes in the back," said Mrs. B. "Plenty of them got two holes."

Well she was right about that anyway. I dug around in there lifting puppy butts until I found the most medium female of all those medium small puppies, black with floppy ears and a brown nose and brown chest, looked like a two-door Pontiac. "Okay," I told the B's, "I'll take this one."

"That'll be twenty bucks," said Mrs. B. "They're usually ten but I got to buy Mr. B's medicine today."

I gave her five. "I'll come by and give you another five if the dog works out."

So I headed down to the Culture House, got to talk to several girls my own age on the way because I was carrying that puppy; they wanted to know if it was my puppy and I told them no, I was giving it to my photography teacher, and they thought that was a strange thing to give to a photography teacher which I guess was true but I didn't want to bother to explain all the intricacies, so I told them that puppy was going to grow up to be a great scientist like Pavlov, of course that effectively split their dualisms and they retreated off the bus.

Kara Ruzci loved the puppy. The puppy licked Kara Ruzci and Kara Ruzci licked the puppy, she rubbed it all over her face and the puppy crawled in her hair. They rolled on the floor. Cute as hell. Made you want to go out and buy a Pepsi-Cola. She wanted to name it Madame Curie or Abigail Adams but in the end settled for Polly Doggerel. We went out and bought Polly Doggerel a hamburger and some french fries and a milk shake and gave her a banana for dessert, that dog could eat three times its weight and Kara Ruzci was determined it should have a balanced diet, not only that, Polly Doggerel had the funniest way of eating you ever saw for a dog, sat back on her butt and shoveled food into her throat with her front paws, in between bites she grinned at you like you were the next Toyota on the assembly line, you could see it pleased the shit out of Kara Ruzci.

So then we took Polly Doggerel to the beach for a little swim and some sun fun. We were having a nice time until the lifeguard came up and said, "You can't have a dog on the beach. Didn't you read the sign? No dogs on the beach."

"This isn't a dog," said Kara Ruzci.

"Well what is it?" said the lifeguard.

"It's a foreign animal."

That bought us about another half hour before he came back scratching his head, probably having worked through the generic categories over and over and got back to dog every time, so we just packed up Polly Doggerel who now looked something like a Christmas cookie with all that water and sand all over her and drove to one of those nearby cheap beach motels, one without a pool because we really didn't need a swimming pool, the Flamingo Haven, so Polly Doggerel could have a shower.

The heavyset woman behind the counter at the Flamingo Haven wasn't too happy about having to choose between us and money, she looked at Kara Ruzci and she looked at me and she looked at Polly Doggerel, she looked back at her black and white portable TV set that had on "Let's Make a Deal" with Monty Hall, she frowned like a mound.

"No," she said. "Not a teenager *and* a dog."

"This is my nephew," Kara Ruzci said, pointing at me, then she held up Polly Doggerel and said, "and this is my deformed baby son who as you can see badly needs a shower and a shave for his beard which he grows all over."

It's a good thing that woman didn't know about checking for the two holes in the back or Kara Ruzci's story would have been shot to hell, though all she'd have to do was give Polly Doggerel a hamburger to show she ate more civilized than a houseplant. So the woman gave Kara Ruzci a key and Kara gave her ten bucks and we went to the room that looked like a converted closet and gave Polly Doggerel a shower and a rubdown, after which Polly Doggerel went out like a light, only woke up once about a half hour later whence Kara Ruzci took her and held her over the toilet and bingo, you'd think somebody'd put a dime in her. I certainly got my money's worth with Polly Doggerel, Mrs. B must have been the world's number-one advanced puppy trainer, must have been all that practice she got handling Mr. B.

Meanwhile I, myself, got to spend time with Kara Ruzci who I was starting to realize was a rather complex individual, being different every time I ran into her, and even I could see that somewhere along the line she'd failed to pick up some rather basic social categories, not that it ever seemed to impede her. Being around Kara Ruzci was starting to make me feel like I did around a big plate of lots of different kinds of food; there was just too much and I couldn't decide what to eat or how much to eat at one time, only the excitement tended to extend a little lower than my abdomen. I was deep into an experiment with the other and couldn't even remember what the tools were, which I knew meant trouble, if you didn't know the tools you had no control over the experiment. I tried to express it to Kara Ruzci after we made love.

"You are my tool and I am your tool," said Kara Ruzci.

"I don't think it works that way," I told her. I couldn't even decide whether or not that was a dualism.

We didn't stay the night at the Flamingo Haven so Kara Ruzci didn't sing to the foot of the bed, though of course I didn't know if Kara Ruzci sat up in the middle of the night and sang to the feet of all beds or just her own bed, but we did take a nap during the middle of which she spoke to the lamp. "Radiator borscht," said Kara.

"You awake?" I said.

"No," said Kara Ruzci. She lay back down. "Go to sleep and we'll have a dream."

Well I lay down next to Kara Ruzci, put my arm around her breasts, something that she liked, and of course thought about pitting the ocean with a frog opener and eating truck tires before I completely dozed off and dreamt I was walking with Kara Ruzci in a cow field. We came to a wooden fence which we crawled through and walked into the forest where suddenly, I can't really explain it, there was some kind of blending, I couldn't see her and I wasn't me, I just felt blended and then I woke up. So did Kara Ruzci. I looked at her and she looked at me and I looked at her and she looked at me. Polly Doggerel woke up and we all played on the bed a bit before getting dressed and driving out to Kara Ruzci's house for a barbecue.

There Kara gave Polly Doggerel the run of the world, not even watching her when she ran out front where the road was, which made me wonder how much Kara Ruzci liked dogs and how much she liked dog cemeteries. Kara didn't mow her lawn back there, she just had a patch cleared out around the brick barbecue pit and a clear patch near the center of the yard where she could nude sunbathe. Every once in a while the grass stirred in a quasi-linear fashion and then Polly Doggerel appeared for her next installment of hot dog with everything, sat back and ate that hot dog like she was hugging a rainbow. Kara Ruzci took photographs in the twilight.

Kara Ruzci wasn't taking pictures of dwarfs and idiots anymore, she was more or less just taking pictures of everything and anything and nothing in particular, not that she'd abandoned humanity as a subject, but humans had become incidental to her images and it didn't really matter whether they were in them or not because what came out of Kara Ruzci's camera had nothing to do with anything out in the world anymore anyways. Kara Ruzci took a picture of a shack and it came out looking like someplace you'd want to put all the babies that died right after they got baptized, everything she shot turned into its very own aurora borealis, it was becoming more and more clear that she had a personal relationship with ephemera. It started to hit me that I didn't know anything about Kara Ruzci and I was suddenly moved to crack a facet of her multifarious complexity, preferably something more in the world of common phenomena.

"So," I said. "Who's Igor Kresky."

Kara Ruzci took my picture. She took Polly Doggerel's picture. She said, "Once I was a young girl who wanted everything all at once but most of all tall boys or short boys but cute boys and certainly sweet boys to come along, and they did, and when I got pregnant Igor Kresky came along and stayed with me until I had the baby. So, sweet, I love him."

"And he has the baby."

"There is no baby," said Kara Ruzci. "I made the baby up."

Just then there was a rumble on the road. Kara Ruzci lived near a dirt stock car track and now pickup trucks pulling stock cars started coming up the road like jelly beans. Polly Doggerel headed right for the street, waited on the lawn for something big enough to squash her flat as a pancake and went right for the front tires.

Missed.

Came out the other side.

Tried again on the next truck but she missed that one too.

"I don't know what it's going to take for her to learn," said Kara Ruzci.

That evening we made love to the roar of stock cars like feeding lions, firecrackers, a squawking loudspeaker. "Spike 32" won the fifty-lap feature. Kara Ruzci sang as sadly as the negative side of night, so sadly that at the foot of the bed I heard the gentle responding sobs.

A Month of
Sunny Dog Days

M E AND STINKY went down to the school yard one afternoon with a basketball so I could teach him the rudiments. Not that I was very good at basketball, among the Dialecticians I was clearly the worst, even worse than Willie with his half of a good hand and bad leg, my job was just to get the ball to one of those other Dialecticians; it was just a racial fact, as Raymon said, and I had to accept it, which I did; I didn't really give a shit about sports. Still, I could do enough things with a basketball to get Stinky started, after all, I did teach him football.

"It's certainly a big ball," said Stinky. He had on a cobalt blue T-shirt with the neck cut out, it did a lot for the scarf.

I held the ball out to him. I didn't give too many people advice in the neighborhood, but I'd always kind of been Stinky's mentor, even back in the days when I was whackin the shit out of him, so it seemed stupid to stop now. "You touch this thing," I said to him, "and you won't have winters off anymore."

"Oh Jarvis," said Stinky. "Now what do I do, put it in there?" He pointed at the rim.

"Right." I gave him the ball and he held it like he was touching the wrong end of a Popsicle.

"Well," said Stinky. He jumped up, practically hopped over the goddamn rim, and dropped the ball through, caught it on the way down. "I really don't see how anybody could miss," said Stinky.

"People try to stop you," I told him. "Only it's not like football, they're not allowed to touch you."

"No one touches me in football," said Stinky. "Unless I want them to."

Well he was right enough about that. We played a little one-on-one, and though Stinky wasn't the best of dribblers, a little too much wrist, wherever he stopped he just jumped up and dunked the ball, I have to admit, it was a little frustrating. Not that dunking was the only thing he could do, as you might imagine he learned a jump shot quick as a bell, had a touch like dry air, his wrist action was excellent for that, went up in the air and hung for ten or twelve seconds till you got tired of pawing at his ankles, then shot that ball like milk on silk, got a look on his face when he shot like somebody who'd just read a big word.

"Think I could make the team?" said Stinky when we were done.

"Not if the world ends."

"You really do have a dry sense of humor, Jarvis," said Stinky.

"Dry as pie," I told Stinky Jinx.

"You don't have to get enigmatic with me," said Stinky. "I know you're smart. But your PR is simply abominable."

"How's Funly doing?" I said to him.

"Oh, it's all rockets now," said Stinky. "This moon race thing. He's building a satellite."

I wondered what kind of satellite, and if Crow had told Karl. The Funsters had been pretty much into fortification up to the Battle of Quebec, kept the neighborhood balance of power relatively stable, but the wrong kind of satellite could really leave Karl in the dust in the arms race.

"You know, Jarvis," said Stinky. "If I decide to play I'm

going to have to talk to the coach about those dreadful uniforms."

"Just make sure you show him your stuff before you talk
fashion," I said.

Well if anybody was going to make a dent in the world of
high school basketball fashion it was Stinky, he already got to
wear his own track uniform and the whole football team had new
uniforms for the fall, rose and baby blue, scarf optional.

Stinky went to see Funly and I dropped by the house where
Joseph had already released his several-pronged attack at altering
the complexion of the household. He didn't get much disability
money for those birth defects but he must have been saving it up
because when I got there he was sitting in the center of the living
room, not up in the bedroom, with an electric guitar and amplifier, an acoustic guitar, and a white German shepherd puppy
that you could tell was going to be a monster because he was
getting bigger every minute.

Joseph knew Red wouldn't want an electric guitar in the
house, Red was already convinced that the Webcor Portable
Stereo was a big enough mistake, especially when Neda was
playing it in the holy room while Red was sitting next to the
Zenith watching everybody watch TV. But Helen always talked
about how Red played the guitar for her when they were young,
and sometimes when they were getting along Red even chipped
in and said, "yeah, I could sing as good as any of these country
singers," and Helen said, "yes, you could," and Red said, "you
bet I could, I could right now," and then he'd think about getting
a guitar, but he never did; we were always moving from one
financial or moral crisis to another and barely had enough for
food most of the time, the Rainbow looked like a mutilated
turtle and we still didn't have linoleum or rugs on any of the
floors upstairs, what little extra Red had went to putting doors
back on or repairing appliances that went down in one-rounders
with Red.

But Joseph had Red psyched to shreds. After the Battle of Quebec and everything leading up to it, including being responsible for losing Bush and Jon in the first place, and having to take responsibility for busting up Funster's bomb shelter, then Helen getting that job, you could see Red had started to feel a little overwhelmed. He used to think he had some control over things, not that he still didn't, it was just apparent he didn't, so Joseph wasn't going to give him any chance for choice, he'd hit him with a confrontation, a gift, and a nuisance, betting that after all he'd been through, and settling into middle age, he didn't have the resilience he used to have for getting him violently through a long number of separate but contiguous events.

"Mrs. B wants the rest of her money," Joseph said when I came in.

"Right," I said. I guess that shepherd must have been one of the big ones she was keeping out back. I checked its butt. One hole. Then he jumped up on me and I knocked him down and he jumped up on me again and I knocked him down so he jumped up on me again and I knocked him down again, this time holding him down by the shoulders though still everything in him was jumping but his body. "Hold on to your goddamn dog," I told Joseph, but he'd put his finger in his good ear. I put the amplifier on top of the dog and that held him pretty good for several seconds. Then Helen came in the door.

She'd been working up at Marycrest now for a week or so as a receptionist at the information desk in the very front office of the administration building, and though it was still too early to get her first paycheck, every day now she got dressed up for work almost as much as on Sundays, dresses and nylons and shoes with heels, you could see it just excited the shit out of her, really, I hadn't thought about how many years she went around the house in her plain housedress with no makeup six days a week and most of Sunday, and now she was getting out of the house and taking the bus up to Marycrest every day and being a dressed-up woman with responsibility outside the home and soon to be making her own money and it made her feel good. But she still had to deal with Red.

So when she got out of work she moved into a mode of major placation and hustled out of Marycrest and caught the first bus home so she beat Red there, not that Red wasn't accommodating, he was coming home about twenty minutes later than usual, probably had himself an extra lunch or something, and then Helen got home and got supper started and did some cleaning so things would be kind of normal when Red came in the door. Of course there was nothing normal about that, Helen never cleaned much even when that was all she was supposed to do.

So Helen came in the door and the dog jumped up on her and she knocked him down and he jumped up on her again and she knocked him down again and that went on for a while until she clobbered him with her briefcase which stunned him for microseconds. "Looks like we have some guitars and a dog here," said Helen. Like Willie she'd obviously learned to separate observation and judgment. She went into the holy room, lit some candles for the Infant like you'd change the Kitty Litter, then went into the kitchen and opened up a can of food smell, something she'd concocted to make the place smell like she'd been in there cooking all day; of course Helen couldn't smell anymore, having lost her smell the morning after the last door massacre, so the place stunk like a shit crypt, just a little worse than Helen's cooking usually smelled anyway, she never really gave a rat's ass about cooking either, I'll have to admit.

Then came Red with his briefcase and arms full of toilet paper samples and bowling ball, and that dog who'd already grown several inches in the last half hour, started banging himself against Red's knees and Red said, "Goddammit, goddammit," which I guess is pretty much what you'd expect him to say, considering.

Of course the dog jumped up and Red knocked him down and that went on for a while until Red got all his stuff put away in the closet and then when the dog jumped on him again Red hit him so hard on the head I thought that dog would suffer ubiquitous mitosis. He hit the floor and did a quadruple split, his eyeballs folded like tents, you could see he was having the first thought of his young life.

"Who belongs to this dog?" said Red. Whatever subtle effects the Year of Two Hundred Books had on Red, it didn't help his English, you'd think the German he knew was influencing him, if he knew any German.

Helen came in the room.

"I don't want a dog," said Red.

"It's a nice jumping dog," said Helen, whacking the dog. She really liked animals and didn't mind kids either.

"He doesn't even have a name," said Red.

"His name's Honky," said Joseph.

"The poor thing doesn't even honk," said Helen. "He jumps."

"I don't want a dog," said Red. "And we aint calling him Jumpy."

Joseph gave Red the acoustic guitar.

"I don't want a guitar," said Red.

"Do you have anything for me?" said Helen.

"I don't want a guitar," said Red. He went over and sat down on his chair next to the Zenith in the front room.

"Did you ever see that commercial on TV," Helen said to me, "where the husband makes his wife a cup of instant coffee and she knits him a sweater?"

Honky jumped on Joseph and Joseph knocked him down and then he jumped on me and I knocked him down and then he jumped on Helen and she knocked him down. He already looked about five pounds heavier than when I came in. He ran over to Red, faked a jump, Red swatted and missed and Honky jumped into him.

"Goddammit," said Red, strumming the guitar.

Honky made another round. Already he'd learned to protect his head by tucking it under his foreleg and throwing his shoulder into your chest, though after a few more rounds of jumping up and getting pounded down he rested by jumping straight up and down, looked like we'd have to cut a hole in the ceiling to keep him in the house.

"Goddamn dog will shit all over," said Red. "I'll be stepping in dog shit every time I turn around." He strummed a few more chords and said he didn't want a guitar and then started playing "There's a Star-Spangled Banner Flying Somewhere," looked like Red really could sing and play the guitar and knock Honky on his can without missing a chord. His singing voice was an octave or two higher than his speaking voice, a little like Gene Autry, except Red didn't do "Back in the Saddle Again" or any Gene Autry songs except for "Rudolph the Red-Nosed Reindeer," which Red sang, oblivious to season, along with "Jingle Bells" and "Easter Parade," "I Walk the Line," "Ring of Fire," "The Yellow Rose of Texas," "When Jimmy Rogers Said Goodbye," and "The Wabash Cannon Ball." By that time Andrew had come down from the bedroom with Crow, and Neda came in, and everybody was sitting around pretty much in awe, we had to admit, Red sure could play and sing, and Red sat forward playing the guitar on the edge of his chair and Honky was in the living room jumping straight into the air, and Red looked at Helen on the couch and started playing "You Are My Sunshine," he just looked right at Helen and played that song:

The other day dear as I lay sleeping,
I dreamt I held you in my arms,
When I awoke dear I was mistaken,
And I hung my head and cried.

"You are my sunshine," sang Red, "my only sunshine. You make me happy when skies are gray." I looked at Helen and she was crying, but Red kept playing all the same.

You'll never know dear how much I love you,
Please don't take my sunshine away.

Over at Willie's the Dialecticians were dancing, dancing, dancing. You can't dance on deaf, that's for sure, so Willie worked up a little mixture of heroin and cocaine which felt a bit like sunbathing on a lightning bolt, certainly made you want to dance. Willie, himself, had begun a cancer campaign, lots of cigarettes and coffee, cyclamates, saccharin, nitrates and nitrites, straight whiskey, though he knew the clincher would be radioactivity. As it was, the pillows in the room were spread to the walls and the Dialecticians were moving to the Supremes, not a drop of orangeade in the place, and all the Dialecticians, even Willie, had on new black leather jackets, a picture of Shiva on the back, DIALECTICIANS in script across the shoulders. At first I had trouble dancing and talking at the same time, because unlike the other Dialecticians my movements were less genetic and habitual, but soon enough I was just plain dancing and not thinking about it. Nonetheless, I couldn't dance like those other Dialecticians who moved like slippers and eels.

"You, yourself," said Willie, watching me watch the other Dialecticians in their new black leather jackets, "are skeptical of fis new turn, I can see."

"You think us Dialecticians will bury ourselves in the convention and the conformity," said Revis.

"We almost got you white leather, to protect your individuality," said Raymon. "But that is a mere synthetic differentiation."

Revco grinned.

"I, myself," said Willie, "cannot tell the difference between a Chevrolet and the end of the world." He gave me my own black leather jacket. "One does not wait to be hunted to hide."

I guess you just can't walk on the razor of reality like Willie did and not be enigmatic sometimes. I put on my new jacket, turned up the collar, pushed my hair back, started shuffling to Marvin Gaye. I thought about deaf, I thought about the other, I thought about our friend Mr. Tony Blanion and what he did or didn't, could or couldn't tell the police.

"Among other fings, our friend Mr. Blanion knows about your camera," said Willie.

It'd been a while since I thought like that about that camera, by now I figured it was *my* camera though it looked like other people figured it wasn't. Of course Karl told me in the first place I shouldn't have stole it or kept it, he said it would be too easy to trace and there he was right again, I had to hand it to Karl, he knew a little about crime.

"Maybe," said Willie, "you should just hit him on the head wif a hammer."

Well I was no longer really interested in using the hammer on our friend Mr. Blanion, if I wanted to drop the nugget on Blanion I had my .22, though it gave me a real sympathy for mass murderers, one of those fundamental contradictions of the world, just because Bobby Hansen accidentally became a vegetable on my account I'd end up killing some creep like Blanion to keep it quiet, then I'd probably have to kill some marginal character to keep the lid on that. Soon enough I'd be at war with society.

Labor Day
with Karl Marxman

"NOTHING YOU can do about it now," said Karl. He was packing up his family for the Labor Day festivities down at the dock where there'd be fireworks and food booths and bands and the Mayor and a ceremonial docking of the brand-new Lake Erie cruise ship, the *North American,* that was supposed to be just like those ocean liners that went to Europe or the Caribbean or the South Seas, only smaller, on which people wined and dined and purportedly sat on the sun-swept decks, in this case on the high seas of Lake Erie as the *North American* made the exciting trip back and forth from Erie, Pennsylvania, to London, Ontario, an idea so ridiculous it was goddamn popular.

"Sometimes this stuff blows right over. You've been clean till now, so the police won't move on you, not on Blanion's story, unless they've really got a case." He rubbed his stubble. "We must have been in his territory."

"You can't fence it?"

"That's as good as keeping it if they're on your tail, besides, they aint after the camera."

No, they were after the person who turned Bobby Hansen

into a potato cake. No use dragging Karl into it, clear as fear. I'd have to get the camera out of Willie's attic too.

Karl got Sophie and Beema and Maggie and Karl Jr. out of the house and threw them in the back of the truck with the dogs and caged birds. Crow flew down from Andrew's window and into the cab, he didn't like riding in the back. "Want to come?" Karl asked me.

Well why not.

So we went down to the dock and listened to the Mayor and the bands and watched the fireworks at dusk, Karl and his family were real big on fireworks, and every once and a while me and Karl took a walk to go buy everybody some ribs or hot dogs or pigs' feet, taking our time, of course, with Karl being real meticulous about pointing out all the sailboats and yachts filled with drunk young revelers circling around the dock in their white boats named *Anabell III* or *Simple Pleasure,* it sure was festive, and then the *North American* came in and landed with lots of streaming lights strung aboard and more fireworks and rivers of rich people coming down the gangplank in tuxedos and gowns and getting into limousines to be carted off to a big party thrown by the Mayor to show his appreciation for all the commerce and other good things the voyages of the *North American* would do for Erie's tourist industry; threw that party right on the flagship *Niagara,* a War of 1812 frigate or some such, several pieces of which were part of the original that Commodore Perry sailed on to defeat the British in the Battle of Lake Erie when he said, "Damn the torpedoes, don't give up the ship, we've met the enemy and they are Mars Bars." Then he went off to bury Mad Anthony Wayne underneath the blockhouse. Though later Mad Anthony Wayne got exhumed. It was a big part of Erie history that nobody cared about, along with George Washington's visit when he was just a teenager; the wealthy folks who came off the *North American* were probably standing around on the *Niagara* passing those same stories around right at that moment.

Of course that wealthy gangplank parade went on for quite some time, and Karl had packed up the family and was just about ready to leave when the very last people appeared on the *North American;* the Hansens, with Bobby Hansen in his wheelchair looking a little bit like those chameleons you used to pin to your chest at the county fair, and they wheeled Bobby Hansen down the plank and the band struck up some combination of "The Notre Dame Fight Song" and "Hooray for Hollywood," and Bobby Hansen, still pretty immobile from the hairline down, showed how he could get around by himself in the wheelchair just by wriggling the front of his feet against the ground, a depressing sight if you ever saw one, though there was a little crowd there getting pretty hepped up about it and along with the band followed Bobby Hansen and his family as Bobby ped-pedded his way all the way down to the flagship *Niagara* to get his intravenous champagne and caviar.

Back at Karl's Karl took me in the basement where he was working on still another cannon, one real similar to the circus cannon only a little smaller and mounted on a base with a swivel.

"It's going to take more than that to keep up with Funster," I told him.

"I aint worried about Funster," said Karl. "We're on the same side."

Crow'd been sitting on the pig but flew over to Karl's shoulder when he heard we were talking about Funster.

"We're going to eat that pig for Halloween," said Karl.

"Fat chance," said Crow.

"Besides," said Karl, "how's he going to put the damn thing in the air?"

"Neda," said Crow.

Well that stopped us both.

"Cough up," said Crow.

Karl gave him a corn curl, looked like everybody'd pretty much succumbed to it, unlike Grandma Funster, Crow was usually pretty reliable.

"Neda and Funly?" I said.

"More info, more corn curls."

"First the info, then the corn curls," I told him.

"He bookends now," said Karl. "All the time he spends with those parrots, next thing he'll probably want rum."

"Yo-ho-ho," said Crow. "Cough up, buddy."

"Forget it," I said.

"He works cheap," said Karl.

"Suit yourself," said Crow. He flew back over to the pig. "Halloween," he told the pig. "Cough up."

Karl showed me his new prize acquisitions, a pair of M16s. "Same kind the Marines are using in Vietnam," said Karl.

"Where?"

"Vietnam."

Didn't make any more sense the second time than it did the first time. "That in Africa?"

"Off Hawaii," said Karl. "Feds are afraid if the Communists take over Vietnam then they'll go to Hawaii, fill up all the hotels with refugees like in *Doctor Zhivago.*"

Well I didn't know dick about *Doctor Zhivago,* but it always seemed to me that Karl carried around a bit of a contradiction, seemed like despite his patriotism wealth-sharing was part of his creed.

"You're going to practice being dumb so long," said Karl, "and then you're going to be dumb."

The next day me and Karl drove out the East Side, through the old Polishtown that was now all black, past the Hammermill and then the GE plants, I once thought they stunk pretty bad but I could hardly smell them now, and out through the working-class suburbs till we finally hit country. Through the trees or between mansions sometimes I caught glimpses of the lake, spreading in all directions into nowhere just like Kara Ruzci said the oceans did, even from the road I could see the whitecaps. Then we finally hit a patch of woods and Karl pulled in, parked the truck amidst a bunch of trees. We got out and walked towards the lake till we got to a cliff, wended our way partway down till we got to the last twenty feet or so where Karl unfurled a thick rope tied into knots every couple feet and we used that to go down to the bottom.

Nice and private down there. There was a short brown beach with lots of driftwood that the cliff cut off on the west, behind us just plain straight-up cliff, and in front lake, lake, and more lake. To the east, just down the beach a ways, we came to a little tree-covered cove, and behind those trees was Karl's boat, looked like an old fishing trawler, big wooden bow, most of the deck enclosed, Karl already had the hull stripped and sanded.

"Runs good too," said Karl.

There was a hatch in the bow and above that Karl already had the mounting for the new swivel cannon in place. Karl gazed out toward where the blue of the sky faded into the blue of Lake Erie. "It's a big goddamn lake," he said. "And we're gonna be the only pirates."

~~~~~~~~~~~~~~~~~Autumn Refrain

T HAT FALL Stinky Jinx became the first high school running back in the history of Erie, Pennsylvania, and probably
the world to go through a whole season without being tackled.
Every week he had his picture plastered all over the Erie *Times
News* sports page; Stinky jumping over the goalpost, Stinky
giving a straight arm, you can imagine how that looked, he
actually had to stop and pose in the middle of plays just so
they could capture him on film, he was so fast that they had to
stop the highlights film on a single frame just to get Stinky in
slow motion. Big Dick sent a press release on Stinky to *Sports
Illustrated* and Stinky got his picture in the back, in the Personality section: "Hootin' & Scootin' Stinky Jinx breaks Erie city
records for touchdowns in a game (27), touchdowns in a season
(194), and forty-six other categories including total offensive
yardage (11,682) and completing the season without being
touched. 'Isn't that the point?' says Stinky. His Dad calls him 'A
real card.' "

Of course South High won the title. People were talking all
over about the heyday years of South when they beat everybody
in sight including teams from Ohio like Massillon and Warren

and Niles who used professional football players who went back to high school at the end of their careers to complete their education, in fact South was trying to schedule everybody in the country including Notre Dame before Stinky got out of school. At the end of the season Stinky went on local TV and got a plaque for being the High School Football Player of the Year, given to him by Lank Ward who'd set a million records in every sport for South High back in the late thirties, Lank gave Stinky the plaque and Stinky gave him a dozen roses, pretty much baffled Lank and the announcer to death. "What a thing to keep *track* of," said Stinky. "What a card," said the announcer. The basketball coach announced that the basketball team would have sunset cream home and mauve away uniforms for the coming season, two days after Stinky, fully clad in South's new football gear, though of course helmetless, appeared scarf afurl and flipping a straight arm in *Vogue.* Stinky was real fond of that picture.

I saw most of Stinky's games down at the stadium, including the one where he scored twenty-seven touchdowns against the local Catholic Prep. They'd been the perennial champions and South hadn't beaten them since Lank Ward left, even Bobby Hansen hadn't turned that around, but that night they didn't have a prayer, not even to the Infant of Prague. South barricaded the backs of the end zones with buses and sandbags, kept wrestlers at every possible exit from the field and alumnae at every entrance to the stadium, just to keep Stinky hemmed in. Around the upper rim of the stadium, where there was a walkway, you could see Bobby Hansen ped-pedding his way around, back and forth, in that wheelchair, must have been real depressing for him having to watch Stinky tear up the field like that in his place, people dropping hot dogs and ketchup and coffee on his head every time Stinky scored a touchdown, which was twenty-seven times that night, still, even if he was down there all he'd be doing was handing the ball off to Stinky anyway so maybe just as well he was hurt and had an excuse.

Nonetheless, every football rally the principal dragged Bobby Hansen out onstage, and Bobby of course, unable to take help from anybody, being so proud, would ped-ped his way out to the front of the stage by wriggling the front of his feet and get a standing ovation to which he responded rather stoically, being unable to move any part of his face. Bobby Hansen sure had fortitude. Bobby Hansen was the kind of person America was built on, I suppose you could take that any number of ways, and one day Bobby Hansen was going to be back out there on the field, if not the football field, then the field of life, and then he'd show everybody. Not only was he now ped-pedding around on his own just by using the front of his feet, when only last Christmas he was totally paralyzed, but just last week he felt a pinprick in his heel.

Well it was still a long way from his mouth.

In truth I had more immediate concerns, namely our friend Mr. Tony Blanion who grabbed me by my leather jacket after the game and offered my nose to his knife.

"Okay rainbow fruit," said Blanion. "This is your second to last chance."

He was certainly a poetic and equaniminous hood, and I could see he was real impressed with my Dialecticians jacket. Of course I, myself, was never too talkative around Blanion.

Blanion extricated a few of my nose hairs with his blade. "You can't throw a bag of wet cats in the air and not expect it to come back down," he said. "I'll settle for five hundred dollars."

"I'll sell the house and car."

"Try the camera, beach ball."

"What happened to Stubie and Gorky?"

"Don't worry about Stubie and Gorky, they're just renting."

I was glad he said that. For a moment I thought he'd gone literal.

"Listen newt tit, I cracked shack up in Glenwood for years. I had the locals on the phone. I was eating police cheese. Now you fucked mud and they want to open my lid."

"Maybe you should get some counseling," I told him.

"You're sellin a boat that don't float, cream beam." He finished up on my nose and was working on my ear hairs. "You got jelly on your floorboards. The fuzz don't want to give me a Christmas present, they want a full bottle, and *you are it.*"

"Just like breakfast in bed," I said.

"Yeah," said Blanion. "If this was breakfast and we were in bed."

Our friend Mr. Tony Blanion could really read a pitch, I had to give him that, in fact I was getting kind of endeared to him, he was one of the few people I could really talk to, even if he did lean a little heavy on metaphor while I, myself, preferred the simile. It would have been nice to think that Blanion was evil, just carve him out of the world and leave everything else healthy, but that wasn't the case; Blanion was simply an urban Zulu and you kind of had to respect him for it, had himself a myth system as valid as anybody else's, sophisticated and clearly operational, unfortunately our phenomenal spheres made bad music when they rubbed.

"The airport's closing," said Blanion. "The next time I see you it'll be for the light bill."

Which was something on the literal level that was getting paid regularly now that Helen had work. Helen had the best-dressed Infant since the founding of Prague. Of course now that Helen had her own source of capital, that holy room was filling up like a water balloon and Red couldn't do a goddamn thing about it.

Then came Thanksgiving. Every year Red planned on not having Bush and Jon over for Thanksgiving and every year for some reason or another Bush and Jon couldn't have Thanksgiving with Uncle Stanley or Uncle David or Aunt Frances and then Helen invited Bush and Jon to have Thanksgiving with us. Then Red hit the roof and he and Helen fought like hell for a week and Bush and Jon came over for Thanksgiving. Boy, Red hated that. But this year Uncle David had some big important thing to discuss with Bush and Jon and invited them down to have Thanksgiving on his farm in Mercer.

Red was happy as a doornail and as usual dragged everybody out of bed and downstairs to watch parades with the giant balloons of Mickey Mouse and Bullwinkle and Popeye, but especially the three personal appearances by Santee Claus in New York, Philadelphia, and Detroit. Red still called him San*tee* Claus and still ran around and poked everybody in the ribs and said, "Look, there's Santee Claus! There's Santee Claus!" at the end of every parade. And Red was looking forward to that one day of the year when he sat *in front* of the Zenith and watched Texas cream Texas A&M and watched the Detroit Lions beat whoever they played, the one day when he sat in front of the TV instead of next to it watching everybody watch TV, when he figured out that Bush wouldn't be there and now he'd have to help in the kitchen.

On top of that, by Thanksgiving Red had nearly exploited every toilet paper market in the tristate area and wasn't going to see an increase in sales without some kind of population explosion. He was facing a dead end. While meanwhile Helen had already got a raise from the sisters at Marycrest and a promotion to Head of Information. Helen was out in the world becoming a fiscal entity and there he was a toilet paper salesman going nowhere. Now he had to help in the kitchen.

For Red, it were symbolic.

I was in there making mashed potatoes that more and more resembled warm cottage cheese when Red came in and decided to put raisins in the stuffing, which of course Helen and Bush never did, but now that Jon and Bush weren't there Red started having lots of nostalgic memories of Thanksgivings at home with Grandpa Whitey and Grandma Emma Loop, good German Thanksgivings where there were nuts and huge pieces of apple and especially raisins in the stuffing and goddammit all he was asking for was a few raisins.

Now usually we spent our time indoors comforted by the continuous ramming of Honky who tended to throw himself headlong into the back of the house, felt a little bit like living in a cardboard bell, but once those two started banging things around in that kitchen you could barely hear him. Finally Helen kicked Red out of there which was just what he wanted so he felt guilty and couldn't enjoy anything, not even the raisins he sneaked into the stuffing. I have to admit, those raisins tasted lousy in there. But we made it through Thanksgiving with nobody dead and we were headed towards Christmas.

Helen's mind worked in mysterious ways. Lately she'd been badgering me and Willie to have the Dialecticians come up to Marycrest sometime and scrimmage the all-nun basketball team coached by the only lay administrator at Marycrest, Dean Hadrian Sullivan, who said he coached the best all-nun basketball team in Erie, if not the world. But most of all Helen was worried that this might be Bush's last set of holidays, considering she was eighty-one and had been through so much the last year, the Cuban Missile Crisis and the Battle of Quebec, just to name two of the more explicit traumas, not to mention living with Jon. This could be Bush's Last Christmas.

And what would poor Jon do without Bush? He and the men had eventually proved too much for the asylum and now all of them were on Thorazine. Jon was okay as long as you left him near a wall or Grandma Funster didn't come over and raise hell with the men, get them off their Thorazine, then they'd start worrying about the Communists again and talking to Jon about it. Other than that Jon was doing pretty good except for long periods when he spoke French and hated himself for it.

Grandma Funster was generally back with the Funsters. I guess we didn't realize it, but back in Grandma Funster's corporeal years when she went chasing me and Georgie Gorky all around the block, she was doing that as much for herself as us, she was just ambulatory from the word go, didn't like to hang around the house, she spent her whole life taking care of Grandpa Funster and all the kids, particularly big Jimbo, and you couldn't blame her for being a little resentful about Grandpa Funster dying and not being dead while she herself was now dead after having lived every minute of her life and then some. "Lobotomy crepes!" said Grandpa Funster, which was tough to argue with.

Jimbo seemed to calm down a little bit after the Battle of Quebec. Red helped him put the door back on the bomb shelter, and Jimbo still had his porch roof sandbagged, but he only manned it on Sunday nights when the flow from what used to be the Greek Orthodox Church behind our yard but was now a black church with too many names and qualifications for anybody to remember started to get heavy in the direction of Dean Danger's Bar & Grill, a process of inevitable accretion if you ever saw one. It started in the morning after the first round of hymns. Red really liked those hymns and he moved the head of his and Helen's bed next to the window so he could wake up on Sunday to those heavenly black voices sifting through the backyard, nonetheless keeping Honky back there the whole time so nobody decided to sift through the backyard in person so as to make a shortcut to 24th Street and Dean Danger's. But after those first hymns that church always lost a couple people during intermission who headed out on the Dean Danger Expressway Business Loop, taking the short route on the way there, across 23rd and up Celebration, and the long route on the way back, across 24th to German Avenue, stopping at the Variety Store for a cigarette or a Hostess Ho-Ho, though some of the younger crowd sometimes stopped off at the Magicians who seemed to have a lot of friends on Sunday probably due to their semimystical persuasion, then down German to 23rd and back along 23rd till they hit the church. Generally nobody used the sidewalks on weekdays, except on Celebration which was a major thoroughfare, unless they were local or drunk, but on Sunday the women and children and the men who walked with their families did, even after it got dark.

But as the day went on people got less and less interested in church and more and more interested in Dean Danger's Bar & Grill and then the Dean Danger Expressway was no place to be unless you knew the tunes, though I, myself, was always recognized as "Red's kid," even by people I never saw in my life, they knew I was "Red's kid" and nodded to me as I walked down the street or one said to the other after they walked by, "Red's kid," which rubbed me a little wrong but allowed me to keep my limbs the way they were originally constructed. By nighttime there weren't many churchgoers left over at Dean Danger's Bar & Grill at all, not any of the really sincere types anyway, though that could just be some kind of cultural dyslexia on my part because even Raymon, Revis and Revco went to church and when I said to Raymon, "How come you go to church on Sunday, you don't even believe anything," he said, "What's that got to do with it," which I guess is the only answer to that question when you think about it; nonetheless once it got late and Red was just about ready to retire in the face of a long week of pushing toilet paper, trying now to expand his territory beyond Buffalo, New York, where he was trying to get the NASA office there to buy his toilet paper for the astronauts even though they told him the astronauts didn't use toilet paper, which Red thought was a pretty good joke, he knew even if they didn't use it up there they'd have to use it sometime, you couldn't throw Red a curve when it came to toilet paper, that's when me and Red took a walk down to Dean Danger's Bar & Grill and waded up to the bar where Dean Danger himself came out from the back looking like a ten-foot bag of bowling balls and gave Red a beer amidst the smoke and masses of dark blue humanity while I went over to a table in the corner and joined Revis and Revco Danger and sometimes Raymon and sometimes even Willie, himself, where we ate hot leftover chicken wings made by Dean Danger, himself. Dean Danger's wife, Tina, didn't work at the bar or grill, she said she spent enough of her day waiting around on men, though sometimes she came over after church and sat in the doorway between the kitchen and the barroom and offered Dean Danger advice about the hot sauce for his chicken wings, among other things, and we also drank beer even though we were officially underage because it didn't really matter that we were breaking the law because back then it was against the law for bars to even be open on Sunday in Pennsylvania but it would have required more than the police department to shut that bar down and besides there hadn't been a police car in that neighborhood since the advent of my consciousness.

Red sat at the bar and ordered Limburger and onion on rye

sandwiches which of course they didn't have at Dean Danger's
Bar & Grill, so sometimes Dean Danger made him a deep-fried
grilled cheese, Dean Danger said he deep-fried everything, he
didn't give a shit, even if he ever did serve Limburger and onion
on rye he'd serve it deep-fried, and a version of that exchange
went on every Sunday night we went over there. Sometimes a
few of the younger guys from down on the Bayfront came by
and patted Red on the back and told him his house wouldn't burn
and Red told them how lucky they were it wouldn't and then
they laughed. It was a big joke that lacked a certain degree of
humor.

Then me and Red walked back to the house, passed the
Magicians' place which by this time in the evening had a longer
line outside the door than for *Ben Hur,* in fact at the end of
the line you were so close to Dean Danger's Bar & Grill you
could still order drinks, and Red said, "Don't think I don't know
what's goin on in there, I know what's goin on in there," what
pissed him off most was that he was busting his butt to sell toilet
paper every day and the Magicians just sat back and let people
come to them, and on top of it all they didn't pay taxes, sounded
like he could have handled it okay if it wasn't for the part about
the taxes.

Red and me still weren't exactly chums, I don't think he ever
got over me being named after him against his will, though I
really didn't have that much to do with it. One time, long ago,
Red and Helen agreed on two things and one was that they were
in love and the other was that they would never name their
firstborn son after Red, that is Jarvis Jr. That was way back just
before World War II, when Red first worked at the Erie Forge.

Red worked real hard at the Forge, in fact he worked too
hard, so the Union sent Derk Delco, the Union Dirty Man, to
fight Red every lunchtime. That went on for so long that Red
forgot what it was like to eat his favorite meal of the day. It went
on so long that the Union Dirty Man started bringing Red a red
rose before every fight. If that wasn't mysterious enough, the
Union Dirty Man tried to follow Red into the Marines but

flunked the physical, then when Red got back to the Forge after the war he learned that the Union Dirty Man died a Marine war hero on Midway in a hushed-up battle called the Great Midway Underwear Massacre in which all the Marines but just a few got rubbed out while only wearing their underwear. Hardly anybody knew about that battle except for Red because he was one of the only Marines who survived it and the last thing he remembered about it he was getting killed.

What else Red didn't know about was that back in Erie Helen's best friend in the war housing apartments was the Union Dirty Man's wife, Dee Delco, a southern girl with red nails and red hair who was one month more pregnant than Helen herself who was pregnant with me. Dee Delco was going to name her baby Derk Delco Jr. only Derk Delco Jr. was stillborn only a few days after Dee learned that Derk Delco Sr. got rubbed out on Midway. Dee committed suicide not too long after and that same night Helen had me and named me Jarvis Loop Jr.

Of course neither of those two ever said a thing to each other about any of that, they just took it out on me, leaving me an unwary by-product of the sociomysterious. And though Red hardly ever tried to kill me over it anymore, I, myself, preferred not spending much time around him, and when we did spend time together it was pretty wordless.

Joseph was now playing his guitar and rumor had it that he was a musician, though he always shut down when he played, closed his eye, plugged his ear, said it was all mathematics, had nothing to do with sound, and listening to him you sure had to give him that. When Joseph was playing the cosmic guitar, Neda listening to the Webcor Portable Stereo, Helen sleeping on the couch under her comforter that she hadn't finished for Bush yet, watching TV, you couldn't turn it off or she'd wake up, and Honky banging against the house, Red could barely concentrate on his bowling ball, though Andrew, who now spent almost every second in the bedroom taking information from Crow and communicating with the celestial levels, said when everybody was plugged in it was like we were on a spiritual booster system.

He didn't use the silver halo anymore, not on his head, he found an old black telephone in a junkyard and wired it up to the halo which he now kept mounted on the porch roof, and of course he'd lied about not needing Joseph to shut down, so when Joseph started playing the guitar Andrew dialed out the mathematical pattern on the telephone and got person-to-person service to the State After, didn't take long before he was Joseph's songwriter. Those two were bound like Pythagoras and sound, according to Neda anyway, and she, if anyone, would know.

Neda had joined forces with Funly Funster in the drive to put a Funster on the moon. First they'd try a satellite, then some kind of animal, then they'd send Funly up for a few orbits. That's as far as they'd got in the planning stage. The only problem was going to be the boosters which would have to be buoyant and reusable so they could pick them up in Lake Erie, though Neda wasn't worried so much about making them as having the facilities for retrieving them. I have to admit, it all sounded a little farfetched.

"Listen," Funly told me one afternoon. "Space makes weird bed partners."

"You can imagine what this will do for my science project," said Neda. "It could mean the state finals."

Funly chuckled. He was really getting one over on Neda.

That fall I had less interest in school than ever, in fact by the time I got to Bush's next Last Christmas it looked like I was proving a detriment to my own graduation. The only interest I had in South High was Stinky who in South's opening basketball game became the first player in the history of Erie, Pennsylvania basketball, and probably the world, to spend more time in the air than on the floor. Us Dialecticians were dancing, dancing, dancing, along with our more recent experiments with life as well as deaf, which led Revis to the theory that Revco's smile was the only eternal entity.

"That," said Raymon, "is a dualism."

"It is a difference," said Willie, "between Revco's smile and killing oneself."

•   •   •

Then there was Kara Ruzci who I thought about all the time when I wasn't thinking about everything else. I spent half my dancing time with the Dialecticians taking pictures just so I'd have something to take into the darkroom so I could relate, because Kara still spent all her time in the darkroom making images that looked like fluorescent amphibians, sent Polly Doggerel out for her own hamburgers, just gave her a couple bucks and put her in the street and she never came back with any change. In the evening, after we were done in the darkroom, we'd ride out to Kara Ruzci's where Kara let Polly Doggerel out to dodge trucks and me and Kara climbed on one of the old shacks in the back of her yard where we sat on the roof and watched the sun set over the lake, then went inside, drank wine, talked about her photographs or my photographs or somebody's photographs, she basically wanted to talk about photographs, then sometimes we had a little deaf, and sometimes not, but we always went to bed, wandering through the maze of her house like rats in Disneyland, until we came to her bedroom where we made love and dreamed together. We walked in woods and bathed each other in cool streams under the warm yellow sun, we spoke to each other without speaking, Kara just looked at me across the abyss of separateness and then I knew to touch her breast or wash her hair. Then Kara kissed my eyes and took my hands and sang to me, Kara would sing, in her strange unknowable voice like the fluted hum of a deep pond, and I felt my own voice rising grudgingly, an oboe of dark wallow, until there was just a single voice, and then only a voice, and I couldn't see Kara Ruzci anymore, couldn't see myself anymore.

But late in the night when Kara woke to sing, I couldn't understand her and there was no blending, only her sad, sad plea and some returning wail from the air. Then I never wanted to dream again. And I did not trust her when she dreamed.

~~~~~~~~~~ The Spanish Armada

I SPENT A LOT of my free time working on the boat with
Karl. We painted the hull and trim, tuned the engine, set up
the wiring, mounted the cannon. Karl wanted to get the boat in
the water before winter and see if maybe we could even make
an autumn strike so we'd have one under our belts before late
spring. Crow came along during most the work but the big
debate was whether or not we should take him to sea, he'd really
increase our yacht spotting range but if somebody connected our
raids to Crow, well the Coast Guard could just float right up to
Karl's front door and that would be that. If we brought him he'd
have to stay in the hold during the fun.

"We can't have you flying around yakking your head off
while we're doin business," Karl told him.

"Corn curls," said Crow.

"You'll get plenty of corn curls."

"Fat chance," said Crow.

"What a card," said Karl.

Crow looked at him sideways.

We didn't license the boat, that's all we needed was to be
traceable, we'd only be going out for business anyways and then

to get caught would be to get caught, a license wouldn't mean much. Karl hooked up a pair of big auxiliary outboards that we hinged to the back and hid under wooden boxes, didn't want to look any more suspicious than we already were, and though we'd have Crow to peruse the area to make sure the Coast Guard wasn't around, and we could monitor the Coast Guard band on our radio to make sure our unwary business associates didn't try to bring in a government mediator, we couldn't guarantee what they'd do once we hightailed, so once we did, the more speed the better. Good thing we got everything done in time because Karl just about busted the bank for those outboards.

We moved out on a moonless night in early October; there'd been years when snowstorms had hit by then but things were pretty mild that fall, me and Kara Ruzci even went to the beach in the middle of September; the whitecaps looked like disappearing moments of snow and the horizon a blue line across a black wall. It was only my second time on a boat. The last time had been the week previous, our test run. I didn't get seasick.

The lights of GE and Hammermill flickered behind us, the city lit up to the west. We kept an M16 in the bow of the boat, near the cannon, and one in the rear by the steering wheel. We had a bullhorn. We monitored the Coast Guard channels. We packed our .22s.

We didn't want to work the Bay, too small, too many boats there, nor get too far west on the lake on the other side of the peninsula, between the city and the yacht clubs. Storms came up fast on Lake Erie so we didn't think anybody'd be spending the night too far away from the beach. At the east end of the peninsula, a mile or so out, we might find some partyers looking for privacy, a morning swim, maybe some waterskiing if the lake was calm. When we got in the area we sent out Crow, after giving him two corn curls. "Yo-ho-ho," said Crow.

Crow came back pretty quick, walking up and down the rail of the boat till the corn curls came out and he'd had several.

"What's the news, dummy," said Karl.

Crow looked askance. He didn't like being denigrated, if

anybody knew that Karl did. Crow bobbed a couple times, started cleaning his wing pits with his beak. "Pew," said Crow.

"Your brother's ruined that bird," said Karl.

"God bless 'im," said Crow.

Well you could see Karl wasn't going to apologize to a goddamn bird, and Crow couldn't care less if we were pirates or shoe heels, to him it was a world of corn curls and simple etiquette. I took the corn curls from Karl and went over to Crow. I'd put a lot of work in on that boat and unlike Karl I wasn't about to give it all up for an ornithological dispute.

I gave Crow a corn curl. "Deaf," I said to him.

Crow looked one way then the other. He hopped back and forth. He hadn't been up to Willie's since the Dialecticians went cold turkey during the Cuban Missile Crisis, and those parrots were lousy conversationalists even if they did have rum, besides that horn music drove him mad. "Cough up," said Crow.

"No info, no deaf."

Crow looked at me then he looked at Karl then he looked at me then he looked at Karl. Then he looked at me.

"Karl's sorry," I said.

"Fat chance," said Crow, and took off, but slow enough for us to follow. Soon we rounded the tip of the peninsula, dark as lark except for a tiny light at the back of a small bay.

"Wonder what that is," said Karl.

"It's a light," I said.

Karl barely looked up from the wheel. "You make a person want to explain things," he said. "But I'm learning not to be that stupid."

Well I didn't need Karl to tell me that discommunication was a racewide disease either. I moved to the back of the deck, near the engine, where all I could hear was the motor drone, all I could see was the wake of the boat like a white scar on the water, all I could smell, from what was left of my ability to smell, was carbon and gasoline. I enjoyed feeling nothing but intrusion.

Soon enough we saw another light, the light of an anchored yacht. Crow came aboard and I hit both his nostrils with a fix.

"Deaf," said Crow.

"That's right," I said.

Karl put us head on to the yacht and I loaded the cannon with a grappling hook tied to a hole at the top of the barrel. When Karl was ready I fired.

If the explosion didn't wake those people up, then that hook sure did when it hit their deck. Karl sure knew his ballistics. There was a bit of screaming and the lights went on and meanwhile Karl pulled us broadside the length of the line while I tied it to the side of our boat then went back and loaded the cannon. Looked like we'd hit a boatful of college-aged Arabs and their girlfriends. I'd heard there were a lot of Arabs at Gannon, the all-men Catholic college downtown, must have heard that from Funly who resented their cavorting around town in German convertibles blasting Sufi Dervishes on their car stereos and littering. I attached our waterproof frogman grab bag to a pulley on the line and sent it over to them.

"Tax man," said Karl on his bullhorn. "This is the way we do it over here." Then he explained to them how we had the Coast Guard bands monitored so they better not try to call for help, or try anything for that matter, or we'd blow them out of the water. I waved from the cannon. Karl showed them an M16.

They were certainly a gracious bunch, spent a lot of time yelling over to us in funny English that they weren't Arabs, they were Iranians, I guess something like being from Cleveland, Mississippi, instead of Cleveland, Ohio, and once that was explained I guess they expected us to tell them everything was okay and go home, like there was some kind of connection between knowledge and good, and maybe there was for all we knew, so Karl reexplained the situation to them which didn't go over so big over there, and immediately their English got worse.

Karl must have had lots of experience robbing foreigners because he simply gave them two-minute notice to cough up or sink, which produced a little conference on that end and then they sent the bag back over to us with fifty bucks and a watch.

"You just can't trust people," said Karl. We couldn't take the family to the zoo on that kind of money. He sent the waterproof frogman grab bag back over and told them to make us happy or we were coming aboard to wipe our butts with their Arabian flag, and of course they made him get it straight that they were Iranians not Arabs before they sent the bag back over with a decent amount of jewelry and $400.

Well if they sent us that much you had to figure there was at least double that still over there, they probably had half the wealth of Irania over there on that boat, but you couldn't spend all night in the middle of Lake Erie negotiating with Arabs. It was just the price we'd have to pay to remain anonymous. So after Karl checked out our booty we told them they could throw the hook over and then all stay right there on deck while we backed away and they all better just stay right there and not shoot any flares or call the Coast Guard until we got turned around or they'd be swimming. So I reeled in the hook and we backed off. They waved. We waved. It was rather pleasant.

Which didn't last very long. Those Iranians had a change of heart as soon as we got turned around. Of course we weren't too worried because by that time I had both auxiliary outboards dropped and we headed for our home berth at about a hundred thousand miles an hour, not quite as quickly though as the Coast Guard cruiser that came caroming out of the little inlet we'd passed on the way to our business transaction, except now there wasn't just one little light flickering in there but lots of lights, looked like somebody was having a party. Anyway now we knew where the Coast Guard station was, no matter how well you plan I guess you always forget something.

Erie hadn't been invaded by Ohio or Canada for a few years and the Coast Guard, by the sound of it on the radio, didn't know quite what to make of a bunch of Arabs screaming about cannons, otherwise we might have drawn a more adamant reaction, though that cruiser was scary enough, being twice our size and apparently gaining. At first we put our lights out but after they sent up the flares it didn't make much difference, felt like we were traveling inside our own little baby lightning storm only orange. They tried to talk to us over the radio, addressing us as the "unidentified vessel," but Karl turned them off because it was too disturbing and I had to agree, we had nothing to say to those guys, it just wasn't one of those situations that you talked out, so soon enough we could hear them squawking at us on their bullhorn, nothing really articulate amidst all the noise of the engines and the popping and sizzling of those flares, I guess they just had more faith in the human ability to communicate.

We might have thrown everything overboard, money, jewelry, M16s, but that cannon was cemented to the bow pretty good. There weren't any whales in Lake Erie to speak of, probably illegal to hunt them anyway, besides we didn't have any fishing gear, we never thought about getting caught and covering up. After all, we were only out on our first little trial enterprise, no big deal, though at present it looked like we'd miscalculated on a few accounts; nonetheless I was barely scared until they started firing the warning shots.

"Not good," said Karl. That was the first thing either of us had said for quite a while.

Karl tried some evasive swerving and had me load the clips into the M16s, but they kept gaining, getting close enough now that we could hear them squawking to "cease and desist."

"I suppose you haven't been in a gunfight before," Karl said to me.

I meant to tell him about the Battle of Quebec but instead I puked, though having done so I felt a little better, even if my stomach didn't quite clear until the bullets started hitting the boat, exploding from the cruiser in neat little cracks and pops, tiny moments of light like minute sparklers, and then a beautiful silence before the thud and crackle against our deck and hull, I could even see them as they came in, like a ball off a baseball bat, I felt like I could hit them back. I heard Kara Ruzci singing.

Karl swerved the boat like crazy but it didn't do much good. "Take the gun with you," he said to me, "and load the cannon. I'll tell you when to let them have it."

In the cabin, on the way to the bow, Crow was having a cigarette. "Deaf," he said to me.

"Easy for you to say," I told him.

He looked one way, then the other, blowing smoke from his nostrils. He looked like the wisest thing since the invention of potato chips.

I picked up a cannonball.

"Bombs away," said Crow.

Well it certainly was an experience of a lifetime. Karl quit swerving and began a wide circle back toward the cruiser, which must have confused them some because for a minute or so they quit firing, though eventually they must have figured we were doubling back because they radioed for more boats and began to cut us off at an angle, which of course is what we wanted, we sure couldn't wait for more boats to get there and we couldn't fire the cannon backwards, seeing as it was on the bow, and we sure didn't want to get in a broadside with them either. They had a big spotlight trained on us from the front of their cruiser and that's what Karl told me to aim for, only a little higher, and he'd have me fire when they were pretty much coming straight at us.

Soon enough the flares started up again, and the gunfire. I don't know what they were thinking, maybe they thought they were on some kind of holiday. If we were the right boat it didn't seem like they'd taken much cognizance of the fact that we hadn't fired back at them, let alone if we were the wrong boat. It got me a little mad thinking that maybe we could have been the wrong boat and there they were firing away at us like we were armed and dangerous, though maybe that's what they wanted to work out on the radio. Nonetheless the inequity of it all started working away on me. We hadn't fired a shot at anybody, we were just running away, and it seemed like if we were running away it was fair enough to chase us but not shoot at us, we hadn't done any shooting, they were going to get real upset when we started shooting back, like that was some kind of major transgression of the social code, shooting back.

Being faster than us and now having an angle they made up

ground pretty quick. Their big white bow came slashing at the black lake, making foam, the sparks from their guns like firecrackers, and the whittling of their bullets against our hull, the drone of the boat like a groan from lake bottom; underneath that, that's where I heard Kara Ruzci's voice, a pale carol of dream that I sang with as I loaded the cannon under that soft rain of bullets and stars and mist of lake.

"What's that noise?" yelled Karl.

"I'm singing," I said.

"Get ready," he yelled.

I sang. And then I saw him, wavering between our boat and the cruiser, standing only a few feet away, standing on the water, a man stood weeping.

"Fire!" yelled Karl.

I aimed for his heart.

I DON'T KNOW what they were expecting but apparently it wasn't the kind of welcoming we gave them. After I fired the cannon we gave them everything we had in the rifles and then headed out fast as bass. That cruiser swerved in forty-six different un-directions, none of them toward us, then stopped cold, it must have been five minutes before one of the crew got off the deck and got on the radio for help. They didn't have any casualties or even any damage, apparently I didn't even hit them, but we sure did scare them right into the floorboards, like it was just their prerogative, being on the side of the law, to go around shooting at people and the last thing they expected was reciprocity.

That night me and Karl dismantled that boat piece by piece, loaded it onto the back of his truck and put it in his basement. The Coast Guard went back and arrested the Arabs, found a lot of pot and cocaine on board, linked them to a drug ring. Speculations were that we were in cahoots with them and crossed them, and not familiar with the thoroughness of the American justice system they called the Coast Guard not expecting to get drawn in, and of course now they were clammed up tight and refused to give up any information about us, only proving what a big-time operation we must be if those Arabs, though they called themselves Iranians, were more afraid of us than the police. From the account the Coast Guard gave of the battle you'd of thought they just fought off the Spanish Armada, sunk one of our ships and the other two got away, frogmen and recovery vessels were out on the lake right that moment looking for bodies, drugs, and pieces of sunk boat, even found a few pieces, said the wood looked like it was grown in Cuba, pretty scary.

Me and Karl split the $400 down the middle because it looked like those Arabian jewels weren't going to be worth too much for a little while, certainly not worth as much as the $6 million worth of drugs, street value, that the Coast Guard figured we made off with; those jewels were hotter than fodder, but added on to the Bobby Hansen money I had left it gave me well over $300 for Bush's next Last Christmas and various other living expenses till me and Karl reconstructed the *Armada* in the spring, plenty of money considering I didn't have to support the family anymore now that Red was selling toilet paper like tickets to the Olympics and Helen was taking over Marycrest.

So I went down to the next block beyond German Avenue on 24th Street to Mr. and Mrs. B's and gave Mrs. B the other $5 for Polly Doggerel.

"She using the toilet?" asked Mrs. B.

"Well yes she does," I told her. "But she doesn't bring back change if you send her out for hamburgers."

"We don't eat hamburgers," said Mr. B.

"Not since Mr. B got diabetes," said Mrs. B.

"Diabetes," said Mr. B. "She's the one should have got diabetes. Just look at her."

"Mr. B is ill tempered since he lost his legs," said Mrs. B. "How's that white dog we sold your brother?"

"He sure was a jumping dog," said Mr. B.

"You're right about that," I said.

"You going to pay for him?" said Mrs. B. "Your brother said you were going to pay for him."

"Well he's wrong," I told Mrs. B. "He gets disability money, he can pay for him."

"Only charged him three dollars," said Mrs. B. "Practically gave him away."

"Jumped too much," said Mr. B. "I couldn't stand all that damn jumpin."

"He was certainly a jumper," said Mrs. B.

I gave Mrs. B three bucks.

"That's a nice jacket you got there," said Mr. B. He lifted himself up on his hands like a little tiny swing set.

"That your girlfriend on the back?" said Mrs. B.

"Looks like a drawing from one of them Egyptian pyramids," said Mr. B.

"That's close," I said.

"Don't Mr. B look like one of them little lawn chairs they got out that sit real close to the ground?" said Mrs. B.

Mr. B raised his cane at Mrs. B but Mrs. B took it right away from him, looked like Mr. B was going to cry. You could see he was having a hard time adjusting to not having any legs.

"He used to beat me," said Mrs. B. "But as you can see, that don't happen anymore."

"I just want to get drunk and die," said Mr. B.

"I don't know if I'd feel good about that or not," said Mrs. B.

Of course I continued to see Kara Ruzci who was beginning to inevitably learn more and more about me. One night after much wine and long tremendous holding of each other that made me feel like she rubbed the softest part of herself against the deepest part of me and put it to sleep, Kara Ruzci gave me those moments of the sweet black nothingness of love, bringing me back again by whispering and singing in my ear some fairy tales she made up herself, during one of those nights I told her about me and Karl, and how I got my camera, and about Bobby Hansen and our friend Mr. Tony Blanion, and even the truth about the *Armada* and the Arabian Lake Erie drug dealers.

"I know," said Kara Ruzci. "You dream about them all the time."

Not all the time. Many of my dreams now, even when I wasn't sleeping with Kara Ruzci, were still Kara Ruzci dreams, even when Kara left for a month to visit Igor Kresky and have a show in New York, we still had our dreams, and nights together, after love, after dreams, after Kara Ruzci rose to sing to the man I knew stood before us at the foot of her bed, I lay awake, because I knew that if I slept I would dream the rest of the night alone, and so I watched her soft face against the dim light, watched the movement of her eyes beneath her lids, watched her lips, her breath, and suffered, knowing that even as I held her, entered her, enveloped her, she eluded me.

Down toward Celebration Avenue, towards Dean Danger's Bar & Grill, in the house before the Magicians', we got some Appalachians, the Ludlows, first whites to move into the neighborhood for some time and even noisier than the Puerto Ricans, though not because of any kind of music, the favorite thing those Appalachians liked to do was have dogfights and they spent a lot of time in their backyard doing just that, having dogfights, and on Wednesday nights their yard was full of towheads and dogs. They had the dogs in cages, and when they were ready to have them square off they stuck a big stick in the cage and harassed the dog till he bit it and then they just picked him up by the stick, took somebody on each end for the bigger ones, and carried him out to the center of the yard where his opponent hung from a stick, then they'd poke those dogs till they let go and went after each other, sounded like something out of the Jurassic Era, and they just let those dogs kill each other unless somebody decided to give up, then he'd stick his stick between those dogs and if he got lucky his dog bit it and he dragged it off, not the prettiest of sights, Helen didn't even want to let Honky out in the yard to witness it.

Karl said they used those sticks because a good fighting dog's jaws locked when he clamped down hard on something. I could see he was pretty fascinated by the whole business. He kind of looked like an Appalachian himself, though he made it pretty clear once the Ludlows moved in that he originated from somewhere inside Boston, explained how come he knew so much about patriotism for one thing, but all this dog renewal made him a little nervous, with Honky jumping around like a beach ball on one side of him, his latest diversion that of snatching starlings in flight, ate them in a gulp, and the Appalachian dogfights going on on the other, Karl felt like he was falling behind in a potentially new inner-city trend. It was hard enough looking across the street at Neda and Funly's rocket rising out of Funster's backyard like a cloud hypo. So Karl went down to Mr. and Mrs. B's and got himself some kind of Tibetan giant wolf dog, looked like a brown abominable snowman, called him Einstein because he had such a big head, between him and Honky it turned our adjacent yards into a meeting of the minds.

Worst part of it all was that the Puerto Ricans and several of the black families on the block decided things had gone a little bit too far in the down direction and packed off and moved farther south to better neighborhoods, something which provoked 24th Street's first neighborhood meeting, held one Saturday morning down at Dean Danger's Bar & Grill at which most of the neighborhood apart from Red and Dean Danger was conspicuously absent and at which nothing was settled but that Dean Danger would only rent the top of his flat to more Puerto Ricans, he'd got real attached to that horn music and couldn't find the records anywhere in Erie.

Then Bush had her Last Christmas.

~~~~~~~~ Bush's Last Christmas

BUSH WAS CERTAINLY an old human being, you had to give her that. Bush had been old all my life and alive all of hers, one of the things she regretted most about living so long, and probably nobody knew that better than Helen who knew Bush from the moment she, herself, was a baby, and in her own quiet way certainly seemed to have the ability to know certain things, not that unverifiable knowledge wasn't already a blight in that neighborhood, so much so that you didn't know who to believe, which pretty much put you back where you started, but Helen didn't have a Crow or a halo or a radio system or hear voices, she was a self-proclaimed sender, not a receiver, that ambiance of denial was enough to make a believer out of you, if not a skeptic, or both, so when she said it might be Bush's very Last Christmas you had to think about it, and that Christmas Eve, after Helen made everybody eat fresh deep-fried perch from Lake Erie and some kind of fried egg stuff stuck back into the shells along with french fries and everything else fried, it was like a regular Polish Dean Danger's, some kind of Catholic tradition, then Helen lit up the holy room and invited everybody to pray, though it was difficult to know whether we'd be praying for it to be Bush's Last Christmas or *not* to be Bush's Last Christmas, which of course nobody was stupid enough to ask because that was too obviously the dilemma, besides I suppose Helen had split that dualism long ago, there was just a certain kind of seriousness with which one approached the world to Helen's mind and issues like Bush's Last Christmas brought them to a pinnacle.

"Rings of Protestantism," said Neda.

But by Christmas morning Bush had survived another year and after talking to her on the phone Red and Helen went off to mass. They'd been getting along okay recently and when they did Red went to church with Helen because church was church to Red. Bush and Jon went off to church down at Holy Rosary to hear mass in Polish now that little fat Pope John XXIII said you didn't have to have mass in Latin anymore, so without Bush and Jon involved we figured Red and Helen would be back in time to catch one of the other favorite rituals of the neighborhood, the symbolic rubbing out of St. Franky Gorky to which his parents Greta and Gary Gorky and living brother Georgie returned from the cemetery where they'd left presents at Franky Gorky's grave and put a candle on the street where Franky got rubbed out by a drunk driver, until, of course, somebody came along and rubbed the candle out too.

But we were wrong. The Gorkys got up and left two hours early.

"You don't know how hard it was slipping in there last night and moving all their clocks two hours ahead," said Andrew heading out the door with a candle and his halo, the Franky Gorky doll with a chestnut for a head stuffed under his arm.

"What if he's at the graveyard waiting for his presents?" said Joseph.

Which made about as much sense as anything else, given the circumstances, you had to figure even if everything was perfect nothing was going to happen, nobody ever heard any of the voices Andrew did anyway, which was certainly as it should be, if anybody else could do the same things and get the same results it wouldn't be very special. Communication was an art, not a science. Given that Franky Gorky wasn't a number it didn't matter how things added up. I tried to figure out about a hundred times whether Franky Gorky was going to be early or late for the symbolic massacre, now that the clocks were two hours ahead, or what it would mean if he was on time. I tried to think how it worked on Daylight Savings Time but it got too confusing, and Andrew never said which direction he changed Franky Gorky's clock anyway. I put on my Dialecticians jacket and went out to the curb.

Andrew had the garden hose stretched halfway down the block and was watering the street in front of the Gorkys'.

"That should freeze up in about twenty minutes, don't you think?" he said to me.

"How did you set Franky Gorky's clock?"

"Two hours ahead of Greta and Gary Gorky's," said Andrew. "Not that it matters. Time has stopped for Franky Gorky."

Now Joseph came out to the curb in front of the Gorkys'.

"You just had a phone call," he told Andrew.

"You take a message?"

"I answered it with my bad ear," said Joseph.

"Probably Jon's voices," said Andrew. "They don't like the mass in Polish." He gave me the hose. "You want to put that back for me?"

"No." When Andrew got cold he turned blue like he looked when he was born, only when he was a baby he hardly had any hair and now he had a hairline like Edju's only thicker.

"Don't be cynical," he said to me. "I didn't ask for this. People don't choose their relationship to the other spheres." He gave Joseph some sheet music. "I'd really appreciate it if you'd play this for me."

It was hard not to accommodate your youngest brother when he was blue and wearing a halo. I put the hose away and Joseph went into the house and hooked up his guitar.

"You need help with anything else?" I asked Andrew when I got back.

"No," he said, "better leave me alone, I'll be centering soon anyway." He patted me on the shoulder as I left. "Ritual is everything to the departed," he said.

The best view was from our bedroom window, where Joseph sat down and memorized Andrew's music while I watched Andrew fix a string to the sycamore tree in front of the Gorkys' and run it across to the telephone pole near Funster's driveway, then he attached that Franky Gorky doll with a horse chestnut for a head to a tiny pulley, kept the string tight with a slip knot on the sycamore tree; all he had to do was release that knot and the Franky Gorky doll would head streetward. He took a life-size head-and-shoulder profile of a Polish grandmother and taped it to the driver's window of a car parked across the street. He let several cars pass, undoubtedly waiting for a drunk. He checked his watch. This whole time business was still pretty much a mystery to me, but why doubt Andrew when it came to mysteries, when he wasn't vague he was wrong.

Maybe he just got cold, he was looking bluer by the minute, because in a little while Andrew gave Joseph the signal to start playing, some combination of "Silent Night" and "Where the Boys Are," and went out and lit his candle on the spot where many unknowable years ago, Franky Gorky bought it; and sure enough, around the corner of 24th Street and Celebration Avenue came a swerving car, whoever was driving couldn't tell a road from a knockwurst, you could see that the biggest problem for Andrew would be keeping that guy on the street till he got to the scene. When he got about halfway to the Gorkys' Andrew released the slip knot.

The Franky Gorky doll moved about six inches.

That put Andrew in a panic. He might have been a major leaguer when it came to the otherworldly but it looked pretty much like all the technological proclivity in the family went to Neda, along with most everything else. Andrew gave that Franky Gorky doll a shove but only got it to move about another foot, and that drunk driver, mistake-ridden as he was, was getting closer every second. Andrew took a look at the approaching car, hesitated, then headed into the street with the doll.

You certainly had to admire that kind of commitment.

Just then, from around the corner of German and 24th, barreling like a loud mouse from the opposite direction, came the Gorkys, Georgie Gorky at the wheel looking like the elderberry who ate Christmas. They must have figured out the business about the clocks and come rushing back to get everything right, putting their stupid juvenile delinquent son on the gas pedal for the sake of speed. Andrew didn't even see them. He got that Franky Gorky doll out in the middle of the street just in time and headed for the curb.

Slipped on the ice.

The drunk driver swerved to avoid hitting Andrew and the Franky Gorky doll so of course hit them both. Georgie Gorky hit the breaks to avoid sliding into the drunk driver, hit Andrew's ice patch and went broadside. BANGO. Andrew went down somewhere in between those two cars.

Boy was Red going to be pissed.

Joseph didn't even come out of shutdown, he just changed his tune from the combination of "Silent Night" and "Where the Boys Are" to a bass note version of "Here Comes the Bride" as I headed out, running into Neda in the hallway.

"What," said Neda.

"I think Andrew sold his pony in front of the Gorkys'."

"Red will really be pissed," said Neda.

"I better go out there," I said to her.

"Patriarch Junior," said Neda. "Let me know what happened, I'm feeling a little self-destructive myself."

Cerebration sure kept Neda cool in a crisis. When I got outside the drunk driver had already hightailed, an obvious veteran of confrontation, while Gary and Greta Gorky nodded in the front seat of their old round Chevrolet, their eyes waddling like ding and dong. Georgie Gorky, a true hard-ass, was puking out the window of the driver's side. Andrew lay in the street on his back, his arms twisted under him, his legs bent like his knees had reinvented bending.

"Pt," said Andrew. He coughed up some blood. I got that

feeling like there was something racing around in me that didn't belong in there, it made me want to cry.

"How do I feel?" mumbled Andrew.

"You feel lousy," I said.

"I'm not blue anymore."

"No," I said. "A little flatter."

"Arms akimbo," said Andrew.

A cold, cold wind swept down 24th Street, and then it got quiet, like a giant ghost had lain belly down on us, silent and cold. The Gorkys leaned quietly against each other in their car. Georgie sat on the curb with his head in his hands. It began to snow, thick dead flakes in the quiet blanket air, and above us Crow circled, slowly, slowly circled, a black message in the snow, raising his wings and offering a simple, stark, "Caw."

Bush's Last Christmas,
Continued

Deaf in the
Past Partial

S OMETIME AFTER THE time I was born but before I was
old enough to know anything because I don't remember any
of it, Red and Helen took some of the money they saved up
during the war from working while having a lot of their expenses
paid by the government and meanwhile renting the house on 24th
Street, before Red ever socked a door off and long before you
could buy a house down there for less than a car, as the case is
now, they took that money and along with Uncle Bif, and Aunt
Jelly who had one little tiny leg from when she had polio as a
child, and invested in a small store down near the Bay on Celebration Avenue and called it the Celebration Five & Dime where
they sold everything in the world including aspirin and white
bread and comic books, cough drops and soda pop and boric acid,
Alka Seltzer and milk shakes, you could even have Red fry you
up a hamburger or grilled cheese on the grill behind the counter
that had swiveling stools in front of it, have yourself a cup of
coffee or an ice cream soda, though you couldn't get a Limburger
and onion on rye sandwich.

Each family was always responsible to have somebody down
there so there'd always be two people in the store though usually

it was best to have Helen with Bif and Red with Jelly because Red always fought with Helen and Bif, not that he didn't fight with Jelly, he did, he just fought with her less because it was hard to fight with somebody who limped around on one regular and one little tiny leg, especially Jelly who got quiet when she got mad and tried to make herself busy around the store so to fight with her you had to follow her around and it was hard to yell at the back of a tiny limping person. Red worked at the Forge and Bif was a janitor at the 7-Up plant and they came down and worked at the Celebration Five & Dime depending on their shifts.

The Celebration Five & Dime had a nice location with the Polish working neighborhoods on the other side of Celebration Avenue to the southeast and a working-class Italian neighborhood where the Irish used to be to the northeast and farther down toward the Bay a bunch of Orthodox Russians. On the other side of Celebration, in the neighborhood behind the store, were a lot of old mansions, remnants of the old Erie Yankees, where nice white Catholic college boys from all around the northwest part of Pennsylvania, from places like Oil City and Franklin and Punxatawney and Titusville, rented apartments while attending college downtown at Gannon. They got a nice mix of people in the Celebration Five & Dime.

Nonetheless the arrangement sometimes made Helen a little nervous. She had her open mind about as open as it could get dealing with Red the returning Marine who at moments seemed like he could kill anything or anybody and sometimes did, the biggest threat being to Jarvis Jr. who Red didn't want to be called Jarvis Jr. and who went around revenging his name upon the world. Though it was all understandable, if that wasn't the worst thing about it, it was all so understandable; Helen was understanding her head off and succeeding only too well, which only led her to try to be more understanding, once you start being understanding there just doesn't seem to be any way to stop, it would be insensibly rigid to just start closing your mind arbitrarily. So when Red wanted to start the store with Bif and Jelly,

Helen went along with it even though Jelly was Protestant and Bif disconverted from Catholicism, and Red, even though he married Helen, didn't go so far as to embrace the One True Church, made her doubt how much Red really loved her, after all Bif was willing to go to hell with Jelly and Red wasn't even willing to go to heaven with Helen, and it looked like in that one little corner of the universe the Lutherans had pulled a coup. Though Helen figured she could always outreproduce Jelly, but that kind of thinking always made her feel petty and tired, besides, sometimes she thought that the only person in the Five & Dime who had any perspective on the whole deal was Jelly who limped around filling shelves saying stuff like the place was doomed anyway, if Bif didn't gamble all the profits away then Red would just get mad someday and blow it up.

"Bif doesn't gamble," said Helen who sometimes ended up in the store with Jelly when Red and Bif had the same shifts.

"Not yet he doesn't," said Jelly. "But now that he has a chance to ruin everything for everybody he'll probably start."

Jelly was certainly a pessimist but that probably came from being brought up Protestant all her life without any exposure to anything else, part of that mystical balance between environment and Providence that created a lot of fuzzy areas; back then Helen didn't have the Infant but her faith was simpler.

One thing Red liked about owning part of and working in the Celebration Five & Dime was that it was lunch omnipresent. Whoever came in there Red was always encouraging them to have a hot dog or a hamburger or six, maybe a milk shake, and Red always lost track of how many or how much of whatever he was supposed to make which put him in the position of giving the customer a little extra and having to eat up the leftover food himself, made him a real popular man behind the counter. Then he'd sit down behind the counter and have long conversations about the war or the great South High football teams of the thirties who went down to Ohio and beat teams like Niles and Massillon who only had one high school in their whole cities with no age limit for playing so started hordes of ex-professional thirty-five-year-old football stars, and the time when Babe Ruth came to Erie, Pennsylvania in the late twenties and hit twenty consecutive exhibition home runs over the wall at Ainsworth Field, he'd just point to where he was going to hit it and then knock it out of the park, hit the last one right over the four-story Roosevelt Junior High School that served as the centerfield wall after he was getting tired and had accumulated his first two strikes of the day, just pointed over the school and hit it there, then walked out of the park to a standing ovation, a pretty big day in Erie and Red saw it, though if you pushed him he'd admit he didn't see it, his dad Whitey did, though Whitey denied seeing it, Whitey Loop said Babe Ruth never came to Erie and if he did it sure didn't make the papers, though everyone knew it really happened, there were hundreds of thousands of Erie-ites who'd seen it or knew somebody who did.

One day when Helen was minding the store with Bif a woman came into the Celebration Five & Dime who had a certain way about her that was real familiar to Helen, she walked like she was born in high heels and wore a tight skirt that made her back end look like a heart, she was blond and no matter what she did with her hands that had red painted nails they looked like little doves, made you want to put white gloves on them to protect them. Bif noticed her right away. He was carrying a case of empty soda bottles down into the basement and bringing cases of full ones back up, usually spent about as much time downstairs as it took to get in a hand of solitaire, but now he was having a harder and harder time collecting the empties upstairs and getting the new bottles into the coolers. The woman went up and down all couple of the Five & Dime aisles several times and Bif was still upstairs. Helen always did wonder about Bif and women, given that Jelly was a little lopsided with that one little tiny leg.

Finally the woman came up to Helen at the counter. "Honey," she said, "you got any of that there Alberto VO5 Hair Spray?"

Well Helen did have some Alberto VO5 Hair Spray, in fact

it was the only hair spray they had at the Celebration Five & Dime, seeing as there wasn't a lot of shelf space the selection process wasn't left to the consumer and hair spray was one of the things Helen ordered, and she, herself, always used Alberto VO5 Shampoo, ever since the war. She tried to remember why she started using Alberto VO5 Shampoo, seemed like a big step at the time, in fact she figured she did remember, she just didn't remember right then with that blond woman with hands like red beaked doves standing in front of her, matching lips.

Helen went over to the wall shelf across from the Luden Wild Cherry Cough Drops and Bayer Aspirin and got the gold can with red and black Alberto VO5 written on it at an angle. She turned around and the woman was right there, she was probably about as tall as Helen if she took her heels off. "Just watchin where you keep it, sugar," she said.

When she paid at the counter she noticed Bif staring from the cellar door and gave him a look that made him walk downstairs backwards. Then she looked at Helen, gave her a feeling like she was living in the wrong tense.

"That's not your husband, is it, honey?" she said.

"No," said Helen.

Several customers later, after Bif came upstairs and saw that the woman had left so went back to spending more time downstairs playing solitaire, Bif came back upstairs and Helen said to him, "Bif, why did you stare at that woman?"

Bif said, "What woman?"

And Helen said, "The blond woman."

And Bif just shook his head and said, "heh, heh," Bif said heh, heh or ha! a lot, which probably came from spending too much time with Grandpa Whitey Loop who said heh, heh after everything and who'd let Bif and Jelly move in with him and Grandma Emma because Bif and Jelly were always broke even though Bif made about as much money as Red, maybe more.

"Painted nails," said Helen. "A southern accent."

"Ha!" said Bif.

"You were staring," said Helen.

"Just a while ago?" said Bif.

"Yes."

"Because you went over and got a can of Alberto VO5 and then went to the cash register and had a conversation with nobody, ha."

Well Bush had always told Helen that some men remained faithful simply by insisting they were; find him in your bed with another woman and say, who's that woman? and he says, what woman? pretends she's not even there until she's out the door and then she really isn't there, then it's his word against yours.

But Helen knew there were things that could happen and things that couldn't happen, unless they were miracles, and she couldn't sell a can of Alberto VO5 Hair Spray to nobody and it wouldn't be a miracle if she did, that would certainly be a wasted miracle if you ever saw one, and she didn't want to fight with Bif about it. She checked the hair spray shelf and it looked like a can was gone, but then she noticed that she forgot to ring up the sale on the cash register and when she inventoried the hair spray she found that she had an extra can, that is if she sold one. And Bif never said another word. The least he could have done if he was covering up was make another attempt to lie about it.

At the Erie Forge Red cut sheet metal. There were only three sizes of sheets he ever had to cut and it didn't take anything but being able to lift the huge sheets and hold them close enough to the blade to get the exact cut, you didn't even have to measure once you learned, you just knew what size and you did it. Karl always told me later that the simplest machines were the most dangerous and then he'd hold up his hand with hardly any fingers to prove it, though who knew where he lost those fingers, Karl liked to hold up that hand to explain lots of things; anyway that was Red's biggest problem too, keeping his mind on his work, especially when they gave him those big earmuffs to wear so he wouldn't go deaf from the banging of the cutting machine and he got to thinking about lunch, though that day the foreman came up to him and told him they were changing his machine and moved him during lunchtime, something that Red really

resented, he couldn't remember the last time his lunch got inter-
fered with, to the machine across from the big furnace and next
to the big sliding garage door where people traveling by in autos
on Greengarden Avenue, which didn't have any gardens nor
much green on it, at least not down there, mostly just a lot of
factories and train tracks, could look in while they waited for the
trains to pass, see the fire spurting from the furnace and the man
with black sweat shoving sheets into the cutting machine and
point and say to their kids who were licking ice cream cones on
their way to the beach, say, "That's why you should get an
education," which made about as much sense as a fence in
Nevada, and the foreman said to Red, "This here's the premier
cutting machine," and Red said, "Premier my ass," made him
think of Stalin, made his mind uneasily premonate, he liked it
better before the war when there weren't so many railroad tracks,
when there were even a couple trees out there, though there was
something he didn't like back then too, but right then, as he ate
his lunch next to the machine and waved at the kids in the back
of the autos while they licked ice cream cones and the trains went
by, right then he couldn't remember what it was, all he could
remember was a dream of bees buzzing in his tent on Midway,
but later, later when he went to work at his new machine, he
heard the first fresh buds of spring bursting on the maple trees.
After that day Red had trouble eating lunch.

And Helen had trouble remembering. Every other day or so
the woman with hands like painted doves and a voice like southern honey came into the Celebration Five & Dime and talked to
Helen, while in between times Helen thought and thought and
then suddenly remembered some significant connection, that
there was somebody else who held her hands like that, and
somebody else who walked on her heels like that, and somebody
else who wore lipstick to match her nails like that, and somebody else who always called her sugar or honey, and then suddenly, out of nowhere, as she was stacking shelves or cleaning the
counter or doing the books, it came to her, but as soon as it did
the woman came in the door for some Alberto VO5 Hair Spray

or Shampoo, or some matching nail polish and lipstick, something the store didn't used to carry but Helen started ordering once the woman kept coming by, and always matching, no matter how beautiful the shade of pink or red or fuchsia Helen didn't order it unless it came in both nail polish and lipstick, but when that woman started talking to Helen, she forgot everything, she forgot all the significant connections, she forgot what was so special about the way the woman held her hands and did her lips and nails, she forgot what was so familiar about her voice; she knew there were things she was supposed to remember, things she wanted to ask, but she always forgot, she forgot who she thought the woman was, she forgot to ask her name, she just talked and listened about most anything and afterwards couldn't remember about what, then she'd always find one extra of whatever she sold, and if Bif or Jelly were in the store, they just never seemed to be upstairs or up front when the woman came around. If Red was in the store she never came at all.

Well you'd think after a while with all that stuff Helen sold the woman, but always counting up and finding nothing missing, that the store'd find itself a little ahead, but every time Helen balanced the books everything came out perfect, the only problem was when Helen went to the bank to match numbers things didn't come out perfect, the store usually showed itself a little behind, and sometimes even showed itself a lot behind, but then just when Helen was about to panic and say something she'd go into the bank and things would be just about even again.

That wasn't something she wanted to talk to Red about. She figured he wasn't taking the money and she didn't want to accuse his relatives, she didn't know how he'd react to that, besides, she didn't think it was something Bif and Jelly would do together, and nothing Jelly would do herself, no, it had to be Bif, in that great unmentioning way men do things it was easier to get forgiveness than permission. Bif was okay as long as you didn't have to trust him, either that or she, herself, was going nuts, or both, or not; once she started thinking about it things only got worse.

Things went on like that into the summer. Red worked at his new cutting machine next to the furnace and in front of the big garage door that looked out at Greengarden Avenue and all the train tracks that headed west toward Bucyrus Erie and Zurn Industries and Cleveland, and east to the GE and Hammermill and Buffalo, and watched the kids bouncing beach balls in the backseats of cars and licking ice cream cones, and he thought about hard salami sandwiches and homemade ham salad sandwiches and baloney sandwiches and liverwurst sandwiches, none of which he could eat when he finally got to lunch because when he sat down to lunch all he could think about was the birds he heard hatching and the grass pushing up from underneath the ground like the hairs of the dead and the sound the honey bees made when they drowned themselves at the bottom of a flower, all of which he heard under his earmuffs at the cutting machine, and the muscles in his arms felt like they'd been beaten by the head of a rhinoceros, and he wanted to tell Helen but he didn't know what to say to her, he didn't know what he'd say. And Helen kept getting visitations from the woman with hands like small birds and the voice like the aftertaste of warm honey and talking about nothing and remembering all the wrong things and selling her the unquenchable supply of makeup and Alberto VO5 and finding just enough money in the store and not enough money in the bank, none of which was witnessed or acknowledged by Bif or Jelly.

I wish I could have been some help in this situation but I was too young, in fact I don't remember any of it because Helen didn't want me with her at the store, in fact Helen didn't like seeing kids in public at all, didn't like them crying at the movies, didn't like them screaming at the zoo or grabbing stuff and crying for candy and toys in the grocery line, no, Helen liked kids at home playing quietly or sleeping then getting old enough to go to school and grow up and become scientists who could read Latin, which was just too much to expect from life, though I doubt it explains anything, but that's why I was never at the store and never knew anything about any of this, not that it would help, Red and Helen spent their lives separated by the chasm of the same reality.

One day later that summer and as usual with Bif down in the basement playing solitaire or unpacking crates, the blond woman came in with her hair up and wearing white heels and a tight white skirt with tucked-in white and black polka-dot nylon blouse and walked up and down the aisles of the store before coming up to the counter and saying to Helen, "You aint got hair dye, do you, honey?"

"Not too many people come in here for hair dye," said Helen.

"Well honey, I do, and I'm a regular customer."

"What kind do you want?"

"Alberto VO5 make hair dye?" said the woman. She sat down on the swivel stool nearest the cash register. Helen couldn't remember her ever sitting down before and she looked to see if Bif might be coming up the stairs but he wasn't. She could get him, she guessed, but the woman might leave, or she could call for him, but the more she thought about it she thought that would kind of violate the implicit contract she and the woman had.

"They don't make it under that name," said Helen. "They probably make it under another name."

"Like Clairol."

"Yes," said Helen.

"Well sugar, why don't you order me some red Clairol." She showed Helen her nails. "Something that matches."

"It could be a while," said Helen.

"I can wait, honey. I'm real good at waitin."

"You could just get it someplace else."

"Now honey, you know how hard it is finding somebody you can trust. This here's where I coiffuse." She looked at her nails though Helen could see she wasn't thinking about them. "I can wait," she said. "I can wait a long time."

Helen went over to the fountain. "You want a vanilla phosphate?" she asked. "On me?"

"Well that would be a real delight," said the woman. "You're real sweet."

Helen squeezed vanilla into the Coke glasses and added seltzer, stirred it. She kept trying to remember something, anything, but when the woman was around it was like she'd never had a thought till she started working at the Five & Dime. She brought the woman the phosphate.

"You got a child?" said the woman.

"Little boy," said Helen.

"Name him after the old man?"

Helen didn't want to say yes and she didn't want to say no. Her head was ringing like a phone with nobody home. "It's a long story," she said, though she couldn't remember the story.

"Always is, sugar," said the woman.

"No one calls my husband by his name. They call him Red."

"Like my nails."

"Yes," said Helen.

"Mind if I smoke, honey?" said the woman. She took a pack of Lucky Strikes from her purse and Helen moved a Niagara Falls ashtray across the counter. She and Red didn't smoke though they had plenty of Niagara Falls ashtrays brought back from their honeymoon. But Bif smoked and he both filled them and cleaned them. Helen wanted to see that lipstick-covered butt left in the ashtray.

"My old man promised me a child for years," said the woman. "Dragged me halfway around the country, went to war, did everything he wanted to do while the time was right. Now it's too late."

"You're not too old," said Helen.

"Not too old. Too late."

"Something happened," said Helen.

"Something always happens."

The woman finished her cigarette and her phosphate. Helen noticed her eyes fix on a deck of playing cards that Bif must have taken off the shelf and forgot to take downstairs with him. "I knew some cardplayers in my day," said the woman.

"What day was that?" said Helen.

"Honey, you should be runnin a bank, not a five 'n' dime."

"I have a little girl too," said Helen.

The woman got up. "Now you order me that hair dye, sugar."

When Red came into the Celebration Five & Dime that evening he felt like he'd spent the day fielding meteors, he had unexplainable cuts and bruises on his arms and his chest felt like he'd failed to digest a bowling ball. Once again he'd failed to eat his lunch.

"What's the matter," said Helen.

"The Chinese invaded Korea," said Red.

"Good thing we invaded first," said Helen.

"We had permission," said Red. "The whole world gave us permission."

Bif was upstairs now. "You look lousy," he said to Red.

"I feel lousy," said Red.

"We should just send them all the 7-Up they can drink, ha!" said Bif.

"Ha-shma," said Red. "They're kicking our asses."

"That's what I mean," said Bif.

"I should go," said Red.

"Where do you have to go?" said Helen. "You just got here."

"To Korea," said Red.

"We should send them Zenith televisions," said Bif. "That'd stop them, ha."

"You can't turn things around in Korea," said Helen.

"Who can't turn things around in Korea?" Red had a feeling he could turn things around in Korea. "Besides, you can't think like that."

"Who can't think like that," said Helen.

"Send them Velveeta cheese," said Bif. "That'll stop them."

"You can't go to war every time the country does," said Helen.

"Who can't," said Red. "I can fight whenever I want to."

"You have to give him that one," said Bif.

"You have children here. You have a mortgage. There's no war housing now. The war housing's filled with negroes." Back then you were supposed to call them negroes.

"I don't care about negroes. I never been hurt by negroes."

"Or Koreans," said Helen.

"Ha, we ought to send them Alberto VO5 Hair Spray," said Bif.

Helen iced him for that one.

"Make it Fudgsicles," said Bif.

Well Red was probably the last person in the world you should tell what to do, and Helen the second to last, or vice versa, so everything was proceeding about exact opposite of best, which was about par, but Red kept thinking about the Forge and all the minute sounds of life and death he kept hearing under his earmuffs, and he felt the soreness in his arms and chest and longed for the simple days of looking forward to and eating lunch, and probably the last thing he wanted to do was go to war but right then he felt like he did during the last war when the Marines were keeping him off duty in San Diego, you just couldn't trust a world that was conspiring to make you happy. And when Helen remembered the war she remembered long lonely train trips across the country and night after night alone waiting to find out that she could continue spending night after night alone, and she remembered blank spaces that she could only fill with death, and all the mysteries, all the top-secret stuff, and it made her think about the mornings of washing her windows outside the housing complex and saying hello to the young mothers and pregnant women, a place full of women and children, and mornings having coffee with Dee Delco, like she'd spent her last several months wandering around in a store having forgot what she came to buy.

"You might not spend this war in Hawaii pitching horseshoes," Helen said to Red.

"Ha, if that was true Red would probably bust this whole place up in a second," said Bif.

Red stuck out his bottom lip. "I'm going to Korea. You can make it with the store."

"Ugf," said Bif.

"Korea," said Helen. "Maybe after that you'll be too old."

"When I get too old I'll use a ball bat," said Red, which is what he always said when somebody mentioned he might get old, which wasn't always the greatest answer but it was an answer.

Helen looked at the Niagara Falls ashtray for the woman's cigarette but Bif had already cleaned it out.

It went on like that for a while. Every time the Marines had another setback Red said he was going to Korea, they'd just have to stop reinvesting in the store while Red was overseas turning the Korean War around and live off the money till Red got back, then they could start reinvesting again and turn the Celebration Five & Dime into a grocery store, sounded pretty good to Red, he'd say he was going to Korea and Helen told him he could go to hell because either way he wasn't coming back to her, Helen figured we could lose in Korea and it wouldn't matter, besides she was afraid to tell Red that somebody was siphoning off the profits of the store as it was, if she told him he was liable to tear the place apart and then there'd be nothing if he left, she figured somehow she'd work all that out herself.

Until one afternoon when Helen was minding the store with Jelly and Jelly said to her, "How come there aint no inventory? Bif's been staying here late every other night doing inventory."

And Helen didn't say anything as Jelly limped down the aisle of Sunbeam Bread and Campbell's Soup and said, "Well maybe it aint inventory he's doin," and limped back up the aisle and said, "and maybe he aint even here." She looked at Helen. "I aint the most beautiful woman in the world," which wasn't exactly true, Jelly had a round pretty face, and she was real short so that little tiny leg wasn't as disproportionate as it could be, relatively speaking. "Maybe Red could take him with him to Korea."

Helen figured it was time to show Jelly the books.

"We're makin money," said Jelly.

"You want to see what the bank says we have?" said Helen.

"No," said Jelly. "I don't want to know nothin. If I find out somethin I'll just have to find out somethin else. He's a man. I got this little leg. He aint leavin me. It's that simple."

Didn't seem very simple to Helen.

When the woman came in that afternoon for her hair color she made Helen sit down and drink a cherry Coke.

"Honey," she said. "You look awful distressful."

Helen looked at the woman. By this time of course she'd completely forgotten about her mornings during World War II when she washed the factory grime off the windowpanes and sills of her barracks apartment and said hello to the other pregnant women and the women with children as they walked by, and she forgot about having coffee in the morning with Dee Delco, and the card games in the afternoon, she'd forgotten all of it, but she sure did feel awful distressful.

"You said you were married," Helen said to her.

"Married as peach pie, sugar, once and forever."

"You're with him now."

"Well honey, I sure don't carry him around in my pocket, but we're married."

Helen looked around for Jelly, but she couldn't see her anywhere. "He fight in the last war?"

"Enlisted, but he flunked the physical. Flat feet. But that cracker stood on billiard balls till his feet looked like cups. He sure did want to fight."

"That story sounds familiar," said Helen.

"It's an old story," said the woman.

"He going to enlist in this one?" asked Helen.

"He don't fight no more honey, he's more ethereal now."

Well this woman could sure use the wrong word authoritatively. She lit a Lucky Strike. "Didn't your old man get enough in the last one?"

"I don't know what he got enough of and what he didn't," said Helen. "He doesn't talk about it."

"Sure are a strange gender," said the woman. "It's amazing

you have any desire for them at all when you think about it. Of course I try not to think about it." She put out her cigarette. "You think he's going to go?"

"Maybe."

"What would you give up to keep him?" She pulled out another Lucky and offered Helen one, which Helen refused, then took, at least when the woman left she'd have that Lucky.

"Sometimes I think he's the best man that ever lived," said Helen, "and sometimes I think he could go to hell and never come back and I'd be a lot better off."

"Well they're both probably kind of true, sugar," said the woman getting up. "You got that hair color?"

Helen gave her the box and the woman paid her.

"Well that's real pretty," she said. She put the change in her purse that matched her nails and lips and the hair color on the box. "How's your little store here doin?"

Helen looked at her and for a moment it was almost as if the woman wavered in front of her, as if she weren't really there.

"You okay, honey?" said the woman. "I'd just like to see this place succeed. You get too many people rubbin the lamp and you never know when one of them's going to take the genie to the racetrack." She lit a match. "You aint smokin, honey."

She lit Helen's cigarette but of course Helen not being a smoker she had a hard time getting it lit. The match went out and Helen concentrated hard on the end of her Lucky Strike that was barely burning. When she finally got it going she looked up and the woman was gone.

That's the first time Helen thought of following her. She put her cigarette out in the Niagara Falls ashtray and ran to the front door of the store, looked up and down the street and saw the woman turn the corner about a half-block away. Helen ran down to the corner but suddenly it seemed like everybody in the world was on the street or driving somewhere because there were people and cars everywhere, then about halfway down that block she saw a truck stop and a woman, it looked like a blond woman, get in. Helen ran in that direction but the truck took off long before she got to the spot. Still, she knew it was a green truck and she thought she saw a red and white decal on the door as it pulled off that said 7-Up.

Well they didn't even have a racetrack in Erie back then, the only legal gambling that occurred was at the Catholic church festivals and bingo games and the odds were so bad it was like putting your money in the basket, the only other time you could gamble at all, let alone on horses, was at the County Fair out at the fairgrounds in Wattsburg, and that was only when the Fair was going on, which just happened to be happening right then, coincidentally with the fact that Bif would be working a double shift that night so Jelly would be closing the store with Red, all of which had Helen thinking about the genie.

That night Red came into the Celebration Five & Dime like a tired bull, his arms ached, his head hurt, his heart felt like a rock in a crock. He'd just spent another day at the Forge dragging himself around like a wet belt and waiting for the lunch that he couldn't eat till he got back to his sheet cutting machine where he found a red rose that reminded him of something only he couldn't remember what, though it made him mad enough to give the earth a haymaker in the equator if only he wasn't so damned tired. But worse than all that, the Marines were now backed up on a little tiny beachhead on the southern tip of Korea and it looked like the only thing that could save the war was for Red to get his ass over there as fast as he could, which of course wasn't going to please Helen too much, but then Helen was a woman and had a mixed-up view of world politics as well as coming from a family which, as demonstrated by Edju and Jon, had an odd way of fighting wars.

So Red felt bad. He came in the store and put his fist in his palm and stared around like a gunslinger. Some things were hard to do but they just had to be done. He looked at Jelly.

"Don't look at me like that," said Jelly. "I got problems of my own."

Then Helen came from the back where she'd just stacked a new part of a shelf next to the Alberto VO5 Shampoo and Hair

Spray with various boxes of various colors, though mostly red, of Miss Clairol hair color.

"I got to go to Korea," said Red.

"Better order some more Hershey Bars and Swisher Sweets," said Helen, "because we're almost out of them."

Then she walked home the twenty some blocks up Celebration Avenue because back then it was safe enough to walk up Celebration Avenue and Helen didn't drive, she never did learn how to drive, told Tammy Turtle the babysitter she was going to have to stay a little longer with Jarvis Jr. and Neda, which was okay with Tammy Turtle, all she had to do was make a phone call and it would mean more bucks, besides she was probably in the middle of hanging from the swing set and having Neda poke her with laundry poles or tying herself up while Neda fed her dirt and rubbed the insides of her toes with tree bark; she and Neda were two sides of the same coin.

Then Helen walked up to the top of Celebration Avenue where it became two roads, the Old French Road which went through Germantown where Red was born and raised, and then out to Fort LeBoeuf where the French once had a fort that George Washington visited when he was just a mean teenager working for the British to tell the French that if they didn't leave the British were coming to shoot them in their eye whites, and Pine Avenue that became Wattsburg Road and went right out to the County Fair, in fact you could catch a bus there while the Fair was on and that's what Helen did.

Helen hadn't ever been to the Fair before because it wasn't the kind of thing her family did, there were a hundred Catholic festivals all over town in the summer that you could walk to, and it wasn't the kind of thing Red liked to do either. Other than work, which he had to do, Red liked to eat, then he liked to play handball or pitch horseshoes or bowl, he was just learning how to bowl, or play softball, all man things that took him out of the house and away from the family except sometimes for softball when Helen got Tammy Turtle to baby-sit and went and kept the official score for the Erie Forge team. She was always good at numbers, though she was also a good athlete, loved to swim and briefly held the girls' city records for the fifty yard dash, the standing broad jump, and the standing high jump, they didn't like girls running and jumping at the same time back then, and sometimes Helen regretted that she didn't get to do anything athletic anymore or even get out of the house away from the kids other than at the store, or even just go out and do something with Red like go to a movie or the County Fair, she'd have to talk to Red about it if he didn't go to Korea and die.

Helen had never thought about going to the Fair by herself before either, she only did it now because of the combination of crisis and intuition which only she could solve. In fact mostly Helen thought that women shouldn't do things by themselves, she thought women should do what they wanted and men should do it with them. There was a formative period in her life when she thought that was the case and those kinds of ideas died hard even in the face of facts indicating it was really just the opposite, except when men did things by themselves.

But now Helen was by herself at the County Fair where she had to pay a dollar just so she could get in and spend money, which didn't make a lot of sense, paying money so you could spend money, the Catholic summer festivals didn't charge you to get in, and this County Fair, at least the front part of it just inside the entrance gate, looked pretty much like a Catholic summer festival with strung Christmas lights down the fairways and lots of booths where you put your money down and somebody spun a wheel, or you tried to throw your money in something or Ping-Pong balls in something or some other kind of balls in something or at something, and there were food booths and amusement rides, though you couldn't get kielbasa or pirogi and there didn't seem to be any bingo, and there were a lot more cowboy hats and a lot more men yelled to her to come on over and they'd win her a Kewpie doll.

Also, there was livestock. Helen left the section with all the food and amusements and game booths and went through a section where people showed you appliances or showed you religion or tried to get you to give money to a charity or the zoo or the museum or the symphony or offered to tell you your weight or your future or your past by reading your head or your hands or your eyes or your tarot cards. At one booth there was the John Birch Society who looked like they were doing pretty good there was such a crowd. They gave out red, white, and blue pamphlets that said the Communists weren't just in Russia and China and Eastern Europe and Korea, they were everywhere and all over the United States, all of which Helen agreed with, including that the Communists were bad, though Helen thought the Communists would be okay if they just believed in God. They didn't have to be killed, they just had to be converted; you pray for people you don't shoot them, you shoot at them and they get mad and then the government sends your husband off to get killed because by that point everybody's just shooting back at everybody else and there's a lot of resentment.

That's what Helen was thinking about when she wandered into the livestock tents, that if the only rule in the world was that men weren't allowed to fight, that men couldn't be violent, it would go a long way toward solving the world's problems. Women and children could get by without rules. Helen got so carried away thinking about all that stuff and watching the bulls and cows and sheep and goats, and especially the chickens and rabbits that reminded her of Bush's pens at the back of the house where she fed the animals before breakfast and after supper, when her father Stanley was still alive and not depressed, and the world wasn't depressed or at war, Helen got so carried away that she forgot why she came to the Fair in the first place until she heard the announcement for the harness racing over the loudspeakers, made her feel tired all over. She couldn't remember when she felt so tired. She didn't want to go over to the harness races and look for the problems in her life, in fact right then the whole thing seemed like a pretty stupid idea, a ridiculous impulse that brought her to the Fair by herself to fight off men in cowboy hats who didn't really want to win her Kewpie dolls while her children were at home with a babysitter after already being at home alone all day and her husband who was about to go off and risk death in Korea was minding the store that would probably be the only thing she had to get by on when he left, though she worked her way back to reasoning that's why she was there, to save the store. How would she save the store?

Boy, Helen felt tired. She hadn't felt so tired since the night she went to the hospital with Dee Delco, the night Derk Delco Jr. was stillborn, the night she found out that Derk Delco Dad's Top Secret Mission was an eternal one, and not so tired again since the night Dee joined them both and she had her first child, Jarvis Loop Jr. She hadn't thought about any of that for so long, yet it felt so familiar, as if she'd never stopped thinking about it.

By the time Helen got to the harness racetrack, where she had to pay another admission charge for the chance to lose her money, there'd already been three races and the fourth was under way. It looked kind of ridiculous, the horses didn't run, they skipped, though it also looked kind of pretty the way they glided ahead of those tiny carriages like water bugs, looked more like wasp racing than horse racing. Helen walked through the grandstands a couple times and it was the seventh race before she found a spot where she could look at the racetrack, beer bar, and betting windows all in a glance. There were only going to be a couple more races anyhow so if she stuck it out at least she could go home thoroughly exasperated and partially relieved. Unfortunately she saw Bif at the winners' window after the seventh race with a face that looked not quite happy enough, he walked away from that window looking at his money and then looking at his race form and then looking at his money before gazing into the air and looking at his race form again. Then Helen saw a red-haired woman come up to Bif and put an arm around his waist. Bif pointed to the race form as the woman led him over to the betting windows and whispered in his ear, she moved around Bif like a cloud around a shroud, reminded Helen of the purple drapes they covered the statues of Jesus and Mary and the saints with in church during Lent, something kind of holy and sexual at the same time, incongruous as it seemed.

Helen didn't follow them, she just waited at her spot until the end of the eighth race when Bif came back to the winners' window looking real happy, he looked at his tickets happy while he waited in line and then he looked at his money happy when he came away from the window. When the red-haired woman came up to him he rubbed her shoulders and kissed her lips and threw away his race form, taking his green cap with the red 7 on it out of his back pocket and putting it on his head and taking the red-haired woman by the arm. But she didn't want to go. She made him pick up the race form again.

There was quite some discussion as those two went back over to the betting windows for the big last race, and Helen could see Bif shaking his head, he wasn't happy anymore, he was reluctant. The whole scene made Helen figure that whatever Bif had lost that night or ever from gambling the Celebration Five & Dime's money probably got won back and then some after that last race, and if it would have been any other moment in Helen's life other than the one it was she would have walked over there right then and taken the money from Bif that would have drawn the store's bank account even with its books, but she didn't, she couldn't move. So she watched Bif place his bets and walk away from the betting windows, and she watched the ninth race go to the longshot of the field, and saw Bif collapse in a heap in an aisle of the grandstand. He took off his cap and the red-haired woman kissed him on the forehead and walked away, began walking toward Helen, walking like she was born in high heels, with nails to match her red lips and red hair, she came toward Helen, and that's when Helen remembered everything, realized everything, and then quickly forgot it. She didn't even remember leaving the Fair and taking the bus home.

That next day Red went to the Marine Recruitment Office during his lunch, but the place was inexplicably closed. He pounded on the doors awhile before giving up, he couldn't figure out what kind of recruitment office would close for lunch during a war, especially the Marines, he was there and look how much lunch meant to him. But when he got back to his car he found a long-stemmed white rose pinned by the windshield wiper to his windshield, a white rose that he brought to Helen at the store after work, and he held her in his arms then while she cried and he felt the deep feeling of ache in his chest that he felt in those first months that he knew her, and those nights in San Diego before he went to war, that feeling that there was nothing in the world he wouldn't do for her, nothing he wouldn't protect her from; he loved her, he loved her more deeply than he had ever loved before.

And that night, the Celebration Five & Dime's bank account rubbed out by his gambling, Bif fessed up to Jelly and Helen and Red, fessed up that he had pretty much cleaned out the chances for the store, unless they wanted to take out a loan, though Red wasn't too big on taking out a loan, he and Helen had already put in the majority of the money to stake the place, money that Bif and Jelly were supposed to gradually pay back with their half of the profits, of course there was the store itself, and the merchandise, though there wasn't much of that left either after Red tore out the counter stools with his bare hands and put them through the mirror behind the counter. Bif and Jelly got out before he tore out all the shelves. "Goddamn place is ruined," said Red.

There wasn't anyplace for the woman with hands like painted doves to come back to to get her Alberto VO5 Hair Spray now.

And there wasn't any way for Helen to support herself if Red went to war.

Though that night MacArthur sailed up the west coast of Korea and established a beachhead behind the Chinese lines, and that was the beginning of the end of the Korean War.

After all that, Red and Bif and Jelly didn't get along so good.

Bush's Last Christmas, Continued

Franky Gorky in the Part Pastel

FRANKY GORKY was the nicest kid in the universe. He always listened to his parents. He shared his toys and candy with other children. Birds sat on his bedroom window in the mornings and waited for him to wake up before they started to sing. Wild animals came up to Franky Gorky and ate out of his hand. Every kid who ever lived on 24th Street heard of Franky Gorky because he was the nicest kid who ever lived in the world.

But he wasn't the smartest kid.

For one thing he never noticed the moon.

Franky Gorky never noticed the moon till one night in December his parents took him outside on a cold night after a snowstorm just after the Feast of the Immaculate Conception and the anniversary of Pearl Harbor, Greta and Gary Gorky took him outside and pointed to the crescent in the sky. Franky Gorky thought it was a funny streetlight. "No," said his dad, Gary Gorky, "it's the moon."

Well Franky Gorky didn't know what to think about the moon, though he wished it was round, and every night after he got put to bed he went to his bedroom window where the birds waited for him to wake up in the morning and looked out at the moon, which, he started to notice, was actually getting bigger, in fact after a while it looked like it was really going to get round. Of course he was a good kid and he knew good kids often got what they wished for, but he'd heard enough fairy tales where people got what they wished for, like King Midas, and it ended up doing more harm than good, lucky for him nobody else seemed to notice that the moon was getting rounder. He wished he could talk to his grandmother who wouldn't tell his parents and always seemed to know about stuff. In fact as the moon got bigger and bigger and one night got so big and white he thought it would suck his bones and maybe the bones of the whole world, something Franky Gorky didn't want responsibility for, Franky Gorky remembered that usually you just didn't get one wish, you got three wishes, and Franky Gorky stared up at the ice death moon and wished it would go away and that he could see his grandmother.

Franky Gorky may have been the nicest kid in the universe but that didn't mean he always did the right thing, even he realized that, and by the time the moon was about half gone again and he started feeling good he figured out that what he should have wished for was that the moon went back to normal, not that it would go away completely. Wishing that it would go away completely was a big blunder, especially since he'd used his third wish on getting to see his grandmother who he found out was coming to see the Gorkys on Christmas like she always did.

So it was a sad Christmas Eve for Franky Gorky when the moon went out. He could barely think about his Christmas toys, and instead of lying awake all night trying to keep from thinking about what he was going to get for Christmas by thinking about the baby Jesus and the Wise Men and how the world was to be saved from Original Sin, he kept going to the window and looking for the moon which he'd wiped out with the abuse of wish, and now all he had left was his grandmother, Grandma Gorky, who was driving in from Buffalo like she did every Christmas, who would listen to him and know what to do.

And Franky Gorky was up like a dart on Christmas morning,

waiting at the front window for his Grandma Gorky, and when she came he did the first bad thing of his life, he ran out of the house without permission and headed across the street where Grandma Gorky had parked because Christmas visitors all over the neighborhood had taken all the parking places on the Gorkys' side, slipped on the ice and got rubbed out by a drunk driver.

That's what happens, said Red, when people take other people's parking places.

That's what happens, said Helen, when you don't look both ways.

What happens is, if you're the nicest kid in the whole universe, then you have to die.

This is what happens when you try to explain something.

~~~~~~~~ **Bush's Last Christmas,**
Continued

" THIS WAS CERTAINLY a wasted effort," mumbled
Andrew. He writhed slightly and I helped him get his
arms and legs out from under him. "Franky Gorky was just a
stupid little kid." He tried to grin and blood slipped through his
teeth.

"Andrew," I whispered to him. "Don't die. Red will really
be pissed if you die."

"You're just thinking of yourself," said Andrew.

Crow was beside us now, tilting his head slowly from one
side to the other. "Deaf," said Crow.

"Don't overreact," said Andrew.

"Thought you were invulnerable," I said.

"Tell me about it," said Crow. "No Saint, no corn curls."

"Karl would give you corn curls," said Andrew.

"Fat chance," said Crow. "Gotta cigarette?"

"I don't like you smoking," said Andrew.

I touched Andrew's hand. Crow was okay, but I didn't want
Andrew to go out arguing with a bird.

Andrew coughed. "Just give me a minute," he said. He stared

143

into the air. Then I heard his throat rattle. His chest lurched. He closed his eyes.

Then he got up. "Let's get in the house," said Andrew, "before Red and Helen get back."

He looked okay. His blue color was coming back and he showed me that he didn't have internal bleeding, he just bit his tongue. The Gorkys already had their car back in the driveway and Greta and Gary were helping Georgie, who looked a little woozy, into the house; he was already on probation for switching peanut butter jar lids in the grocery store so the Gorkys were happy to get out of there with a few bumps on their car.

"I went down before they collided," said Andrew. He stripped the Polish grandmother silhouette from the car in front of the Funsters' and picked up the Franky Gorky doll, took him a couple minutes to find the horse chestnut head. "Who's Dee Delco?"

"You tell me," I said.

"I tell you too much already, and you never listen."

Inside Joseph had Honky jumping through a Hula-Hoop and Neda was finishing the last volume of Will and Ariel Durant's *Story of Civilization,* the whole set of which she'd got for Christmas.

"Pretty cursory," said Neda. She never talked to Joseph or Andrew and they never bothered much with her, they all may have lived in the same house but they were on opposite ends of the trick photograph.

"Did he see Franky Gorky?" Joseph asked me.

"He's just a stupid little dead kid," said Andrew. "Just do me a favor and don't give him my phone number."

That's when Red and Helen got home and Bush's Last Christmas got under way for serious. Up to that point, at least before Andrew's little hoopla with the Gorkys, Franky Gorky included, things had gone pretty well. Me and Neda and Joseph and Andrew all got sent to Midnight Mass which none of us went to, though as I said, Helen did make us all sit around the table before we left and eat deep-fried Lake Erie perch and deep-fried crushed-up hard-boiled eggs put back in the half shell and deep-fried everything else, although everybody did get to have one glass of Mogen David wine. Helen and Red each had two and Helen threw up. After we all got back from not going to Mid-night Mass Helen had fresh baked hot smoked Polish ham ready, topped with cloves and pineapple slices that Red never let any-body eat but himself because he said they were too greasy, they'd make us sick, even he had to eat a loaf of bread to soak up the grease in his stomach, and we ate that fresh baked hot smoked Polish ham in big thick juicy slices with mustard and fresh ground pure horseradish on seeded rye bread, I had to admit, it was a tolerable experience, even if I was wishing I could be spending Christmas with Kara Ruzci, looking in her eyes and whispering, "love, love, love," and touching her somewhere in the crease between her thigh and her butt where her skin was so soft I couldn't imagine how she walked around in it. Meanwhile Red ate so much horseradish it came back up his nose and made him cry and he sat there at the head of the table with his red face and red hair and a big grin with squinty eyes with tears coming out of them until he recovered enough to take another bite and do it again. Red sure liked his horseradish.

Other things were going okay too. Red scored his big toilet paper contract with the NASA office in Buffalo, New York after all, got a Christmas bonus for it, and Helen got another raise and a promotion to the dean's office where she was the assistant to the dean's executive secretary. They gave everybody money to give everybody else Christmas presents, which we did. We all bought each other flasks and roach clips and water pipes and sat around in the living room drinking Kool-Aid and blowing bub-bles and clipping socks together while Red frowned under a jacket, a sweater, a sweatshirt, and two flannel shirts that were all too small for him, though he did have a little Kool-Aid from the leather-covered decanter I bought for him, you could see he didn't know what to do with a decanter and neither did I.

Helen got several dumb things of her own but most impor-tantly Red bought her a new Philco refrigerator which Helen was happy about for about two-and-a-half minutes while she thought about how nice and big it was and how we really needed a refrigerator since Red socked the shit out of the last one. But Helen was a bit too analytic for her role on earth and pretty soon she wasn't so happy about getting a refrigerator because she said, "I'm Norma Jean the appliance queen." Both Red and Helen got quiet. Just shows how gifts can fuck up a Christmas.

It all made me worry about what I was going to get Kara Ruzci who was off in New Jersey with her Italian family eating deep-fried smelt and deep-fried dough wrapped around anchovies and deep-fried everything else only all Italian things, of course, and then leaving it on the table so all the dead people could come down and eat the leftovers, that sure was a spooky idea, even with all the purported contact we had in that neighborhood with the departed and my own firsthand experiments with deaf, none of that seemed to strike me as spooky as that business of Kara Ruzci eating deep-fried Italian everything and leaving the leftovers for the dead relatives. Maybe it was just because it had to do with Kara Ruzci who certainly had her macabre side, though I didn't mind her absence half as much as I minded that I wasn't in her dreams; it just hurt me like crazy that she could make love and blend with somebody else the way she did with me, and I knew she was doing it. For one there was that guy she sang to every night right in front of me, and who knew who else, maybe even that tuna Igor Kresky, it all just made me crazy and made me want her all the more, I was getting so desperate I was thinking of taking the problem to Willie.

Anyway, I didn't know what to get her for Christmas, she sure didn't need another dog, made me wonder how Polly Doggerel was handling the trip to New Jersey; Kara Ruzci's parents probably didn't let Polly Doggerel eat at the table like she did with Kara, probably didn't even let her eat with the dead people, Kara probably had to send her out for hamburgers.

Well as good as everything had been going, when Red and Helen got back from Christmas mass things were kind of grim. You could tell that Helen had the whole mass to think over her refrigerator because she kept looking at her old winter coat like it was a goat, and as much as Red liked to keep secrets from himself, the threshold of another Last Christmas at Bush's with Jon and David and Stanley and their families sitting around and acting like he was some kind of subhuman even though he did more for Bush than any of them made him go to the closet for his bowling ball, reminded me I should have bought him a bowling ball bag instead of a leather-covered bottle. The worst part of it was he felt obligated to go, you wouldn't catch him dead not going, there were even a couple of years before Helen realized that Bush probably wouldn't live to see another Christmas that Helen herself didn't want to go, not that she said anything, she just drank Mogen David wine for breakfast and puked, made perfect sense, and Red made her go. Those were dangerous times; when Red felt virtuous you knew he was on the verge of tremendous destruction, so this year after being so generous about the refrigerator I figured it would have been better if he hadn't gone to church.

Myself, I hated holidays with the family because it was hard to get a fix.

But none of that stopped us from loading into the old Studebaker Rainbow and heading for Bush's where once again, packed into Bush's tiny living room, sat Uncle Stanley and Aunt Sylvia with their faces like shovels and all their kids with faces like shovels, particularly Audrey Mary Pell who sat next to her fiancé Archibald Strong who sat there smug as a rug with his card-trick potency in his triple-piece suit, and Uncle David and Aunt Eleanor and their two sons and two daughters up from their farm in Mercer of whom Uncle Stanley said about every half hour, "Look at those complexions, like peaches and cream, can't beat living on a farm for good complexions, ayah, yah, yah," and Uncle David would agree, "ayah, yah, yah," and Uncle Jon would come in from the kitchen and throw in a few ayah-yahs because the three of them grew up ayah-yahing together and Christmas was their big chance to get together and do it. They had their Carling Black Labels and their knees crossed and they lifted their beers off their knees and uncrossed their knees and then recrossed them the opposite way and said "ayah, yah, yah," and of course Joseph and Andrew got in there and pushed a couple of Aunt Frances' pinheads off the couch and put the warm Pepsi-Colas that Jon had given them on their knees and then took them off and then uncrossed and recrossed their knees and got right in there ayah-yah-yahing with the rest of them, Aunt Frances letting her kids get pushed around because she felt so bad about Helen marrying a working-class German Protestant while she had Uncle Harvey Stano, the Pontiac low-level management dream provider who was sending all her pinheads to private Catholic schools. Anyway Uncle David and Aunt Eleanor's kids' complexions didn't look like peaches and cream, they looked more like strawberry cream cheese with chives.

So there was about a billion shovel faces and pinheads packed into that tiny living room in Bush and Jon's apartment even before we got there, and though Bush had walked about six miles up to Marycrest to have lunch with Helen a couple times, worried the hell out of Helen, Bush now being eighty-one, the rest of us, particularly me and Red, hadn't seen Bush and Jon since the Battle of Quebec, that little altercation being something Helen's side of the family took a dim view of even though none of them ever drove Bush out to North Warren to visit Jon at all. The only person on that side to go out there was Edju and that was to leave Jon off there in the first place, not that it was a totally misguided expression of familial love but nobody on that side of the family really thought Jon was nuts, not even Edju. Even if Jon did fight like an angel for nobody in World War II, Edju didn't fight for five different armies in World War I, so those two had to carry the family's nonfighting record all by themselves. No, the only person who thought Jon was nuts was Red and of course Red was absolutely right about that which put him solidly in the vast minority. Still, Red brought Jon a bottle of Johnnie Walker Black and Jon looked at him like a shy horse standing on a golf tee and said, *"Merci beaucoup,* Red, *mais ne pensez pas que je vous aime,"* which nobody understood except

Neda, not even Jon, the men picked up a little French while they were in Quebec and fed him lines.

"*Tu es fou,*" said Neda.

"Thank you, Neda," said Jon. I guess he was only talking French to Red.

Bush brought out the chocolate and whiskey. "How's your fat stuttering friend?" she asked Red. You could see she really liked Red, he was the only person who drank whiskey and ate chocolate with her, and before the Quebec thing he used to pick her up on Saturdays and take her shopping for groceries all around town because Bush knew where all the bargains were and wouldn't buy anything anywhere if she knew it was cheaper someplace else, but now she couldn't walk around the whole city carrying kielbasa and chickens and she couldn't afford a cab. Too bad he was German and Lutheran.

Red didn't say anything to her, he just took a bite of chocolate and downed a shot of whiskey. Only Bush and Jon and Red and Helen and me and Neda were in the kitchen, everybody else was in the tiny living room drinking Carling Black Label or warm Pepsi-Cola and ayah-yah-yahing like mad.

Bush gave me whiskey and she and Helen had a little stare-off.

"That's not good for him," said Helen.

"It's good for somebody else?" said Bush.

"Red," said Jon. "*Je vous veux partir. Je déteste votre existence.*"

"Say that in English and I'll knock your goddamn block off," said Red.

"There's a nut in this room," said Jon, "and I'm not going to say who it is."

"*Mange merde,*" said Neda.

"That's right, Neda," said Jon. "Your father is a dangerous man."

"I'm trying to think if I can remember everybody's birthday," said Helen.

Well we all knew Helen could remember everybody's birthday.

"My own mother is a traitor," Jon said to Helen. "You don't know what it's like living every day with someone who will betray you."

"And cook and clean for you too," said Bush.

"If you loved me you wouldn't allow Red in here," said Jon.

"Because of you," said Bush, "I had to pay four extra dollars for the ham, a dollar more for chicken, and buy my duck's blood separate from the duck. You want Red out, learn to drive a car." She gave Red more whiskey.

"I can drive," said Jon.

"They won't give you a license because you're nuts," said Neda.

"I prefer walking," said Jon. "Besides, sanity is not a qualification for a driver's license."

You had to give Jon that one.

"I'd rather ride," said Bush. "It would be nice if someone in my family drove."

"Stanley drives," said Red.

"Stanley has a family," said Bush.

"You should take the bus," Helen said to Bush.

"*You* should take the bus," Bush said.

"I do," said Helen.

"Then don't tell me." She looked at Red. "Why don't you drive her to work?"

"I don't want him to drive me to work," said Helen.

"You don't want me to drive you to work?" said Red. You could see he'd never thought about it, but now that he had he felt guilty and no sooner than Red felt guilty he got defensive, why should he have to drive Helen to work anyway, especially since she didn't want a ride, which hurt his feelings, her not wanting a ride.

Jon held up his right baby finger and for a moment, just at the very tip, maybe it was the way the light hit it, it shimmered, like it wasn't quite material. "You'll be sorry when I'm invisible," said Jon.

Just then Uncle Stanley came into the kitchen. "Come out

here and watch Archibald's card tricks," said Uncle Stanley.

Well Jon's finger seemed to have regained its materiality and Bush had to get work done in the kitchen anyway so we packed into Bush's living room to watch Audrey Mary Pell's fiancé, Archibald Strong, whose family owned half of Erie, Pennsylvania, perform card tricks, card tricks, card tricks, while Audrey Mary told us the story of how Archibald had his hand mutilated by a faulty water faucet when he went to get a drink of water one night all by himself in the bathroom, and it looked like he might never regain use of his hand but he flew to a specialist in West Germany who performed miracle surgery and gave him therapy that involved doing card tricks all hours of the day, good thing Archie had the time to do them, and now Archie's hand had recovered miraculously because of his discipline and passion, it was the first really big challenge of his life, it being difficult for rich people to find challenges, and since then Archibald had sued the faucet company for hundreds of thousands of dollars and realized that card tricks were a lot like business and could teach you a lot about life. Us Loops gave Audrey Mary Pell a standing ovation for her story, last Bush's Last Christmas she'd left out the parts about the German specialist and Archie being in the bathroom all alone, the business about rich people having a hard time finding challenges and all that nice homiletic stuff at the end about business and life, she'd probably been workshopping that story with the Strongs a little bit, but you had to hand it to her, it was an improvement.

"So how's it like business and life," said Andrew as Archibald Strong held the deck out to him and had him pick a card, any card at all.

"It has to do," said Archibald, "with the dimensions," he paused and made a frown, you could see he was trying to keep it simple for us, "the area between facade and reality."

Archie gave us a look to see if we were all comprehending but all the Loops were looking at me, they knew I was a Dialectician, even if Red and Helen didn't let me wear my jacket over to Bush's, and Archibald was treading in dangerous territory I'd already transcended, though the way I saw it, for me to take on Archibald Strong in the field of popular epistemological concerns would be like Babe Ruth playing Little League, he was an otter out of water and anybody could have him. I just nodded to Neda and sat back, one thing about Neda, no issue was too small for her to take on, she, herself, had transcended being petty.

"I don't get the spatial metaphor," said Neda. "Why reify space to draw some specious distinction between facade and reality, like where's facade if it's not analytically a priori part of your definition of reality."

"Pardon?" said Archibald.

"Let's say you're holding four sticks," said Neda. "It doesn't matter where you're holding them or in what combination, you're still holding four sticks. Just change that to fifty-two cards, four suits, thirteen denominations."

"What the hell's she talking about. Sticks!" said Uncle Stanley. He looked over at Helen and Red. "What's sticks got to do with cards."

"She's just saying it's a dumb trick," said Andrew. "Anybody that knows the trick can do the trick. It bores us."

"It's fascinating!" said Uncle Stanley. "Don't let them talk like that," he said to Red and Helen.

Well Red didn't understand a damn thing about what was going on except that Neda seemed to be making a fool out of Archibald and thus Helen's side of the family, which was okay with him, and Helen didn't like rich people, though she never said anything about it, we all knew she didn't like rich people.

"Archie can take care of himself," said Helen.

Archie blinked twice.

"Well let's see you do the trick," Uncle Stanley said to Neda. "Ayah, yah, yah."

"Neda can do anything," said Helen.

Neda took the cards from Archibald Strong. "See this deck," said Neda. She showed it to everybody, fanned the cards, folded them behind her hands. When she opened her palms they were gone.

Archibald Strong smiled wryly. "Well," he said. "Some combination of the fifty-two cards, though certainly all of them, are on your body."

It was good to see he got the simple part of the explanation. "Wrong," said Neda. "You're sitting on them."

Archibald was certainly surprised to find those cards under his tweed-suited butt, and the room got quiet as a candle, not a yah-yah in the place, felt a little bit like the Cuban Missile Crisis without the Cubans and the missiles. I don't know what would have happened if Edju and Aunt Elizabeth hadn't burst in from the kitchen where they must have slipped in while Neda and Archibald were having their ontocardial dispute.

"Oooh Neda, so very much you, so Neda, Neda," said Edju. He still spoke worldese like French cheese and you still couldn't understand a goddamn thing he said, except that Neda was still so very very much Neda, which you had to give him.

"What a delightful trick," said Aunt Elizabeth. She still sounded like the Queen or would have if any of us had ever heard the Queen, but we all figured she was just translating for Edju.

"Hello, Uncle Ed," said Neda who was the only person in the world who seemed to communicate with Edju other than Stinky Jinx who could match him oooh for hoot, and was the only person who called him Uncle, which he liked, you could always tell, because he gave her money.

"Mmmmm oooh Neda mmmm oooh," said Edju, giving Neda a $20 bill. "So girl nice umm very."

"And you've become so very beautiful," said Aunt Elizabeth.

Well you had to give them that too, Neda looked like the most beautiful girl since the invention of postpubescence, looked like she, and Joseph who'd shut down on the couch next to Andrew as soon as the philosophy started, had got every bit of looks that Red and Helen had to offer, Andrew looking more like something that hatched in a Cleveland sewer, and then me whose most edifying physical attributes lay in the realization that they were so forgettable, kind of just the obverse of the tip of Jon's little finger which you remembered because you couldn't see, though at least we weren't shovel-faced or pinheaded like our cousins.

Bush was in the doorway now so all sixteen billion of us were in that tiny living room.

"My Last Christmas on earth, you'd think I'd be spared," said Bush.

"Esther? Esther? So? So?" said Edju, which was Bush's name before she was Bush.

"You're taking a trip?" said Aunt Elizabeth.

Jon held up his little finger, or pretended he was holding up his little finger, it was hard to tell because you couldn't see it. "She betrayed me in Quebec. She could pay dearly."

"I already have," said Bush. "For chicken, duck, and ham."

"Jean, mmmm, so *très beaucoup,* so *très beaucoup.*" Edju was proving he could fail to make sense in any language whatsoever.

"After all, she is your mother, Jon," said Aunt Elizabeth. "And sometimes things have to be done for your own good."

"You can conquer the world using that excuse," said Jon.

"Well it wouldn't be the first time," said Neda.

"Look at Eastern Europe," said Jon.

"I have a sister in Poland," said Bush. "So she stands in line for kielbasa, at least they pay her medical bills."

"Mother!" said Jon.

"Mmm, Esther, so no, so no, mmmm very."

"The toilet paper there is like cardboard," said Aunt Elizabeth.

"I'm afraid we're going to have to have you watched, Mother," said Jon.

"For eighty-one years I've been dying to get watched," said Bush.

Edju came up and shook my hand, peering from under his hat. "So Jarvis, mmm, so very, mmm so very, big, big boy, man, hmmm?"

"He graduates from high school this year," said Helen.

"You used to have to go to high school to graduate from high school," said Red.

"So no?" said Edju.

"Audrey Mary was accepted at Bryn Mawr," said Aunt Sylvia. "We agreed with the Strongs that she should at least get two years in before marriage."

Of course then Aunt Frances who looked just like you took Helen's bad side and doubled it had to talk about all the universities her pinheads were attending and how well they were doing, made me think a college degree must have been easier to get than a driver's license, though I hadn't got one of them yet either.

Well eventually things settled down and Bush started bringing the families into the kitchen in shifts for Polish sausage and duck's blood soup with homemade egg noodles, boiled chicken, and beer-basted ham. Those of us left in the living room had to watch the Celtics plaster somebody on TV or watch Archie Strong do card tricks, card tricks, card tricks, which should have been a lesson to Neda and Andrew that you don't hit bricks with sticks, particularly gold bricks, it was just another rendition of the biggest asshole always wins, which if you think about it explains a lot in terms of vertical relationships in the social megalith.

Of course our family always went into the kitchen to eat last because Bush always served up Christmas dinner in chronology of birth and Helen was the youngest, though the only thing vaguely chronological about it was that we always ended up last, because Stanley's and David's and Frances' families alternated all the time, sitting around Bush's crowded kitchen table with Jon sitting at the head in a rocking chair picking at food to go with his scotch and coffee and Thorazine while everybody talked about the Communists or that new little fat Pope John XXIII or both. Then we got called in and Jon got up to take a walk between the refrigerator and the table, a distance of about six feet, though he was pretty good at that kind of thing, besides the refrigerator was one of his favorite conversationalists and he had to worry about his now already disappearing thumb which made him able to hold his scotch glass between his opposable un-appendages the way a flower holds a hummingbird. Of course

Edju and Aunt Elizabeth had already eaten, otherwise they probably would have got in there before we did.

"How come we're always last, Bush," I said when we got in
there.

"Don't take it personal," said Bush.

"The first shall be last and the last, first," said Jon, levitating
his scotch above his palm.

"It's a religious issue," said Neda.

"Think of all the anxiety everyone else goes through," said
Helen, "trying to figure out when they're going to eat."

"You get to eat with me," said Bush, pouring me and Red
some whiskey, along with herself.

Red stared at his whiskey. You could see he liked things
better before Bush clouded the issue with ambiguity.

"Take advantage of it," said Bush. "This could be my last
night on earth."

You had to admit, Bush didn't look so good, she looked like
she could die any minute and be the last person to know.

Bush poured sweet wine for everybody and we toasted her,
because for all we knew, it could be her very last Last Christmas.

After that Bush cleaned up some and then all Helen's brothers
and sister and in-laws came into the kitchen and me and Neda
and Joseph and Andrew had to go sit in the living room with
our shovel-faced and pinheaded cousins, and of course Edju and
Aunt Elizabeth went in there with the adults, so you had to
assume they were going to talk about money, which they did,
I just happened to get the seat at the doorway between the living
room and the kitchen so I heard.

Turns out Uncle David's farm down in Mercer wasn't making any money, he said small farms couldn't make money growing things anymore, so what he needed to do was plow under
all his land and just use most of it to grow grass and sell hay and
the rest of it to graze dairy cattle, that way he wouldn't have any
overhead and all he'd have to do was sell the milk and become
a rich dairy farmer. The only problem was he didn't have any
money to buy cows. The only loan he could get was the kind

where they matched what he already had to buy cows and he didn't have any money to buy cows so he couldn't get any money to buy cows, it was just one of those evils wreaked upon him by modern bureaucracy, the Communists, and the Jews.

"Why don't you go to the Strongs for a loan," said Red.

"That's who won't give him the money," said Bush.

Everyone was sitting around Bush's little table except for Jon who stood facing the refrigerator and said, "If everybody in the family who has a job lends David a thousand dollars, that gives him six thousand, twelve with the match loan."

"Hmmm, so, very very, very very," said Edju.

"You can say that again," said Red.

"To whom, exactly, are you referring?" said Aunt Elizabeth.

Well he was referring exactly to Red and Helen, and Edju and Aunt Elizabeth, and Stanley, and Aunt Frances' husband Uncle Matt. Aunt Frances was studying to be a nurse but she wasn't making any money, and out of that six thousand the only thousand directly related to David was Stanley who was making more money as a chemist than anybody but Edju, and the person most intimately related to Uncle David, Uncle David himself, wasn't talking about contributing anything.

"David's got to contribute," said Helen. "The Lord helps those who help themselves."

"What if you can't help yourself?" said David.

"Then the Lord doesn't help you."

David eventually agreed to throw in a thousand of his own but Edju still wouldn't kick in unless David paid him and Aunt Elizabeth back as soon as the loan came through, which left him with fourteen thousand minus two thousand so back to twelve thousand which is what he thought he needed in the first place to buy a herd of cows. Then Helen said she and Red could only give him a thousand, which was a thousand more than they had as far as I knew, I could hear Red imploding as far out as the doorway, it was just something you picked up on living with Red, every bone in his body was telling him it was the wrong thing to do and the last thing he wanted to do and probably the stupidest thing to do and so must be right, besides, David was the least offensive of all Helen's brothers, he sat around and ayah-yahed with everybody but he seldom made anti-Protestant statements like Stanley or condescended about his kids like Frances or hated his guts like Jon, most the time he just kept down on his farm and raised kids that looked like walking cottage cheese with chives.

Nonetheless, that pretty much put an end to Bush's Last Christmas. Everybody kind of funneled out of there pretty fast and Red and Helen didn't say a goddamn thing to each other in the car on the way to our annual visit to Grandpa Whitey and Grandma Emma Loop's house which was now Uncle Bif and Aunt Jelly's where Uncle Bif met us at the door and said, "Hope you didn't bring any meteors with you this year, ha!" referring of course to Karl's cannonball which last Christmas landed right in his yard. Then Uncle Bif led us into his living room with the giant fat Christmas tree that went up to the ceiling and took up half the room where Aunt Jelly was limping around on her little tiny leg serving everybody their favorite drink as long as it was 7-Up. And there in her big fat chair with her giant mountain self and apple pie head was Red's mother, Grandma Emma Loop who never forgave Red for marrying Helen and adding to the proliferation of Catholics, and in all the years we'd come to see her on Christmas never ever said a goddamn thing to Red or any of us, and Grandpa Whitey Loop who sat in his rocking chair in front of the TV looking like a tiny Pillsbury Dough Boy with baggy clothes on saying, "hope you didn't bring any meteors, heh, heh," he just didn't give a shit about anything anymore, and on the couch was Red's older sister, Aunt Tilly who had two wandering eyes that made her look like one of those African chameleons just before they got eaten by the snake on one of those nature shows, and next to her our legendary Uncle Lefty Limburg who was brought up just down the block in Germantown and married Aunt Tilly and was the only man in Erie, Pennsylvania who could throw a softball underhand at over a hundred miles an hour in his day, could also put a curve or a drop on it. And Red was the only human in Erie, PA and probably the world who could catch for him, and if there was anybody in Erie and probably the whole world who could hit the ball as often and as far as Red it was Lefty, who even though he looked like a piece of beef jerky was probably the most famous amateur athlete in town outside Lank Ward and now Stinky Jinx, though he always said that really the best athlete the city ever had was Red, and Red had to admit, he was right.

Next to Aunt Tilly sat Bif and Jelly's daughter, cousin Nancy who was looking at me like one of those Yellowstone bears on Walt Disney, in ten minutes she'd be banging on my windows.

Back in the master bedroom, off to the side of the living room, was the older children set, old Bif-boy Jr. back from his stint in the air force in Sacramento, and Tilly and Lefty's twins Sweety and Sweaty Limburger, which was Lefty's last name, Limburg, though like hamburg, you just couldn't say it without adding that "er." They were all back there playing Scrabble where Neda immediately swept in to demolish them. Joseph and Andrew set up camp under the Christmas tree and used Uncle Bif's movie camera to produce and direct a porno movie from the Nativity scene figurines, it sure didn't take much to keep those two entertained.

This was the year I didn't let cousin Nancy take me up to her bedroom, I pretty much had all my psychosexual impulses set on Kara Ruzci and even the thought of anybody else made me think that life was one mundane mud moment after another without even the purpose of worms, I had my heart and self set on the return of Kara Ruzci from Hoboken, New Jersey whence I planned to put her face between my hands and look at her until eyes became spies of the inner light and we united, I was even thinking fondly of Polly Doggerel.

Soon enough Uncle Bif had the whiskey out and poured it in anybody's glass who had 7-Up in it, patting me on the back and saying, "I'd like to take a few movies, but look at those two under the Christmas tree, ha! by the way, didn't I give those two some toy 7-Up trucks last year, next year I'll have to get them some condoms, ha!" though this year he didn't get anybody anything, which was only right, while Uncle Lefty started telling stories about when he and Red were kids and did things like replaced all Grandpa Whitey Loop's little cooking pumpkins in his garden with giant pumpkins and Grandpa Whitey put them all in the Model-T the next morning to cart them off to the County Fair in Wattsburg, never said a goddamn thing to anybody, like they'd quadrupled their size in one night, "giant pumpkins, heh, heh," said Grandpa Whitey Loop, he didn't even give a shit back then, and the time they stole all the potatoes from Arnold Zutefeffel's garden and just replanted the green stalks, had a big potato roast, and the time they crawled up a tree in Zutefeffel's apple orchard to steal apples and Zutefeffel caught them, stood at the bottom of the tree with a German shepherd dog and a shotgun and Red dropped the whole burlap bag of apples right on Zutefeffel's head, knocked him out cold and put him in the hospital for weeks, gave the apples they didn't eat to Grandma Emma Loop who made apple pies of which she took two to the hospital for Arnold Zutefeffel.

"Zutefeffel, heh, heh," said Grandpa Whitey Loop.

And Uncle Lefty said, "Well how about that time you came home drunk and fell down the basement stairs and landed in all your homemade ketchup and all the bottles popped like there was target practice going on down there and Emma ran down to the basement and thought you were dead."

"I wished he was dead," said Grandma Emma Loop.

"Dead, heh, heh," said Grandpa Whitey, you could see he didn't give a shit about any of those stories or even being dead.

"The way you two talk about being dead," said Aunt Tilly, her eyes moving like she was playing the spoons.

"Oh, Grandma never wished Whitey was dead," said Jelly.

"Don't bet on it," said Grandma Emma. She looked like the world's largest canned Bartlett pear.

"The way Red and Lefty talk," said Helen, "then they expect their own kids to be angels."

"That's right," said Tilly. "These two."

"Times were different," said Lefty. "Right, Red?"

"That's right," said Red. "Times were different."

"They were different for Hitler too," said Helen.

"Hitler, heh, heh," said Grandpa Whitey. "That's a good one." You could see Grandpa Whitey didn't really give a shit about Hitler.

"Hey, no talking about Hitler or Shakespeare in this house," said Bif. "I got enough trouble, ha!"

Well that hurt Helen's feelings a little bit, she liked talking about Hitler because he was paradigmatically evil and whatever you said about him in that sense had to be absolutely true. Of course Bif was always fucking up by trying to keep everything irrelevant, which probably being the absolute true way to approach the world got him in all kinds of trouble, not that Helen took everything seriously but she did have the world demarcated and as far as she was concerned Hitler was right down there with the devil. Given Bif's disconversion from Catholicism and ultimate doom she could see why he didn't want to talk about Hitler.

"Let's talk about that new little chubby pope," said Bif. "Boy he's a cute little guy, ha!"

"Bif, don't talk like that," said Jelly.

"We all believe in the same God," said Tilly. "That's what that new little chubby pope is trying to say."

"That like eating from the same quiche?" said Jelly.

"It's like waking up and finding all your little eating pumpkins gone but just one gigantic pumpkin there," said Grandma Emma. "Then what do you do?"

"Take it to the Fair, ha!" said Bif.

"To the Fair, heh, heh," said Grandpa Whitey.

"Times were different," said Lefty. "That explains a lot of it."

These Protestants could sure handle a theological issue. They might not have had a leg to stand on but they were professional dancers, it was evident that that was their irreconcilable difference with Catholicism, it had something to do with that dance metaphor and that's why Willie had us Dialecticians dancing in the attic.

"Listen," said Bif. "Let's all the men go into the kitchen and stand around and drink shots and wait for a meteor, ha!"

"That wasn't no meteor," said Red.

"Ha! Right," said Bif.

"Heh, heh, right," said Grandpa Whitey.

Well it didn't matter. Bif got Neda and Bif-boy Jr. and Sweety and Sweaty Limburger out of the master bedroom so Bif-boy Jr. and Sweaty could join Red and Lefty and Grandpa Whitey and me and Bif for beer and shots of whiskey in the kitchen where we could talk about the women, ha! while leaving Helen and Neda and Tilly and Sweety and Jelly and Nancy in the Christmas tree room where they could talk about us, either that or watch Joseph and Andrew make their porno movie. We didn't talk about the women anyway, Uncle Lefty went to South a few years ahead of Red and Lank Ward and he was pretty excited now that Stinky Jinx in his sophomore year was leading South to the championship of everything, at present basketball where South hadn't won a championship for years, though this year they were challenging the local Catholic Prep who always had two platoons of Polish giants that they stuck on the floor four at a time along with some little Italian to handle the ball, it was the same system that the public schools in town used only they put four blacks on the floor with some little white Protestant handling the ball, only Prep played basketball like a military drill team and once they got the lead you might never see the ball again, besides they played defense like giant buzz saws, they could shuffle overgrown Polish-Catholics in and out of the lineup all night.

But South had revolutionized Erie basketball that winter, they had a black kid handling the ball and Stinky Jinx playing forward where you'd normally expect to see a black. Stinky could steal the ball from one of those Polacks without them even knowing it, like killing a dinosaur, and once he had the ball scoring was academic because even when he occasionally missed he could follow his shot without coming back down.

"Too bad that Bobby Hansen kid got hurt," said Uncle Lefty, "then we might have two white kids out there. He wasn't a bad ballplayer."

"He's Catholic, for one thing," I told Lefty.

"No kiddin?" said Lefty. "You know him?"

"No," I said. "I never met him."

Just then there was a roar that shook the earth, and outside a faint glow of orange that came through the windows on all sides and shined on the profiles of Bif and Lefty and Grandpa Whitey and Sweaty and Bif-boy Jr. with his air force crew cut, and Red whose fists clenched with some power that muffled the room, and in the Christmas tree room Helen was on her feet and Tilly and Jelly at the windows saying, "what, what," while the roar receded and rose again like a great wave of red night, and we now, like cats following the sound of a dogfight, followed Red out the door into the glow.

And there, in the air, a needle of gold tearing the black sky and obliterating the stars, a white trail of smoke shining like the tail of God.

Bif looked at Red. "Meteor?" he said.

"It aint no goddamn meteor," said Red.

"Maybe it's one of them comets announcing the birth of Jesus," said Aunt Jelly.

"It's not a comet," I said.

"Maybe it's The End of the World," said Aunt Tilly, her eyes looked like they'd just scored two touchdowns.

"It's not The End of the World," said Neda. "Not for us." You could tell from the way she said it. Funly Funster'd jumped the gun and was headed for outer space.

A Book of Dreams
Jimbo

"F-F-F," SAID Jimbo Funster. "Sp-Sp." He couldn't get it
out.

"If we sit out tomorrow night," said Neda, "we should be
able to spot him and get him on the radio."

"I thought it was a s-science project," Jimbo said. "N-Now
he can't go ice fishing with me."

"He pulls the trigger over Australia and he's in the Lake,"
said Neda.

"N-Neda," said Jimbo. "B-Bring him down. Betty has got
l-lots of Mars Bars."

Neda gave him the palms up.

"You c-can d-do anything, Neda," said Jimbo. "L-Look how
you got that fish out of my trunk."

"The trick isn't getting up there," said Neda. "Believe me,
people have been up there."

Jimbo's stomach growled and he looked up at the dark sky.

"He's got enough food. And I'm using his waste material to
power the oxygen recycling system. And he's in a retrograde
orbit in case the reentry system fails, or he's afraid to use it."

"How l-long?" asked Jimbo.

"June." Neda shrugged. "July."

Back home things were pretty quiet. Helen fell asleep on the couch under the comforter she was still crocheting for Bush's Last Christmas and Red sat next to the TV watching her with his bowling ball on one side of him and a ball bat on the other. Last Christmas after he returned Karl's cannonball Red had to go out and squelch a street riot with his bare hands. One recurrence per Christmas was enough for him and he'd be ready for the second. Next to him "Ishmael and the Night Visitors" or some such TV Christmas show was on, I could hear the Three Kings singing "Thank you, thank you, thank you-thank you." From upstairs I heard the faint strumming of Joseph's guitar. Neda headed up there with her copy of the *Mahabarata*.

"Pretty quiet tonight," I said to Red. I don't think I'd said boo to him, or contrawise, since the last time he took out all the doors. His chest heaved a little bit and for the first time ever he looked a little old.

"Look at your mother," he said to me.

"You want a beer?" I said.

"No," said Red. He never took his eyes off Helen. "They can do anything, her and Neda."

"Why don't you go back to reading," I said to him. "I thought you were pretty happy when you were reading."

"I'm happier when I'm happier, and sadder when I'm sadder."

"I don't know."

"That's right, you don't know." He looked at me. "Look at your mother sleeping there. She used to fall asleep like that with you in her arms. I came back from the war and she slept like that with you."

Well that was something I wouldn't touch with a crutch.

"You don't go to school," Red said to me. "How you going to graduate if you don't go to school."

"I'll get by."

"You'll get by. What're you going to do with your life."

"Maybe I'll become a thief," I told him. "Rob from the rich."

"Don't tell me things I already know and don't want to know," Red said. His chest heaved again. "I graduated," he said. "I could have gone to college, your mother too."

"I know."

"Look what it did for me."

"So tell me I have to graduate."

"Tell yourself you have to graduate."

Red certainly got enigmatic on Christmas night. And the way he was repeating everything I said made me worry it was in our genes.

He was back gazing at Helen. "The rich buy my toilet paper," he said.

I went in the kitchen for a beer but he must have thought I went upstairs, because when I got back he'd crossed the room to kneel in front of Helen, his head in her lap, though she hadn't awakened, he knelt there, rocking silently for some time, then taking her in his arms, lifted her and carried her upstairs.

I followed him up after I finished my beer. Andrew was still awake, just taking off his halo when I got into the room.

"I just talked to two dead Soviets on the phone," said Andrew. "They got sent to the moon right after *Sputnik* in 1957, so Funly isn't the first."

~~~~~~~~~~ # A Book of Dreams
Funly

NEXT NIGHT ME and Jimbo followed Neda into the Old Maids' Field where she pointed out Funly's capsule crossing the sky, it was a pretty dim little thing, you couldn't see it at all on the horizon, and given the lights of the city even in the center of the sky it looked like a needle crossing a haystack.

"Let's get inside," said Neda. "We'll only be able to reach him for a few minutes."

She had everything set up in that corner of the Funsters' basement that Funly used to use for his espionage activity.

"Lot of nice stars out here," said Funly when she tuned him in. "What's *Sputnik* look like?"

"A very tiny antelope," said Neda.

"I'm going to blast it out of the sky," said Funly.

"That would take weapons."

"I'll ram it."

"F-F-Funly," said Jimbo.

"Dad!" said Funly.

"Grandpa's n-not eating," said Jimbo.

"That's because Grandma's with me," said Funly. "I couldn't fit Grandpa in here."

By then Grandpa Funster had dragged himself into the basement. He looked like a hanger with not enough clothes on it. Deaf might not have killed him but it sure didn't do much for his health, which was, of course, just the opposite of Grandma Funster who it did wonders for in every way but the corporeal.

Grandpa Funster crawled up to the microphone. "Roast Ann Arbor," said Grandpa.

"I'd like to land this thing right in Khrushchev's lap," said Funly.

"Polka iron," pleaded Grandpa Funster. "Lestoil!"

There might have been some other important things to discuss but Funly's capsule faded out of our range.

Back at the house Karl and Crow were having a cigarette on their porch.

Karl came up and shook Neda's hand. "That was some light show last night," he said.

"It was nothin," said Neda, and you had to believe it was true, it probably would have been difficult for anybody else in the world to walk around able to do anything they wanted but it wasn't for Neda because she'd been a genius so long that she was a genius at being a genius. Besides that, of course, Neda was beautiful, she was the most surprising and gorgeous maneuver that matter ever pulled on form, probably because of the way she snuck up on it the way she did, starting out so fat and mean, but now she had a physique that brought human men to trembling, eyes bluer than the thought of blue and only blue, lips that made you think honey was a bad example of sweet, and a look on her face that made you sure she invented Einstein in her spare time.

Crow flew onto Karl's shoulder and of course out of somewhere Neda had a corn curl for him.

"Thanks, sweet," said Crow. He put his beak into his chest feathers and came out with a piece of chocolate caramel that he gave to Neda. "Sweets for sweets," said Crow.

"You're the only animal in this neighborhood who knows how to treat a woman," said Neda.

"Tell me about it," said Crow.

"Funly really on top that firecracker?" said Karl.

Neda shrugged, as far as she was concerned Funly shouldn't even have been up there, there was supposed to be a rat or a rabbit or a newt in that space capsule, not a Funly Funster. He'd jumped the gun and now it was his business, he could talk to Jimbo and Grandpa Funster on the radio, what's done's done.

"It's Funly all right," I told Karl.

"Shit," said Karl. "Makes you think anything could happen."

"Fat chance," said Crow. "Gotta cigarette?"

Neda gave him one of her Pall Malls.

~~~~~~~~~~~~~~~~ ## A Book of Dreams
Stinky

A FEW NIGHTS later I went down to the big City Auditorium to see Stinky Jinx lead South High in the Erie Christmas Tournament basketball finals against the Catholic Prep, and of course by this time Stinky had even started to get national attention so that place was packed tighter than a Vienna sausage and probably smelled worse if I had any sense of smell left, which I didn't, I'd followed Helen's footsteps and mysteriously been abandoned by the olfactory, which meant half our family could now kiss smelt and never know the difference. Nonetheless I could still pick out the Jinx family in the reserved section with their mauve and silver banner-scarves, in fact that was the big deal at South now, to bring your mauve and silver Chanel No. 5 scented scarf to all the games and wave it every time Stinky scored, which happened a lot, of course the team themselves all wore them around their necks during warm-ups, they all looked like Stinky now except that he was white with a crew cut and eye shadow and his scarf had sequins. Big Dick Jinx spotted me and waved to me from his seat, he gave me a lot of credit for getting Stinky started in the right direction.

Under the basket where South warmed up I spotted the

Dialecticians in their jackets and shuffling their feet to music that sounded like some combination of "Sweet Georgia Brown" and "Roll Out the Barrel" and collecting residue while Stinky sprung in the air and tipped the ball in with his left foot. There wasn't any sawdust around so I guess he didn't need his parachute. Up on the second deck, in front of the cheering section, Bobby Hansen was ped-pedding his way back and forth on the cement walkway inspiring the masses with his tenacity, even from down where I was standing I could see that now he could move his whole foot, he'd build up speed till he got to the wall and bounce off the bottom of his pads and turn around in the opposite direction without losing a bit of velocity, like a cat in a swimming pool. I had to admit, it made my heart jump, though I figured if he'd shown half as much school spirit a year ago he'd have been here broken leg and all and wouldn't be the vegetable he was today.

Well Stinky finally caught sight of me and bounded over.

"Hoo-hoo!" said Stinky Jinx. "This is a lot like bal*let!*"

"You look good," I told him.

"Certainly better than those guys," said Stinky, pointing down the court. "Can you believe what some of these teams wear?"

"Sports tends pretty conservative, Stinky." I noticed that his silver eye shadow actually sparkled and he noticed me noticing.

"Isn't it amazing. Mom gave it to me for Christmas. Goes on wet. I got some gold too." He started hooting gently to himself like a tiny, tiny train. "What *is* the attraction here tonight?" he said.

"Maybe all the Catholics came out to see Prep."

"Do you think they'll pray? We don't get to pray."

"You don't seem that upset about Funly this time," I said to him.

"Oh Jarvis, Funly's just got to get it out of his system. He's such a wild kid. Anyway, at least I know where he is this time."

The buzzer sounded and Stinky had to go over to the sideline, though before the game started he snuck into the Prep huddle for the prayer, then gave their coach Bill Rafferty a big kiss right on the ear, none of which went over too big over there. The game got under way with Stinky clearing the tip and then taking a pass which he caught in the air at the top of the key where he spun and took a backwards jump shot that of course went in. You had to let Stinky do that stuff as long as he promised to stay on the court, because his attention span was bad and he got bored with the fundamentals.

"Hoo-hoo!" said Stinky.

And the stands lit up with hoo-hoos! like a million Daffy Ducks.

Though the game didn't turn into a runaway because Rafferty had his Polish trees and one little Italian sit on the ball, which worked okay till it got near Stinky, then you couldn't even see what happened. Suddenly the ball would be on the other end with Stinky rising over the basket like a quarter moon to drop it in like you'd drop a cupcake in a Halloween bag. By the time that Prep team started avoiding Stinky completely they were already down by ten.

"You should hear those guys," Stinky said to me as he ran out hooting for the half. "Their values are so topsy-turvy!"

It was pretty clear he'd forgotten that he scored twenty-seven touchdowns against those guys in the fall, which wasn't as jubilant an occasion for them as it was for him, even if Stinky was absolutely bipartisan about it.

Well there's nothing like halftime at a big ball game to get you sinking deep into your thoughts. I started thinking about Kara Ruzci in New Jersey and how good it would be to see her when she got back. All I'd want to do was take her clothes off and nuzzle into her breasts for a year or two, then give her the Christmas present I hadn't bought yet, and then she could teach me to drive her car and maybe someday we could drive it to California or New York City and see the oceans with their long salty waves. Maybe someday soon I'd have to drive to New York City or California and stay there if Bobby Hansen kept getting his feeling back in his extremities, or if our friend Mr. Tony

Blanion decided I'd had my last chance and it was time to go to the police and show them the remains of my turkey dinner, namely that potato Bobby Hansen.

In fact thinking of Blanion reminded me that Blanion usually caught me after these big athletic events and I might be getting my rent notice of life within the next hour or two, then I'd have to become a mass murderer or leave town. Though the more I thought about it I didn't think I could kill Blanion. This whole Bobby Hansen thing was just a big accident and the only other times I'd come close to hurting anybody was in self-defense against people I couldn't even see. I started looking around, but I didn't see Blanion anywhere, he'd probably wait till after the game anyway and then slip out of some crack too small for a shadow.

What I did see was Bobby Hansen up on the second tier cheering runway padding his living feet to one of South's new cheers, "Hoo-hoo! They just want to *grab him!*"

I looked for Willie and the Dialecticians, but it appeared that Willie, himself, had managed to dissipate in his usual way and the rest of the Dialecticians of course immediately lost concentration and went off to experiment with the other in the form of some cheerleaders from Ashtabula whose team lost the consolation game. I went over there anyway.

"We are giving these female humans some of the consolation," said Revis.

"Yes," said Raymon. "We were under the basket dialecticizing the theory and now we are having some of the praxis."

Revco gave me a nice dragon grin and moved closer to his cheerleader.

"So do not make with the condescension," said Revis.

"Because," said Raymon, "we are proselytizing the dialectic."

"And contemplate the piercing," said Revis, "of certain dualisms."

"Which you, yourself, have occasion to praxis," said Raymon.

"Yes," said Revis, "when your praxis is not in New Jersey."

One thing about those Dialecticians, you sure didn't have to say anything to them to get their response, except for Revco who seemed preoccupied with the dualisms his cheerleader was presenting him, until she looked up and said, "Hey, you're a white Dialectician."

"You guys have a lot of work ahead of you," I said to them.

"Praxis, praxis, praxis," said Raymon.

"One cannot sit in the field like the cat," said Revis.

"Because it is not a hunt," said Raymon.

"Nor," said Revis, "is every day your Christmas."

"So one finds intelligence," said Raymon, "in many places."

Revco looked up and grinned at me. "Such as Ashtabula."

The teams started coming out for the second half just then and Stinky ran by and said, "Hoo-hoo! I think I'm going to make a foul!" I guess he just learned it. It had always been tough to teach Stinky the more subtle aspects of athletics, not because he wasn't a smart kid, it was just that his own sensibilities were a lot more delicate, it was like trying to teach butterflies about boulders, though maybe the topsy-turvy values of those mean Prep guys gave him some insight, he might have learned some of that kind of stuff in football if he'd ever been tackled.

So when the second half began Stinky went out and started fouling like a wild turkey until he got four on him and the coach pulled him from the game. He got the hitting part right, and he sure enjoyed waving to the referee and the scorer's table, but he didn't like sitting down, and South's coach, big fat old Barry Barfoni who'd been raised from the bliss of mediocrity by this whole Stinky business, was turning into a puddle trying to explain to Stinky about the five-foul rule.

Meanwhile, out on the floor, you could see the rest of the South team really relished the opportunity to play without Stinky. Not that they didn't appreciate all he'd done for them in terms of liberalizing the uniform situation and the kinds of shots you could take, because with Stinky on the floor it didn't matter what you did, Stinky just dangled over the basket and put your shot through the net like so much fresh-squeezed orange juice, but this was an opportunity to show their own stuff, stuff that was pretty extravagant and undisciplined. Though it had its moments of beauty, it also had its pockets of disaster.

So soon those giant tree sloths from Prep had themselves back in the game, though I have to admit, I sympathized with those South kids, they were having a good time and who wanted to win a ridiculous high school basketball game anyway if it meant playing the game like a power lawn mower. Even so, South didn't have its best players out there. The Dialecticians, themselves, were the best players in Erie, PA if not the world, though they probably didn't think about it in those terms, I knew that, if nobody else did, which made their nonchalance even more quintessentially a split of that dualism. Those Dialecticians weren't even watching the game.

Barfoni got Stinky back in the game with Prep a dozen points ahead and playing basketball like electric Chinese checkers till Stinky came in and stole the ball, left his feet at half court and floated around three tree sloths, slipped that ball through the net like you'd imagine a girl slipping into a slip, an act of pure gentility and finesse. You could see he was done fouling for the night. Then he wouldn't let them bring the ball in. Wherever they passed it he simply slid over there just a little faster than you could think about it and silked it out of their hands, rose in the air like a summer morning and dropped that ball through like the first winter night.

And I can't explain it, but just then something stirred in me, it just seemed like Stinky's movements had *the end* written all over them, like somehow or another he and I shared some razor edge of denial, like something out there in my unreal world had been sliced open, but I was still in that moment before the skin opens and the blood streams out, and way before that other moment when the pain comes. Not like Stinky was counting baskets or wanted to win, he was simply teetering on the edge of understanding something he didn't want to know about and didn't plan to, and wouldn't. But I saw it, I saw that big numb split in the world as clear as fear. It was probably how Willie saw things all the time.

I never thought I'd ever want to see anybody win anything, my whole view of competition was that anybody who entered it deserved to lose, but in those last few seconds when Prep had the ball and the lead I wanted to see Stinky take that ball away and win the game as much as I'd wanted Willie to beat up Blanion, I wanted all those Catholic prayers, even Helen's, to go down in front of the firing squad of the absurd, and every desire that anybody ever had to win something, or hold on to something, to be crushed by Stinky Jinx who I saw in that moment as the vision of everyone who knew nothing about the world and wanted nothing to come of it.

So when Stinky stole the ball again with ten seconds left, when he rose above the basket like a phoenix and a snowflake to place the ball through the net, I had a moment when the world balanced between idiocy and peace.

They called him for charging.

Prep won the game.

Well it wasn't a league game anyway, just a tournament game, South would play Prep at least a couple more times that year, though for the moment it was apparent those Prep guys saw this as some kind of adequate revenge for that 173–12 shellacking they took in football. Nonetheless Stinky got the MVP trophy which Big Dick Jinx got out of his hands pretty quick before Stinky gave it away to some spectator who looked like he needed to water some flowers, and a dozen roses which he gave to his mom. I shook Stinky's hand and he gave me a kiss on the ear while Big Dick patted me on the shoulder and said, "Don't worry, we'll get 'em next time, now that Stinky's got this foul thing straightened out," and Stinky said, "Hoo-hoo! What a thing to keep track of!"

·   ·   ·

The only thing left for me to do now was walk home without donating my nose hairs to our friend Mr. Tony Blanion. I figured if I stayed away from him he'd never get to give me that last warning, maybe I could baffle him with a dilemma of criminal ethics. Besides, it was the one-year anniversary of my accidental complicity in the vegetablification of Bobby Hansen and I had some unjustified premonition that if I avoided Blanion tonight I'd profit by some kind of informal one-year nullification clause. Maybe I could convince him, after all, we did share a kind of unique form of agile discommunication.

I didn't figure I could outguess him, so it was just my duty to do the sneakiest things. I slid into a big crowd of Prep cheerleaders and fans and followed them back to the Prep locker room where they were going to wait at the door for their victorious tree sloths, then slipped into the back hallway and down a long corridor till I found an unlocked door, a janitorial supply room with a high, small window that I climbed some boxes to and out of, had about an eight-foot drop which wasn't much once I hung out the window by my hands. I looked around the small alley to get my bearings, then headed toward downtown, opposite 24th and Celebration. I couldn't have handled my escape more perfectly so I wasn't surprised when a shadow stepped out from the side of the building.

"Smack Jack," he said lifting a cigarette. "Got a light?"

Well I did, and why shouldn't I give him a light, I killed flies because they'd kill me if they could. I lit the match for his cigarette. It wasn't Blanion, just somebody who Blanion would look like in twenty years if he didn't become a cop.

"Needs a quarter for coffee," he said.

And I gave him a buck, why not make everybody lucky.

But I still had a two-mile walk ahead of me even if I took a direct route, which I didn't, if Blanion was going to follow me he was going to have to walk the walk to talk the talk. I headed west toward the suburbs and hitched a ride out to the amusement park by the beach that was shut down for winter from a guy who had hair over his ears and I'd never seen a guy with hair over his ears. He told me he looked like a beetle and if I'd been Red and had the Year of Two Hundred Books behind me I'd have told him he was reading too much Kafka, but I didn't know anything about Kafka and still don't, I just had him let me off and then walked a mile north toward the lake before crossing the road and hitching another ride in the opposite direction south of town, out by the Old French Road. Then I hitched another ride back into town from a Prep alumnus whose younger brother was a third-string tree sloth on Prep's basketball team. He was happier than a monkey wrench about Prep's big win over South and said that Prep now had proof that Stinky was the product of some Russian genetic experiment, why else wasn't he black and why else was he in some obscure town like Erie and not Philadelphia or somewhere. I told him that I lived right next door to Stinky Jinx and I knew for a fact that Stinky didn't exist, he was just some figment of Prep's imagination, manufactured from guilt. Needless to say, we didn't understand each other.

But it all kept my mind off things, which allowed me to generate the idea, by the time I got to German Avenue, not to go home at all, but go over to Willie's. Not that it made things any easier if Blanion was centrally located, the neighborhoods around there were lit for crime, lots of light on the corners where you could be spotted and none in the center of the block where you could be nabbed once your direction was established. So when I got to German and 24th I headed in the opposite direction from both my house and Willie's, figuring if Blanion spotted me he'd have to guess which one I was going to, and I also decided to run so I'd either screw up his timing or make him chase me.

I got about two yards before I was up against a tree with a knife at my throat.

When I saw it wasn't Blanion that solved the first problem. He tried to keep me at bay with the knife while rifling my pockets but I grabbed his wrists. This guy was all lips and nose with eyes buried somewhere under his forehead.

"Hey," he said. "I'm robbing you."

"Where you from?"

"Let me go, I'm robbing you."

"You're not robbing me."

"I am," he said.

It was turning into a real intellectual encounter, probably could have the same conversation with a bank president if we took the opposite positions, except that this guy was swinging that knife around like a melting ice cream cone. Not that he wanted to stab me, I could see I'd already taken this whole robbery business a step beyond his plans, he didn't even know how to hold a knife, even I knew you were supposed to attack underhanded. I started feeling sorry for this guy, trying to rob somebody in our neighborhood. I let go of his wrists and he backed off.

I took a five out of my pocket. "Go to a bar," I told him. "Pick out a drunk who's dressed real good and follow him to his car."

Well that got him thinking, although that wasn't saying much, he was like one of them Christmas toys that came without the batteries.

"You keep this up around here," I told him, "and somebody's going to shoot you."

Well I had him intellectually surrounded and physically at a standoff, even if he did have that knife, besides, I was offering him money, even if that did imply I had more, that would have required an inference. He looked me up and down a couple times and took the five bucks, slunk off walking backwards like one of those baby turtles from Woolworth's. I kept an eye on him too, you never knew about shy dogs.

Once I couldn't see him anymore I decided that given all I'd been through it was a bad idea to take the sidewalks to Willie's at all, so headed down German a half-block then cut in and went through all the backyards. It was an all-black neighborhood and they hadn't started keeping Doberman pinschers and dark German shepherds yet so I cut a pretty silent swath to the back of Willie's house where I slipped real quietly to the corner by the back door.

There, leaning at the front corner of the house with his hair like a greased spook, slouched our friend Mr. Tony Blanion, smoking a cigarette and pondering his reflection by streetlight in the blade of his knife. Apparently he'd made a lot of good guesses that night but he'd come up one short. I just stood there watching him for a while, the back of his head glistening like an obsidian moon. That night the path of innocent misdirection had led me straight, and like Stinky, in my own thwarted way, I'd become an MVP. I was looking ahead.

I ducked into Willie's vestibule.

A Book of Dreams
Deaf in the
Afternoon

" THE BAD ASS laughs last," said Tony Blanion.
Which you had to give him, considering the circumstances, he certainly had me hammerlocked with his knife in my
ear, and he was digging around in there pretty good.

"I hope that's smaller than your elbow," I told him.

"You got earwax, Mr. Income Tax."

"Remind me to buy you a gun next Christmas," I said.

"Then you better buy it tomorrow, frog lust, because I'm
recalling your credit card," hissed Blanion. I could see he was
pretty upset about all I'd put him through to arrange this meeting.

"You know," I said to him, "we are in a friend of mine's
house."

"That nigger's next on the shit list."

"Can we be practical for a minute?" I said. "The police can't
pin this Bobby Hansen thing on you, or they'd have done it
already."

"Soup's simple," said Blanion. "I just like opening cans."

"How dumb do you think I am?"

"Pretty dumb, cookie feet. You still got that camera at your

181

girlfriend's, you left footprints like fresh mints all over that place, and fingerprints, Mr. Clean, talk better English than the pope. Bobby Hansen gets one look at you and his feet'll be parakeets."

"You're just a bad guy," I said to him. It was silly not to give him his due.

"It's a matter of principle," said Blanion. "You can contemplate it in your prison cell between butt-fucks, fun-bun, because tomorrow your life is a dull knife in a dead house, far away."

Well Blanion was as bad and mad as I'd ever seen him, a guy like him made you want to think about the relationship between evil and poetry, even with a knife in your ear, though as he pointed out, I'd have a lot of time for that later. As it was he took a pretty good slice out of my ear and pushed my face into the wall. By the time I got turned around he was gone.

I sopped up my blood with my shirttail and sat there on the floor in the corner of Willie's vestibule for a little bit. I felt kind of sad about things but I felt pretty clear about them too. This was an experiment, neither with deaf nor the other, but the tools were pretty clear; Jarvis Loop was about to start a whole new life and only had a couple hours to say good-bye and refuse to explain himself.

I took the back stairs all the way up to Willie's room in the attic and of course he wasn't there so I left him a note.

> Willie: Good thing the world is bigger than the self. See you in transition.
>
> Jarvis

I was pretty proud of that note. Willie probably already knew everything anyways.

After that I went home. Found a grocery bag and put in a couple pair of jeans, a couple T-shirts, a couple sweatshirts. I had a set of clothes on, including my Dialecticians jacket, so I'd be pretty much set for a month. I took a last look at Joseph and Andrew, sleeping on the floor like the ding-dong brothers, Joseph with a finger in his good ear and Andrew with an earphone hooked up to a transistor radio hooked up to the halo out on the porch, probably should have been using a tape recorder but I wasn't going to wake him up to tell him. Neda had her light on, probably translating *Finnegan's Wake* into Hebrew or something, so I didn't bother to go in there, nor Red and Helen's room, I'd never been in there with the two of them in bed together before and I didn't plan on starting any trends just because I was leaving for good. The funny thing was how odd I felt about those floors up there with no linoleum on them. Now that Red and Helen both had jobs maybe they'd do something about that, maybe Helen would finally get carpet in the bathroom, maybe they'd get an electric heater in there or something so Helen wouldn't have such cold anemic winter feet.

Downstairs I left Helen a note and put it under the Infant's candle. "You know what to believe and what not to believe," I told her, and that's all I said, it didn't matter that it was wrong, it was just a stab of dim Nite-Lite words in a dark world of hallway to the bathroom, I knew about Nite-Lites because I'd seen them in some of those rich houses I broke into.

Then I walked out to Kara Ruzci's. It was a long cold walk and I liked it. Her house was out on the first ridge of hills above the city, and from spots on that road you could look over Erie and see all the lights stretching east and west and stopping abruptly in a line on the north which was the lake. The snow belt started up there on that ridge too, so there were piles of snow along people's sidewalks and driveways, and lawns like simple white sheets. Of course Kara'd been gone for a while, and wouldn't be back till the New Year, so I shoveled her driveway and sidewalk so as to not leave any footprints. I was sure they'd be watching her place now, as well as Willie's, and Red and Helen's, they'd probably even be checking their mail for out-of-town letters, particularly ones that came from suspiciously faraway places like Vancouver, Canada where I was headed eventually, after I got to California.

Inside Kara Ruzci's I got my camera, and my .22 which I hid there without telling her, and looked around for anything else of mine that could incriminate her. I didn't find anything, though when I started my letter I figured that it could end up incriminating her too if the police got there before she did, though that was just too much incrimination to worry about; Kara Ruzci didn't know that much about me unless she knew everything, and in that case it would be the same.

I wrote her:

Dear Kara Ruzci: I love you. There are dreams and dreams and dreams, and in some dreams we will meet and I will wash your hair and hold your breasts and the whole world will be nothing but your skin against mine, and maybe at night you can sing to me. For me now there is only this great wrenching, and now I love, I love you, and never want to love again. You must buy Polly Doggerel a hamburger for me. I love you forever. Merry New Year.

Jarvis

I'd never said I'd loved her and now I couldn't get enough love in that note to communicate. I called the bus station and found there was a bus heading west for Chicago at dawn. That left me a couple hours to sleep and I slept dreamless for those two hours, awaking in the fading night and calling a cab to take me to the bus station. I made Kara's bed, took a last look at my letter, then went out to the bottom of the driveway to wait for the cab.

The only other city I'd ever been in was Cleveland, and that was only to the stadium to see the Browns and the Giants with Red and Stinky and Big Dick, but now I was going to get a big dose of other cities, starting with Chicago. I stared out that bus window at the dead grass of the winter freeway and wished I'd had time to talk to Karl about criminal escape strategy, but I didn't, I just figured once the police didn't find me in Erie they might start checking the buses coming out of there. So I'd spend a day or so in Chicago before I got back on the bus. By that time they wouldn't be checking every bus in Chicago and I'd catch a streamliner straight out to San Francisco from there. By then I'd have lots of time to plan things out, not that a plan ever did anybody any good.

Right about then I wished I had some whiskey, something to cut the nerves and let me sleep, something to make me feel good about escaping, because it sure was good to escape, good to see that wound of phenomena open up and see what side of it I was on; it sure was nice to know I'd be seeing those long ocean waves against those wide white Pacific beaches in a few days, or see them crashing against black jagged cliffs, just like in Lake Erie, only longer and bigger, waves and waves, and maybe in the East it would be a horrible cold winter, and ice would cover the lake in giant frozen waves, and Kara Ruzci would go out to the peninsula with Polly Doggerel and climb atop a frozen dune and stare out at those waves. She wouldn't have to think of me.

~~~~~~

IN CHICAGO I didn't feel like leaving the bus station. I'd only been on the lam for part of a day, in fact I didn't even know if they were looking for me yet, and I was already tired of being chased. I didn't see any police around there, except for one who seemed to be checking his beat, and there wasn't anybody standing around the buses when people got off or standing with the bus drivers when people got on, so I figured there wasn't anybody looking for me. I picked up a newspaper because I was so bored I was ready to read anything until I thought about actually reading it, maybe I could read the funnies or even the sports, and I got a Cleveland *Plain Dealer* because Cleveland was closer to home, and bought a ticket and got on the next bus west.

Things got flat as a mat and I must have read everything in the paper but the front section before I got the idea to look and see if there was anything in there about me being wanted, must have sifted through a dozen pages before I saw it.

SUSPECT SOUGHT IN ERIE SLAYING

Well I'd figured Bobby Hansen was set for a relapse, but the way he was bouncing around town on those newly recovered feet of his, I didn't think he was ready to make the transition from vegetable to cadaver. Looked like I got out of the water just in time, though I really didn't like the idea of Bobby Hansen being dead, it changed a picture which was grim enough already, made me think maybe I should go back and try to explain myself, and might have got off the bus right there to do it if I didn't realize the idiocy of such a rational impulse. You had to get to the bottom line real fast when you were considering spending the rest of your life in jail, it wasn't like explaining yourself to the principal, as if that ever worked either, I wasn't even a juvenile anymore. I couldn't even look at that article, I just folded up that paper and put it under the seat next to me. I had to figure things out. What was the experiment now, and what were the tools.

But I finally fell asleep.

Woke up somewhere in Iowa with some old unshaven guy next to me who looked like he'd smell bad if I could smell. He was reading my newspaper.

"Sure is an unusual way to die," he said. He grinned at me. He didn't have teeth and he looked just like skin on a skull. "Wake up dead in bed with your head split open." I didn't say anything and he just kind of worked his mouth a little bit. "Probably the Mafia."

Looked like deaf was everywhere. I looked over at the paper and he pointed to SUSPECT SOUGHT IN ERIE SLAYING.

AP—An Erie youth was found dead in his own home early today from an apparent blow to the head. Anthony Lawrence Blanion, 19, of Erie, was reported dead on arrival to Erie St. Vincent Hospital after his father, Louis, found him in bed this morning suffering from a severe head wound. Police believe Blanion was struck with a heavy object, possibly a hammer.

The Marriage of Heaven and Hell

"THEY CAN'T figure out," I said to Willie, "how somebody slipped upstairs to his bedroom without being noticed and split his head open."

Willie lay back on his pillows. He smoked a cigarette, made me realize that he and Crow started smoking around the same time. He fiddled in his toolbox. "I, myself," said Willie, "would not be figurin such. It is not somefing to fink about."

"Blanion's dead," I said to him.

"That would seem to be what everyone is assuming," said Willie.

"He's not dead?"

"You are having," said Willie, "an overreaction, when fis is your lucky day."

I looked to where Willie kept his tools and there was his hammer, looked unmoved and clean as a tooth.

"You, yourself, have still the addiction to causal efficacy," said Willie. "So you are barking in the wrong ballpark."

"You didn't hit Blanion with the hammer?"

"It is like the same side of two different coins," said Willie.

"Except they're really different sides," I said.

"And no coins," said Willie.

"I'm getting obsessed with issues," I said to him.

"Fis is somefing which happens," said Willie, preparing a hypo, "to human beings."

Willie brought out a bottle of Jim Beam and we sipped that while sitting there experimenting with deaf, all a little at a time so as to remain coherent enough to exchange enigmatics, though soon enough I wasn't thinking about what I was talking about, which I have to admit seemed like a real healthy state of affairs. I was thinking about the very first time I walked out the door by myself, it must have been early because I didn't even walk so good at the time, Helen was off in the house doing something and the front door was ajar, I just headed out without a thought in my goddamn head, the world looking like a new paper napkin, probably the first and last time in my life I ever really saw anything, then Helen came and got me, hard to tell if she was more scared or mad, when she picked me up I thought she was going to crush me to deaf, then she held me upside down by the ankles.

"Rhine wine," said Helen. "You got meat feet. Don't you ever scram, lamb, or I'll turn you into jam."

That was unusual talk from Helen. That's when I saw, while hanging upside down there, the man Kara Ruzci sang to at the foot of her bed, I knew it was him, though as soon as I tried to put him into some kind of cognification he disappeared, gave me the notion I had a whole bunch of realities I couldn't do anything with because I couldn't think them, though every time I started thinking about something else I saw that man again. I'd say he was middle-young and handsome and had a deep black look in his eyes except that I can't remember a goddamn thing about him, I just swung there like the bottom of a clock and there he was, ticktock, looking at me like I was the inside of a tomato soup can. Then there was Willie.

"Good fing the self is bigger than the world," said Willie. "Otherwise there would be no place for the world to hide."

·   ·   ·

"It was nice of you to leave me a note," said Helen. "But if you're going to spend the night out, why don't you just say so."

"It wasn't that simple," I told her.

"I can imagine." She lit the candle in front of the Infant and gave him a pat on the crown. "He's been doing well recently," she said to me, "don't you think?"

"He's an ace," I said.

"You laugh now," said Helen. "But no one leaves the Church for good. You'll be back."

"Red's lucky," I said to her.

"Your father will convert someday," said Helen. "It's inevitable." She got out her rosary with the water from Lourdes in the medallion. "Want to say the Rosary with me?"

"No."

She knelt down at the table below the Infant. "Looks like Willie finally hit that Blanion boy with the hammer," said Helen.

I didn't say anything to her, I just watched her there, bowing her head. "Holy Mary," said Helen, "Mother of God, pray for us sinners, now and at the hour of our death."

Amen. I got to Kara Ruzci's house before she did, put my camera back and got rid of the note. Now that I'd suffered the purgatory of our potential separation my love for Kara was like fire in a gas can, I had flowers waiting for her as well as champagne and a white linen dress from India which was of course too big, besides she never wore dresses anyway, though she did that night, she put it on immediately and loved it even though it pretty much made her look like a very nice fish wrapped in newspaper, and we danced around the living room drinking champagne while Polly Doggerel very neatly unwrapped and shoveled down the dozen or so McDonald's hamburgers I'd bought for her on the way over, along with a milk shake and two bags of french fries, before going out to sit on top a snow pile to bounce and bayoo at the rising stars.

I couldn't keep my hands off Kara Ruzci.

"This is certainly a new intensity," she said as I clung to her ear with my mouth and she gave me a wide angle lens for my Nikon. "This will help you get more space out of the same room."

I was convinced that intensity would help me get more space out of the same room. I would believe anything. I took off her new dress and brought her to the floor and kissed her everywhere. And when I entered her that night I couldn't move, I thought I'd burst, and Kara Ruzci held me between her thighs as I sobbed within and around her, her insides moving around me like a muscular velvet vise, and she said, "Shhh, don't move, shhh"; we lay one inside the other for hours and yet hours into the night, hours on the edge of coming, until after finally exploding inside her I lay broken on her breast. "Shhh," said Kara Ruzci. "Shhh. It's only the beginning." But when I raised my head for her eyes there was something in them very cool and far away, and I felt like there had been nothing between us, that there was some great gulf of past life and worlds of different worlds.

That night I slept a black sleep and did not dream. And when I awoke to the low trill of her night-dark voice I remembered how I missed her in that blackness. I tried to hold her as she gazed out to that other place and sang to him. "I love you, Kara Ruzci," I pleaded to her. "I love you." But it only moved her to a deeper, sadder song, a sound like a dark mirror, and from the other side of the room rose a sorrowful moan like a great bone cracking in the center of the world.

"I've got to find him," I told Willie.

"It would seem to me," said Willie, "that you are finding him all the time, and fis is the problem."

"I never get to talk to him," I told Willie. "I want to talk to him."

Willie rubbed his chin with his bad hand. Despite all his experiments he looked as healthy as a chocolate bar, his skin, in that warm attic, whistling with residue, his muscles like brown round butter. "You are going to talk about the weather."

"I have to find out who he is."

"And you will do fis by talking."

"Maybe I should hit him on the head with the hammer."

Willie looked over to the hammer and the toolbox. "You cannot solve everyfing wif the hammer."

"Some things," I said to him. I tried to look at him real hard, like I could see right through him to the whole Blanion thing, but he was impenetrable.

"You cannot hit him wif the hammer," said Willie.

"Why not. Is he a dream?"

"I, myself," said Willie, "do not know anyfing about the dreams."

"You know everything," I said to him.

Willie walked over to his pillows and the toolbox, dragging his bad leg slightly. "Everyfing is connected," said Willie. "But not how we fink it is connected. That is the experiment."

"And what are the tools?"

"I, myself, am not the plumber of the soul." He smiled at me lopsidedly and sat down on his pillows, getting his toolbox.

"Take me to see him."

"Because I must," said Willie. "Everyfing points to it, and so it is a kind of doom."

"Everything is a kind of doom," I said to him.

"No," said Willie. He prepared the hypos. "Fis is not the same fing I always give you."

"What is it?"

"It is not the same fing." He shot himself up first. "You cannot take the hammer."

"Okay," I said. "No hammer."

While he found the vein in my left arm I kept my right hand in the pocket of my Dialecticians jacket, feeling the warm blue metal of my .22.

But not too much happened. We sat there for a long time on the pillows collecting residue. Every once in a while I looked at

Willie like I expected something to happen and he grinned a little and nothing happened. I was expecting a little more transformation.

After a little bit more Willie stood up and said, "Do you have money for the bus?"

"We're taking a bus?"

"Sometimes," said Willie, "you have to take the bus."

I suppose we could have caught the bus over on Celebration by Dean Danger's Bar & Grill, but the buses didn't run as frequently over there so we walked up German to 26th. The sun had gone down since I'd gone over to Willie's and now it was dark and cold. Everything looked the same, maybe a little more deserted than usual, though of course it was hard to say, after all it was a cold January night, the stores wouldn't even be open downtown and that's the only place this 26th Street bus went.

"We going downtown?" I asked Willie.

"Yes."

"He lives downtown?"

Willie didn't answer me.

"He hangs around downtown?"

"We are not looking for him," said Willie. "We are looking for you."

Willie certainly had a way with ambiguity. The empty bus came and I paid our fares and we walked down the aisle and sat near the back. It had been a while since I'd been in a bus at night and I liked looking at all the inner and outer reflections in the windows. Willie sat quietly with his arms folded.

"Listen," I finally confessed to him. "I don't really know what this guy looks like. I don't see him when Kara sings to him, I just hear him sometimes."

Willie raised one eyebrow.

"I just think I've seen him a couple other times, but as soon as I think about it he disappears."

"When you see him you will know, or you will not know, or you will fink you know and be wrong," said Willie. "I have read that to know you do not know is fis big fing, but sometimes you fink you do not know and you are wrong. I, myself, fink fis whole knowing business is too much like swimming on the wrong paf of the woods."

"So?"

"So you will not use your gun. Fings go in one end and come out the other looking very different."

"Shit," I said, my hand sweating on the .22.

"Exactly," said Willie.

I looked away from Willie to the reflections in the windows and at that moment resented everything in the world, because it was all too far away. The only thing that was real to me was that gun.

"Myf and metaphor," said Willie.

"Where are we," I said to him. "Are we—" I hesitated. I knew there were words I couldn't use with him. "We're not still in your room. Where are we?"

"On the bus," said Willie.

That was just too obvious to be satisfying. "I'm deep into an experiment with the other."

"Fis is true," said Willie. He rubbed his chin lightly with his bad hand. "I, myself, do not prefer experiments wif the other, they are too fraught wif the passions and the dualisms, and one is apt, as are you, yourself, in the confusion, to choose the wrong tools."

The bus came to the end of its route and we got off at Perry Square, the park that sat between the business district to the south and the dock bars to the north on the Bay. It was senseless to walk near the buildings for a shield because the wind came right up the street off the lake. I followed Willie a couple blocks till we came to a bar called The Mermaid and walked in, no problem, even though we were both under age. There were a couple groups of people in the back and a few men at the bar, though nobody struck me as the person I was looking for. We drank Koehler Beer and Jim Beam and in a little while a woman who looked both a little well-dressed and a little run-down came in, perused the place, then came up and asked us if she could help us with anything.

"That is not, at present, the nature of our experiment," said Willie.

Her eyes narrowed. "There's a black girl outside," she said, but when that didn't arouse anything she left. I looked at Willie and he looked at me and I looked at Willie and he looked at me. I looked at Willie some more but it didn't seem to faze him.

"This is some experiment," I said.

Willie looked into his beer glass. "What is the experiment and what is the tool."

"I think I'm the tool."

"You are not the tool," said Willie. "And the gun is not the tool."

Well for the first time in my life I was about to give up on Willie when there, at the other end of the bar, looked like he just appeared out of thick air, sat the man, with a clear fashionable drink, a dark suit, and hair like a sparrow, a gaze on his face as he looked into the bar mirror like he'd seen everything there ever was and didn't want to see it again, which at first made me feel a little sympathetic, but I immediately realized that's what made him feel so superior, made him think he could come into Kara Ruzci's bedroom while I was sleeping with her, after I'd made love to her, and sing his sad fucking wailing. I hated him. And seeing him made me hate him all the more.

I turned to Willie but Willie was gone. I looked at the man again, and looking at him made me feel all the things I'd never felt, one of which was that if somehow I could talk to him, if I could find out who he was, explain myself, maybe he'd understand and leave me and Kara alone, maybe he'd stay in his own world, his dream world or his bar world downtown off the 26th Street bus.

I got off my bar stool and walked down the bar and sat beside him.

"What are you drinking?" I said.

He moved his head as little as he had to to catch my eye. He barely smiled. "You don't exist," he said.

I called the bartender over and told him, "Give him what he's drinking," and ordered another round for myself.

When the man got his drink he raised it to me. "You don't exist," he said. His eyes were dark and reflected nothing.

Maybe he didn't know he was talking to a Dialectician, but that wouldn't fly if all it had was wings. "Who are you?" I said.

He sipped. "I don't talk to myself."

"Well I got some suggestions about some other things you shouldn't do but do anyways," I said.

He looked at me then, a glimmer of something rising from deep within his self-absorption, and then fading back. He looked again to his drink. "How did you get here?"

"I took the bus."

Now he drank down and I ordered him another, more convinced each minute that he was the man who sang to Kara, and knowing more than that, that there was a time when he held her, when he parted her legs with his waist and cupped her mouth with his, silencing her screams with his own. And now he wouldn't leave her. Now he came back again and again.

"Who are you?" I said.

"An angel, a brother, the devil on his last reincarnation. And you, you are brand-new, a soul released from a cactus with a million lives to go."

"I'm not interested in mixing metaphors with you," I told him.

"Fight or not, she is mine, and she has always been mine."

"Leave her alone."

"She is mine, and she has always been mine," he said.

I grabbed him then, and made him look at me, but there was nothing in his eyes but blackness.

"I don't even know who you are," he said, "unless I have seen you somewhere in a dream."

"Kara Ruzci loves me," I said to him. "I sleep with her. I love her. And you haunt her in the night. And you haunt me."

He turned away. "Leave me alone," he said.

"If you come to her again I'll kill you."

And that made him smile. He did not show his teeth, but he smiled.

"I'll kill you," I said.

"And she will follow me, and you will lose us both." He called the bartender over. "Give the young man a drink," he said.

I turned it down. The man made a low noise, like the sobs that came from the foot of Kara's bed. "You don't pity me?" he said.

"I hate you."

"I pity you," he said softly. "I pity you very much."

My hands sweated under his pity. He moved from his stool and went to the door, stepping outside. I followed him, but he turned the corner and was gone.

I caught a cab for Kara Ruzci's.

And found him there in her driveway, watching her house like an eye. When I called to him he turned but said nothing, then walked up the drive. I followed him around the garage to the back of the house where he stopped, eyeing the wall to Kara's bedroom. My hand warmed the gun.

Ignoring me, he stepped forward, his face to the wall, and it was then I heard the song of Kara's fluted voice, wordless and sad. I felt as if a steel rod had entered my back and emerged through my groin, my knees buckling as I heard the man begin to sob to the bedroom wall. Kara's voice rose to meet his as the man's tears shimmered around him under the moon until he shone like crystal and wings burst from his back, sweating like a new moth's, whitened. He raised his arms as Kara came through the wall and he held her. Then he spread his wings and they rose above the house as if lifted by a gale and disappeared.

You don't, at first, feel the pain of a bullet, barely its thud, so I didn't feel the stake inside me until after they'd gone. My blood ran down the protruding tip and into the ground where it pinned me kneeling, and kept the blood neatly running from me into the snow. So this is what it feels like, I kept thinking, this is what it feels like, but couldn't keep my mind on what this was. I wasn't growing stronger so pushed against the rod to tuck my feet, and when the first nausea passed, stood, and came free. I had no interest in what or how I'd been impaled, I only knelt again and waited for Kara and the man to return.

Which they did, long later into the night, out of the eastern sky, a moth of light in the false dawn. The wind rose as they came over the house, and then went calm again as they landed at the wall to Kara's room. She left his embrace and went through the wall. The man pulled in his wings and turned. It was then, without rising, that I shot him in the chest. He fell, but I could see his breath in the air as I got up to stand over him. On his face, he had the most quizzical smile, before I blew it away.

Then it began to snow a blizzard. When I left there was no sight of the man or my blood. I left no footsteps, and in the now moonless night, had no shadow.

The Marriage of Heaven and Hell, Continued

HELEN GOT promoted again at Marycrest to Head Secretary to the Dean, Dean Hadrian Sullivan, Marycrest's one and only dean who kept a close clamp on any potential dean proliferation up there, according to Helen, and she got a raise in salary, made a bundle more than Red, though not nearly as much as the dean. Which irked her a little because she pretty much ran the school; organized the teaching schedules, worked out the college's annual budget, ordered food for the cafeteria, mediated hierarchy squabbles among the nuns, gave out the janitorial assignments, signed all the documents that Dean Hadrian Sullivan himself was supposed to sign, and just as well because Helen knew a lot more about them anyways, and decided who got to see the dean, which was nobody, because Dean Hadrian Sullivan spent all his time coaching Marycrest's all-nun basketball team which was the best all-nun basketball team in Erie, if not the world.

That all-nun basketball team was his passion, though he always gave Helen a lot of credit for everything else. When he introduced her he always said, "Meet my head secretary, Helen Loop, she runs the school," and Helen always said, "If I run the school how come I don't get paid to run the school?" which everybody took as a good joke and an admission that Helen didn't run the school which, par for the course, was absolutely wrong, though Dean Hadrian Sullivan always answered her, he always said, "Because I'm the dean, you could apply for my job, you certainly have the experience, but I wouldn't give it to you because you don't have the credentials," a very funny light-hearted joke that was really deadly serious.

Red had pretty much saturated the toilet paper market. Everybody everywhere pretty much had his toilet paper from Toledo to Wheeling to Utica and that was as far as he was going to drive in one day. He didn't like staying away from home, he'd got his fill of that during the war, but you could see it bugged the hell out of him that Helen made more money, because there he was so mountainous and agile he could play Ping-Pong with bowling balls, and so personable he could sell snowmobiles to Central Americans, not to mention all his artistic sensibilities which did him about as much good as wet wood. But he saw himself as a failure, after all, he'd been working since he was old enough to smell, something which only made things worse for him around that house. Everybody else in the place had lost their smell completely and Red would have had us all at the doctor if he didn't hate doctors so much; Red was always saying the place smelled like decay or sweat or germs or burnt fudge and who could argue, none of us could smell a fucking thing and if Red was right we were probably all better off. Though you had to give Red a certain amount of credit, considering that he was the only person who could smell in what was according to him a stinky house, and that after working all his life, his wife, after having four kids, went to work for less than a year and ended up with more money and authority than he'd ever see, you had to give him credit, he'd barely smashed a goddamn thing yet. He just spent a lot of time next to the Zenith flipping his bowling ball like it was so much popped popcorn and watching Helen as she slept on the couch under the afghan she was crocheting for Bush's next Last Christmas. Then on the weekend he'd take some of his toilet paper bonus points or some money he'd saved and come home with a Maytag washer or GE dryer or Hoover vacuum cleaner or Westinghouse dishwasher or Singer sewing machine or Amana Radar Range or Sunbeam iron, then he'd stand in front of Helen beaming like the moon on the Caribbean and Helen'd give him a peck on the cheek, be happy for about ten seconds, and then get real depressed, which is exactly not what Red needed while he was trying to carry on the facade of the great provider. No, Red didn't get it and Helen wouldn't explain it, so Red walked around the house looking real hard at the doors. You could see he was waiting for the first warm spring day, which, you had to hand him, was a subtle evolutionary step in his emotions.

He quit selling toilet paper. Went out and got himself a job as a door salesman. Must have figured everybody else in the world had the same inclinations when they got irritable. He probably sold a hundred doors the first day because he came home with a Waring blender for Helen, though this time she didn't even get happy for ten seconds, she just went up to bed, about a half hour later she was up there puking in the bathroom.

"It's that goddamn operation," said Red. "She's not a woman anymore." He got his bowling ball out of the closet and looked thoughtfully at the maple tree that had started to grow back together pretty good since the last time he blasted it. You could see he was thinking that maybe just a few more household appliances, maybe an electric knife or a rotisserie would get Helen over the hump.

Well that's when a door slammed upstairs, and you knew from the slam of it, because it was an old slam, though one we hadn't heard for a while, that Neda was coming down for a face-off. Not that Neda even liked Helen; Neda didn't really like Helen much at all, but there was getting to be less and less room in the house between Helen's holy objects and Red's appliances, on the level of ontology if not simple volume, and despite and added on to everything, Neda had to look at Helen every day, like I had to look at Red, sometimes things were just that simple.

Maybe Red didn't fear anything in the whole goddamn

world, but if there was one thing that had an effect on him it was that slam. Red turned to the stairway as Neda emerged. He put down his bowling ball.

"Why do you think she's up there puking?" said Neda.

"Your mother pukes easy," said Red.

"For Christ's fucking sake," said Neda. "Put some carpet up there."

Red walked over and brought his fist down on Neda's head, just enough to knock her out cold. He looked over at me, into the front living room, but I wasn't going to give him half a reason for conversation let alone argument because he'd been looking for an excuse to kill me ever since I was born and I was too close to being the hell out of there for good to blow it on carpet in the bathroom after I'd spent my whole life getting splinters.

So he went upstairs and had it out with Helen. There was nothing he hated worse than her puking unless it was making him feel responsible for her puking, he just had too much conviction in his innocence to not feel guilty about it. So he went up there and argued about her side of the family, mostly Uncle Jon and all the stuff he did for Bush while that whole side of the family shunned him, even Bush, just like Helen did after he bought her all these wonderful appliances. Then he started about the thousand he and Helen gave to David to buy cows that they were probably never going to see again. You could hear Helen puking through most of this, though she raised her head out of the toilet long enough to call Red a heathen and offer the Loop antithesis to Pelkowski economic failurism, Uncle Bif, the synthesis of which was a bunch of sounds that made you know that Red was holding Helen's head in the toilet.

That was real bad planning on Helen's part.

And you had to give Red his due, sometimes he was just a bad man.

So winter or not he was downstairs just a few minutes later and knocked out all the doors, saving his last and best for the front three that he took out with three straight overhead rights, bam, bam, bam, and headed right over to Jimbo Funster's just like the good old days; those two probably had quite a time distracting each other considering all the distraction Jimbo needed now that Funly was orbiting in space. Helen came downstairs when the noise was over, stepped over Neda and changed the Infant's diapers, put on a new set of underwear and robes, black with gold trim, lit her candles and went to work. I got Neda on her feet and took her up to her room.

"Helen must have figured you were just taking a nap," I said to her.

Neda lit a Pall Mall and let the smoke ease out of her nostrils. "You can't blame Helen for being nuts," she said. "Or Red." She pulled Jim Beam out of her underwear drawer where she used to keep her Mars Bars. "Helen's family's rotten to Red. They'll never see that money they gave Uncle David. Jon is nuts."

I drank some Beam and Neda did too, but I didn't say anything. I was at the point where I didn't have anything to say to Neda anymore.

"Helen's not the only person in the house with cold feet," she said to me.

"And Red's not the only one who can put carpet in," I said.

"Exactly," said Neda. "That's why he's the only one who can put carpet in."

That's why I'd stopped talking to her. If there was anything Neda hadn't figured out right, it would have been news to God.

Well you'd have froze your ass off that night if you didn't go downstairs and sleep near a radiator, the whole goddamn family was down there staking claims and making tents around the radiator of their choice with blankets or cardboard boxes or whatever else they could get their hands on, except when Red came home he got Helen and the two of them went upstairs and slept together in their room. Helen always said Red made enough heat in bed to heat Winnipeg and I guess that resolved a lot of their differences when it got cold out and Red knocked out all the doors, besides, he needed a lot of comforting on those nights after he'd broken all the chairs or punched out all the appliances or knocked all the doors out because seeing his house in such shabby condition got him real depressed, made him feel like he was living in a slum, though of course Helen could always suggest we move if she wanted him to go outside and beat up on the pear tree. Anyway, they slept upstairs and everybody else grabbed a radiator; they weren't a pair to doubt their children's adaptivity, something you could mistake as some kind of neglect if you weren't perceptive.

Next day, even before Red's new door company delivered its truckful of new doors, I was upstairs with Red putting in the new carpet and holding all the tools he didn't need. I got to hold the screwdriver and the pliers and the monkey wrench while Red measured out the carpet lengths, cut them, and tacked them to the floor. He had a white handkerchief around his head to catch his sweat because anytime he worked he sweated, it didn't matter that there was only one radiator up there and even *with* doors on the house it must have been about a minus six thousand degrees not counting the wind chill, and of course I had to stand, he wouldn't let you sit down on the job, you had to stand there holding tools apropos for a truck engine job while he crawled around on the floor tacking carpet, then of course when he moved you had to move with him, he didn't like you getting too far away, you might have a lapse in attention.

"You see what I'm doing here?" said Red.

"Yes."

"Pay attention."

"I think I got to shit."

"Don't talk like that in the house when your mother's here."

"She's downstairs."

"You take a shit you'll never come back."

"You need the monkey wrench?"

"Not yet."

"You're never going to need the monkey wrench."

"I'm going to need it. Give it to me."

"For what?"

"Okay then, hold it."

"I'm going to take a shit, Red."

Red looked up for a second. "You smell like decay."

"It's because I have to take a shit."

"You don't smell like shit, you smell like decay. You been boozin?"

"No."

"Don't tell me. You're turning into a goddamn boozer."

"Maybe I got a cavity."

"Don't get any cavities. I don't want anybody getting sick. I don't want anybody getting in trouble. I don't want any boozin. And stay out of the bathroom. I got everything laid out in the bathroom, you go in there you'll mess it up."

"Red," I told him. "This is the last time I'm going to help you do something."

"You think it's the last time," said Red. "I get too old I'll get a goddamn ball bat."

Well you didn't want to push a discussion with Red beyond the ball-bat stage, considering he'd almost drowned Helen in the toilet and everybody had to freeze and not take a shit for two days so we'd have carpet upstairs, maybe Red himself didn't know how to receive a present but he sure made you grateful for what you got.

Not that it took much around then to make me grateful. Our friend Mr. Tony Blanion had joined Grandma Funster and several other notables in that neighborhood who now only spoke to selected individuals like Andrew who most importantly weren't the police. Blanion was as dead as lead and I didn't have a thing to do with it. And Bobby Hansen had a relapse. All that bouncing around during ball games and rallies and proving things with his feet must have been too much for him because he'd recently returned to the primordial innocence of total vegetable, the only thing moving in Bobby Hansen was brain waves which were probably having a free-for-all up there now that they were freed of the responsibility of lugging him around. Of course it was a sad, sad thing in some ways, but I had to keep it in perspective, it was me or him. "Bobby Hansen," said Helen to me one day when she got done meditating with the Infant, "is a lot like Job."

"What is the experiment," Job asked the Lord, "and what is the tool?"

Helen started writing letters to Bobby Hansen and his family and sometimes I sat down with her and chipped right in, told Bobby Hansen ambiguous wonderful things about the life of the mind. Helen even kind of befriended the Hansens and sometimes after work went over to Glenwood Hills and had a cup of coffee with Mrs. Hansen and Bobby, though Bobby, himself, didn't have any coffee, if you wanted to feed Bobby Hansen you had to kind of open his face up like an oyster shell and put things inside to dissolve, but Helen had coffee and Mrs. Hansen had coffee and talked about how hard Mr. Hansen had it being a loan officer down at First National Bank, the same bank, it wasn't difficult for Helen to note, that she worked at for a little while during World War II which the Strongs owned and where Archie Strong worked, though I guess you really couldn't say he worked there, you had to say he was kind of affiliated, and where David Pell just got his matching loan to buy cows and cow milking machines for his farm, in fact Mr. Hansen was the president of the loan office and if there was one thing he hated more than dealing with people who didn't deserve loans it was sometimes breaking down and giving them loans and then they never paid them back, no, you just didn't make any money loaning money to people who didn't have money.

Well Helen was nuts but she was no dummy, so one day I took a hike up to Marycrest and went over to the Hansens' with her after work, looked Bobby Hansen right in his active eyeballs, told him how much everybody missed him at school, even explained to him Red's theory about how you couldn't have two great running backs in the same backfield, tried to give him some credit for creating Stinky Jinx, though I could see Mrs. Hansen regarded all that pretty dubiously. Then Bobby Hansen's eyes started bouncing like fumbled footballs and he started to drool so we had to go.

Me and Helen didn't talk on the bus on the way home, though when we got off on 24th and Celebration she held my wrist for a minute and looked me in the eyes.

"You're bad," said Helen.

"No," I said to her. "You're bad."

"No," said Helen. "You're bad."

After talking things out like that I guess we both felt better.

Though Willie, himself, wasn't looking better, he looked a little pale in his pillows, and though it was as hot as usual in his attic he wasn't collecting much residue. He pushed himself up a bit, kind of like Jim Bowie when people came into his sickroom at the Alamo, and rubbed his chin with his bad hand.

"I see you are not wondering why you are not stuck in the ground somewhere," he said.

Well I have to admit, I'd been trying not to think too much about it. I'd been with Kara Ruzci a couple times since I'd last seen Willie and though she seemed to suffer an occasional unspecified moment of abstraction, like she'd momentarily misplaced a piece of self, we got along better than ever and loved each other with such passion I thought our eyes would break, then we fell asleep and dreamed we held each other asleep in our dreams. Only once, deep in the night, was it broken, when she awoke and sat up, her eyes like landed wasps, her face listening. "I feel like I'm waiting for something that already happened," she whispered to me. "To fall in love with me," I said.

"Some things happen and some things don't happen," I said to Willie. "And sometimes what happens and what doesn't happen happen at the same time and you can't tell them apart."

"The happening and the not happening," said Willie.

"Yes."

He reached behind him for his toolbox. "Fis is true and wrong."

Being a Dialectician it didn't take me long to work out the other logical possibilities, even though I knew each conclusion dictated some antithesis and of course more that Willie had anticipated long before he said anything. I watched him prepare his hypo.

"So do not be finking that what happens first is the cause," he said to me.

He found his vein and I got ready as he prepared my experiment.

"He doesn't come back anymore," I said. "That's all that matters to me."

"But not all that matters." He put the needle in my arm and emptied the hypo. "Somewhere there is a wound."

"If you know so much," I said to Willie, "why don't you tell me."

Willie sat back again on his pillows. "Maybe before you were born," he said to me, "you knew somefin."

One thing I didn't know before I was born was how to drive and one spring afternoon I went down to the Culture House to see Kara Ruzci and she came out of the darkroom and said, "Happy Birthday!"

"It's also my birthday," I told Kara Ruzci.

"No," said Kara Ruzci. "It's *my* birthday."

"And Khrushchev's birthday."

"It's also Khrushchev's birthday," said Kara Ruzci. "But it's a very special day of which you have no understanding."

Well it was true I didn't have much understanding in general, I guess it seemed to me that understanding always implicated explaining and knowing and planning, not that I had any evidence around me to indicate it or that it was the reason I didn't operate on that particular disc, I guess Kara Ruzci kind of understood that, there certainly was a condensed thread of world splitting that Kara Ruzci operated on, so amidst all that, that day was the day Kara Ruzci decided to teach me to drive.

We waited for Polly Doggerel to get back from lunch and then got in Kara's green Ford Falcon and drove to the hardware store where Kara Ruzci bought a hundred thousand feet of industrial tape and thick foam rubber which we taped all over the inside of the car, the floor and seats and dash and steering wheel, and then all over the outside of the car, over the roof and hood and trunk and fenders, we even put foam on the hubcaps, that car had foam on everything but the lights, tires, and windows. Then we foam-rubbered our legs and arms and torsos and necks and heads, just left a little open space for face and the bottom of our feet and my fingers, Kara Ruzci, herself, foamed her fingers because she wasn't going to be driving, and then we foam rubbered Polly Doggerel because as good as she was on the open road dodging trucks she was pretty much at my mercy in the Falcon, though she took it pretty well, looked like Polly Doggerel saw it as an opportunity to experiment in weightlessness, made me think I was maybe a latent carrier of the disease, and she spent a lot of time that day floating upside down in the backseat in foam dog shape grinning at me in the rearview mirror like I was the next Christmas turkey.

"Okay," said Kara Ruzci when we were all foamed. "Let's go."

That Falcon only had two gears, forward and reverse, and I was amazed how little the road got once I sat behind the wheel, though we'd pretty much doubled our size on the outside and halved it on the in and Polly Doggerel didn't make it too easy when she floated up into the front seat, and as Kara Ruzci said, we didn't have to worry about hitting stuff, you either hit stuff or you didn't, that's how you had to approach driving, the worst that could happen was you hit stuff and we were as ready as you could be for that, so of course I hit as much as I could, particularly at four-way stop signs, though some of the larger vehicles tended to put us into prolonged bouncings which pretty much made everybody in the car weightless, and at certain busy intersections, once we started ricocheting, that could go on quite a while. Nonetheless, once I got that out of my system I started getting around pretty good, whence we stopped at a State Store for one Kara Ruzci armful of champagne, chilled by taping it to the roof, put a child's snowsuit on Polly Doggerel, right over her foam rubber, made her look a little bit like a negro eskimo, good thing for her it started to snow, and headed for the zoo.

That snow added a whole new sense of inability to my driving and by the time we got to the zoo, in transit having tied a rope to Polly Doggerel so she could go out the window and space-walk for a bottle of champagne, we were all pretty giddy with weightlessness. There was about four inches of snow on the ground and we had that whole quiet zoo to ourselves, got Polly Doggerel in free for being under twelve, and took turns holding Polly Doggerel as we made footprints in the snow under the full blank white falling air, went from cage to cage showing her all the other kinds of animals who were caged for being so wild as to not have the discipline to avoid extinction. You couldn't see much of Polly Doggerel underneath all that foam rubber and snowsuit except for her eyes like raisin pies and grin like the last wiener dealer in the world, but for Polly Doggerel, as she understood it, for her kind it was either the cage or the grave or both, and so she had to live like Achilles on a picnic, maybe that's why she liked the big cats the best, Polly Doggerel didn't talk much but when we went inside and Kara Ruzci held her right up to the lion's cage, that dog didn't even blink when that animal took a swipe at her.

"What do you think of that?" said Kara Ruzci to Polly Doggerel's black nose.

Polly Doggerel yawned and said, "arf," like barf or scarf, or suicide, or semicolon, rather stoic.

Kara Ruzci figured she was just tired from all that floating and champagne.

Next thing we picked up a couple of pizzas, Kara Ruzci didn't cook much, the inside of her refrigerator looked like she'd been saving cheese for Napoleon, and went out to Kara Ruzci's snowland where she turned on the heat full blast and we ate pizza and drank champagne and played strip poker, which took a long time considering all the stuff we had on and the fact that Polly Doggerel was much more interested in the pizza and champagne than the card game, nonetheless she finally won, which left me and Kara Ruzci dead naked to lefts, exactly where we wanted. We made love there on the floor and then went to her bedroom and made love, only to sleep and dream of making love and sleep and dream of making love, deeper and deeper into dream and love, waking only to hold her beneath me and press myself into her; that night we loved and loved as no one has ever loved, with no distinction between sleep and dream and wakefulness and love, I came into her and she into me, a marriage of day and night and all the time in between, and an end to everything I had ever been before, to whatever I was before that love. In some morning when we finally came away, we looked upon the fields and fields of immaculate snow. "I am your love and you are my love," said Kara Ruzci, and I loved her with such pain I thought the center of me would split, yet that pain was all that held me to the earth.

STINKY JINX LED South High to the city title in basketball that winter, that tournament game to Prep was the only one they lost, revenging that in the first rematch 77–13, and in the second, when Coach Barfoni pulled Stinky in the second half, 58–36. That kind of beneficence of course produced nothing but disdain from that Prep crowd, they made it known all over the Erie *Times News* and both Erie's TV stations that they'd nail Stinky and South in the district title game, and Barfoni, not having won a basketball game let alone a title since Lank Ward left South in the thirties, turned Stinky loose for the whole game, so they beat Prep 110–8 in that one, so of course after the game there was a big riot, raised a lot of fuss in the town about ethics in sports and nobody at South gave a rat's ass because they had Stinky for another two years. The only worry around there was keeping Stinky from getting too ethereal. He was picking up a tendency to not come back down on the floor after he scored, made it a little tough for him to get back on defense, and occasionally he got so high above the basket and unveiled so many balletlike moves up there that he forgot to shoot at all, or sometimes even missed when he eventually decided to drop it through. Of course if South had the lead like they usually did it didn't matter much.

By the time South beat Pittsburgh Fifth Avenue for the Western Pennsylvania championship, Stinky started to get some attention, and after the state title game, even though Stinky drifted off somewhere into the ceiling lights of the Harrisburg Farm Show Arena after his first basket, took the whole first half of searching the rafters and catwalks up there just to find him hooting to himself behind the scoreboard, it was pretty clear that it was going to be impossible to bury Stinky's talents, even in Erie, PA. Big Dick was on the phone every second he wasn't in his Buckhorn Potato Chip truck, arranging Stinky's enigmatic interviews that he kept down to one a day in which Stinky generally hooted softly and talked about flower arrangements. Anybody with shoe polish for a brain could see he'd taken sports about as far as it could go in terms of accomplishment as well as fashion so of course nobody saw it, particularly Big Dick. On top of it all, I knew Stinky missed Funly. That spring Stinky went through track season breaking records like potato chips, with all the élan of a sleepwalking gazelle.

"I told you this sports stuff wasn't all it's cracked up to be," I told Stinky. Big Dick was on the phone arranging interviews and we were watching the finals of the Miss Pennsylvania contest on the TV.

"Hooo," said Stinky. "Just hooo."

"Stinky, what about *Sport Magazine* next Wednesday?" yelled in Big Dick.

"Can't you get something with *Mademoiselle*?" said Stinky.

"What a card," said Big Dick. He told the phone, "Wednesday's fine."

"Look at them," said Stinky pointing to the TV. "They're not any better off."

"Miss Pennsylvania never wins," I said to him.

"Well look at them," said Stinky. "Their coiffeurs and cosmeticians should be shot." He looked at me. "A desert of the imagination."

Well Stinky sure could bring the warm out of you with his planet-shattering innocence, even if he was the greatest athlete in the history of Erie, Pennsylvania if not the world. I gave him the best I had. "It's a pluralistic universe," I told him.

"It's a mediocre universe," said Stinky.

"Maybe that too."

"Oh hooo," said Stinky. "Hooo, hooo, hooo."

Well there I was, simmering in the milk of human kindness with Stinky Jinx when I should have been covering my ass, because while I was in there with Stinky, Helen came home from work an hour early, extricated Andrew and Joseph from the bedroom, and packed them in a taxi for the Hansens'. I don't know how she got those Hansens to buy that pie, though I guess if your kid's a vegetable you're willing to try anything to elevate his status, even if everything is equal and holy in the eyes of God, so there was Helen setting up shop with Andrew and Joseph at the Hansens'. She even had the Infant over there. I guess they threw around some incense and a couple prayers, then got down to the real stuff and had Joseph shut down and turned Andrew loose on Bobby Hansen. I, myself, as a Dialectician, was no novice to the ephemeral realms, and though open enough to accept unusual phenomena, I knew a ridiculous idea when I saw one. A WATTS line to the dead is one thing and making paralytics walk another, that's as plain as rain, a whole new ball game, hardball with the saints.

When Helen came back with Joseph and Andrew, they didn't take a taxi home, they got a ride in Mr. Hansen's new station wagon, she had a grin like Ho Chi Minh, something that would have told me something else if I knew who Ho Chi Minh was, but I didn't, so I didn't catch wind of anything until she put the Infant back on top his cabinet in the holy room and lit enough candles to bake a cake in there. I went up to the room and found Joseph and Andrew.

"Bobby Hansen is a mobile unit," said Andrew.

"I think it was just mental," said Joseph.

"Fundamental mental," said Andrew. "Just guilt or something."

"He's walking," I said.

"And talking," said Joseph.

"What did he say?"

"Nothing of interest," said Andrew.

"He's not the brightest guy in the world, you know," said Joseph.

"Besides," said Andrew. "He's got amnesia."

"You didn't cure that," I said to him.

"What do you want?" said Joseph.

"Miracles?" said Andrew.

Well things hadn't looked so simple and clear since I almost shot Bobby Hansen in the first place. Looked more and more like I had a soul like the Mystic Writing Pad, put whatever you want down, lift the cellophane sheet, and bingo, it's all gone, just some little tiny traces left over on the cellophane about as meaningful as gnat shit. I felt so good about things I even went to school one day. Of course the place was buzzing like crazy about Bobby Hansen being back, and him having spent the last year and a half as a vegetable there was a lot of talk about making him repeat his senior year, everybody having seemingly forgotten that universal law about having two stars in the same backfield. I guess the Hansens kept the whole business about Andrew pretty quiet because everybody attributed Bobby Hansen's miraculous recovery to his tremendous willpower. I saw Bobby Hansen in the hall carrying books for eighteen different girls, went up and shook his hand, told him how glad I was he was ambulatory. He didn't know me from a flapjack.

But one person who did recognize me was the principal who I wouldn't have recognized except that she introduced herself to me and took me in her office, a stuffy little place with too many clocks, and proceeded to explain the adult world to me. She had a rather linear and conventional way of looking at things, also made a few disparaging comments about my attitude. They had a way of dealing with people like me, she said, they graduated them and got them the hell out of there. Good news was coming on like nuns.

Even Kara Ruzci had news for me. "I'm pregnant," said Kara Ruzci.

"Is it my baby?" I said.

"No," said Kara Ruzci. "It's *my* baby, but you are the father."

"I'm pretty young to be a father," I told Kara Ruzci.

"You're not young for nothing," said Kara Ruzci, which I had to admit, made absolutely no sense. "How do you like August?"

"I like it warm," I said.

Kara Ruzci hugged Polly Doggerel who'd taken so well to astronaut training she tended to move rather weightlessly at a moment's notice.

"First I'll meet your parents and then you'll meet my parents and we'll get married in August on the Feast of the Assumption and Polly Doggerel will have a young baby sibling for Christmas."

You'd never have guessed that Kara Ruzci had such a talent for conventions and logistics from just looking at her, and I had to admit, it was a good thing that pregnancy came along because the way things were going up to then it was looking like I wouldn't have any excuses, outside the ontological, for not taking control of my life. So quick as a boxcar I dragged Kara Ruzci down to 24th Street for dinner with the family.

All in all I figured Red and Helen would be pretty happy I was going to graduate, and probably pretty happy I had a girlfriend, which would preclude any chance of my homosexuality; I didn't exactly mature early, never had a wet dream till I was deep sixteen, and didn't even care about girls until Kara Ruzci. Helen had been checking my sheets for cum for years, even asked me once how come I didn't have cum on my sheets and I didn't say anything to her. So Red and Helen had to be feeling pretty good about everything occurring and about time. Though the fact that Kara Ruzci was a little older than me by about seven years and more pregnant by several months was going to kind of give them the absolutely correct feeling that everything was sort of happening all at once.

Helen made pork chops, which was a bad harbinger because there was never enough pork chops for Red anyways and now we had one extra person. You could see him eyeing that pork chop plate, when it came to pork chops Red didn't discriminate between creed, sex, or color, it was just a simple matter of pork chops, and of course then he went so far as to do exactly the opposite of what he really wanted, Red had a tendency to do that, and when Helen passed him the pork chop tray he didn't even take one, he passed that tray right over to Kara Ruzci on the far end. He almost shit when she took two. And now there was me and Neda between him and the pork chop tray on one side of the table and Joseph and Andrew and Helen on the other. Kara Ruzci held that tray for me and Neda, then passed that tray the other way around. That was not a household in which to give up your rights. Red wasn't going to blow up while Kara Ruzci was there so we all took two or three, even Helen. Red got the last two pork chops and watched the potatoes. He grabbed a half-loaf of white bread and had himself a bread sandwich, ate it down, mfff, mfff, made everybody feel a little safer, Red with his mouth full.

Nor was that the kind of household where you waited for the end of anything, so I started right up and told everybody I was going to graduate.

"Downright normal of you," said Joseph. But nobody else even lifted a head from their plate, which was okay with me, I'd lived little enough to know the blessings of being ignored. Then Kara Ruzci told them we were going to get married which didn't get a rise out of anybody either, though Helen did stop shoveling pork chop for a minute, you had to eat fast around there because you didn't exactly have hegemony over your own plate once somebody else got done, especially eating next to Red, and between those bites Helen said, "What's the rush?"

Well there wasn't really a good answer to that one. Helen finished her second pork chop and took the third one with her as she went over to her dish cabinet arabesque, we always had dinner in the holy room when we had guests, and put a tiny pair of earmuffs over the Infant's ears and turned his face to the wall. She looked at Kara Ruzci and the corners of her mouth made an effort to go up or down but instead just kind of stretched out more straight. I don't think she knew she was doing it but her right hand went down and held her belly. I wondered what she wondered about Kara Ruzci. She must of known with Kara being as old as she was that I wasn't the first person in there, and with a name like Ruzci things could only be worse if Kara was a divorcee, which I guess she was old enough to be. Nonetheless you could see Helen's eyes register the geometric symbolic expanse of it all in seconds, then resolve; Helen could reconcile a crocodile in her bathtub and do the most practical thing in the world with it, you had to give her that.

Red finished eating and got his bowling ball, stood at the head of the table spinning that thing on one baby finger, then rolling it down his arm and over his neck and out the other arm and spun it on the other baby finger, which pretty much said it all. I could tell he liked Kara Ruzci okay, and though he didn't like the idea of me fucking around, or worse her fucking around, at least we'd done it with each other. He had lineage beating with every heartbeat, though he'd certainly be disappointed if it was a girl and he'd probably kill me if it was a boy and I named him Jarvis, and the idea of being a grandfather didn't strike him so hot either; he was too young to be a grandfather, he'd figured he wouldn't be a grandfather until he was too old and had to use a ball bat for everything. On top of all that, as much as Red loved me he had to hate me, or vice versa, and I was about to leave a real void there, already he was eyeing Joseph and wondering how good he could hold tools. Of course Neda was deep into her campaign of the New Nice Self and just smiled at Kara Ruzci like she was the very last Mars Bar, and Andrew, well Andrew'd been to the Temple, after bringing Bobby Hansen back he just had nothing to say to anybody, the burden of supernaturality was a big pain in his ass.

I guess there just wasn't anything for anybody to say.

Red slipped that bowling ball down his chest and down his leg, spun it on his toe and kicked it behind him, caught it on his heel and flipped it into the living room, must have put a spin on it because it took a right angle when it hit the ground and went back in the closet; the only thing he couldn't do with that ball anymore was make it come when he called. Then he got his guitar and we all went into the living room where Red played and sang "The Yellow Rose of Texas" and "When Jimmy Rogers Said Good-bye," he looked at Helen most the whole time but sometimes he looked at Kara Ruzci, and he sang "I Walk the Line" and "Back in the Saddle Again" and "Rudolph the Red-Nosed Reindeer," he sang "The Old Wooden Cross," "There's a Star-Spangled Banner Flying Somewhere," and "Beautiful, Beautiful Brown Eyes," he sang that one right to Helen even though her eyes were closer to black, and then he sang "You Are My Sunshine," he looked at Helen and then he looked at Kara Ruzci and then he looked at Helen again and then he looked at Kara Ruzci, and when he sang, "And I hung my head and cried," he made you want to cry, made you feel like whatever you loved was the only thing in the world and it was doomed.

Well we drove all the way across the Pennsylvania Turnpike to Hoboken, New Jersey in Kara Ruzci's green Ford Falcon with Kara Ruzci pointing out bald eagles all along the way; I said, "Where?" and she said, "There," and I didn't see anything or saw something that sure wasn't an eagle and said, "I don't think that's an eagle," and she said, "It's an eagle"; it was tough to argue those kind of points with Kara Ruzci. And we had to stop every twenty minutes so Polly Doggerel could pee and get a hamburger while Kara Ruzci took photographs of everything, there wasn't a thing Kara wasn't interested in unless it was important, took us seventeen hours to get to Hoboken; nonetheless, Kara Ruzci's parents weren't appreciative.

Kara Ruzci's father was a zoo refurbishing mogul. He'd got in on the ground floor when he inherited a small hardware store and general house repairs service from his father who came over on the boat from southern Italy during World War I, though the Americans drafted him and sent him back over there where he surrendered to the Austrians and met his wife, who was now Grandma Ruzci, in an opera house in Vienna where he was kind of a prisoner and kind of a janitor, he was a little vague about exactly what the situation was, though Grandma Ruzci wasn't Austrian, she was from Milan and had gone to Vienna to study opera. Anyway they came back after the war and lived in Newark where Grandpa Ruzci bought a horse and wagon with all his savings and made a lot of money moving people out of town at night without them knowing it for the Mafia; he said they put a gun to his head, made him do it, but they paid him well, so when he got enough money he set up his hardware store out of which he also went out and repaired your house or car or tractor or horse or whatever was broken, he didn't care. Now he was a million years old, he made Bush look like just a baby old person, and all he had left of him was two big giant hands that hardly worked and two giant clomping feet, nothing in between but some stuff to hang clothes on, took all his strength just to lug his hands and feet around, so mostly he just sat around and drank dago red and cheap whiskey and lolled his head and said, "nyaa, nyaa," with a very intelligent look in his eye, he could say "nyaa, nyaa" in more ways than anybody I ever met, though Grandma Ruzci gave him a lot of shit for it. She was kind of roly-poly like ravioli, of which she probably made the best in the whole world, not that I ever had it before then, other than Chef Boyardee, which I would have said wasn't bad up till I had hers. She carried a picture around in her bras of when she was thirteen and studying opera in Vienna, that's how old she was when Grandpa

Ruzci found her and married her and brought her to America, she was posing in that picture with some kind of giant guitar that looked like a squash, and she walked around showing that picture to everybody, including Grandpa Ruzci who'd probably seen it a few thousand times, and saying what a mistake it was to come to America with Grandpa Ruzci where all she did was cook and have babies and now Grandpa Ruzci was old and useless and all he said was "nyaa, nyaa"; Grandpa Ruzci had a very special "nyaa, nyaa" to answer that.

Nonetheless all that set up Kara's dad, Grandpa and Grandma Ruzci's oldest son, Louie Ruzci, with his very own hardware store and home repair service, though Louie Ruzci was very big on saying how he became a millionaire after starting out with nothin, I guess it just depended on where exactly he thought he was starting out. Which I never felt like delineating. He wasn't the subtlest of fellows, he worked like hell and saved and invested his money and read *The Wall Street Journal* and got into zoo refurbishing just before this whole natural-habitat zoo movement got hot, pointed to his head when he said that, research, anybody can make money in America if he's smart, like Louie was, and most people weren't, looked me kind of hard in the eye when he said that, old Louie Ruzci really had a thing about I.Q. and dollars, and he was the first person I ever met who wore a toupee, made his head look pretty much like an Oldsmobile sedan with wood paneling, not only that, Louie Ruzci didn't even really like animals or give a shit about zoos.

"You think I like zoos?" Louie Ruzci asked me, he chewed a cigar but he never hardly lit it.

"Maybe."

"Maybe what?"

"Maybe you like zoos."

"I don't like zoos," said Louie Ruzci. "You don't have to like what you do. In fact nobody likes what they do. That's your first lesson. You don't make money doing things you like. You spend money doing things you like."

"He likes to argue," Mrs. Ruzci whose name was Barbie said to me, she looked like one of those big fat dill pickles only with a dress on.

"Not really," said Louie Ruzci. "People don't like to listen. They want to talk. You don't learn anything while you're talk-ing."

I looked across the room where Kara Ruzci was busy listen-ing, though you could see she wasn't listening to Louie, in fact I'd never seen Kara so disebullient, I guess she'd heard that listening business a lot of times over the years.

We weren't over at Louie and Barbie Ruzci's, which was some big home on a hillside out of town with sprawling acres of lawn and then woods, we were right in downtown Hoboken at the little house that Louie bought for Grandpa and Grandma Ruzci, sitting in a small stuffy living room with big padded chairs everywhere. Me and Kara and Louie and Barbie were in there along with Grandpa Ruzci who was so deep in a big thick chair that all you could see of him was his clomp feet and giant hands, every once in a while you heard a couple of nyaa nyaas come out of there so you knew he was still alive, and Grandma Ruzci was making delicious sounds in the kitchen, you could see the heat in there, probably would have smelled pretty good if I could have smelled, though sometimes she bitched about how hard she was working and how Grandpa Ruzci was good for nothin and she should have done something else with her life other than cook for him for fifty years, then Barbie Ruzci got up and went into the kitchen to help her and Grandma Ruzci chased her out and said, "Send that good-for-nothing husband of mine in here to help," and Grandpa Ruzci said, "nyaa, nyaa," from deep within his chair and somehow despite those huge hands and feet that he dragged around without having anything else to drag them with, he got up and went in the kitchen and Grandma Ruzci chased him out, said it was too late. That went on for quite a while while we waited for Kara's younger sister Louise and her husband Arnold who had four kids already and one more on the way, Arnold used to sell insurance but now he was a foreman for

Louie Ruzci, and he and Louise, babies and all, sold Amway.

But they weren't there yet.

"What do you do for a living?" Louie Ruzci asked me.

I told him, "I go to high school," which was only a lie in that I didn't attend.

"Are you one of Kara's students?" asked Barbie Ruzci.

"In a way," I said.

"He's too linear," said Kara. It was nice to know she could talk in front of her parents.

"Yes," I said. "My pictures all turn out parallel."

"Photography isn't a profession," said Louie Ruzci.

"Teaching photography is a profession," said Barbie Ruzci, looking at Kara.

"Teaching photography is not a profession," said Louie Ruzci.

"Louie likes to argue," said Barbie Ruzci.

"I don't," said Louie. "Other people like to argue because they don't listen."

"Nyaa, nyaa," said Grandpa Ruzci, rather sardonically.

"What are you doing after high school?" Louie said to me. He took his unlit cigar out of his mouth.

"I'm going to retire."

"You think that's funny," said Louie. It took him a while but I could see he was finally wondering what I was doing there with Kara. "My daughters should get married," said Louie.

"One did," said Barbie, you could see she was the more observant of those two Ruzcis.

"I'm going to," said Kara.

"Find men who'll take care of them."

"Sounds good to me," said Kara.

"Me too," said Barbie.

"Me too," I said.

"Nyaa, nyaa," said Grandpa Ruzci.

"You were always good for nothin," yelled in Grandma Ruzci. "Don't tell me who takes care of who."

"I'm getting married," said Kara.

"You don't want to struggle all your life," said Louie.

Just then Louise and Arnold and their four kids came lopping in, they looked like a whole family of those Thanksgiving parade balloons only eating hot dogs, those kids looked like four different sizes of bloated mice. Polly Doggerel who'd been playing outside came floating in with them grinning like a Samurai, and though she tried to remain pretty inconspicuous by staying low to the ground, sometimes she bumped into Louie's shins.

"There's something wrong with your dog," said Louie to Kara.

"But what could it be?" said Kara Ruzci.

Not that any of that fazed Polly Doggerel, she got eyeball to eyeball with one of those mice, mesmerized him, and took his hot dog.

"Hey, cut that out," said Arnold to Polly Doggerel, who right away looked him in the eye and in about six-and-a-half seconds took his hot dog. "What the hell," said Arnold.

"There's something wrong with that dog," said Louie.

"It's a protein deficiency," said Louise. She had the manner of a dark beach ball in the Coney Island of life. "She needs vitamins," she said to Kara. "I got some vitamins in the car if you want to buy some."

"She needs some french fries," said Kara.

"There's nothing wrong with her," said Grandma Ruzci from the kitchen door. "My little Carmen used to do that all the time, and he could sing *La Traviata* like an angel. She just needs a little spaghetti."

Polly Doggerel's eyes turned into brown lights.

"Nyaa, nyaa," said Grandpa Ruzci.

"What do you know," said Grandma Ruzci. "You used to beat poor Carmen. He used to make him eat hot peppers to keep him from singing."

"Nyaa, nyaa, nyaa," said Grandpa Ruzci.

"There's something wrong here," said Louie Ruzci.

"Nyaaaa," said Grandpa Ruzci.

"I'm getting married," said Kara Ruzci.

Polly Doggerel took Louise Ruzci's hot dog.

"What the hell," said Arnold.

"Let's eat," said Grandma Ruzci, and Grandpa Ruzci charged into the kitchen, hands and feet first, where he set up a glass of beer and a glass of whiskey and a glass of dago red in front of everybody, one thing he could do with those weighty balloon hands of his was handle booze, though it was real apparent that those Ruzcis, except for a select few, or should I say one, Kara, had balloonitis in their genes, if not elsewhere as well.

Grandma Ruzci passed around spaghetti with red sauce, ravioli stuffed with meat and spinach and cheese, some kind of rice with chicken in it, big rounds of hot Italian sausage that Grandpa Ruzci made himself, along with dago red wine, that sausage was the only thing that wasn't a fucking noodle, but it was all the best food in the world and those grandparent Ruzcis wouldn't let you get half of anything done without filling you up again. And Polly Doggerel got her very own amounts of everything, only on the floor in an aluminum pie dish; that was a bit of a dilemma for her, so finally Kara went over and put the dish on a box so she could sit up and eat with her hands which was a little sloppy but Grandma Ruzci didn't have any hamburger buns. For dessert we had blackberry pie, chocolate cake, spumoni ice cream, some kind of cold cream-filled donuts, and six different kinds of Italian cookies.

"This was certainly a great meal," said Kara Ruzci. "I'm getting married."

"Eat some more," said Grandma Ruzci.

"Grandpa Ruzci poured some more booze and said, "Nyany-nyaa." He was happy.

"I couldn't run my business like this," said Louie Ruzci. "Too much waste."

"You don't run the business," said Barbie Ruzci. "I run the business."

Good thing Louie wasn't listening or that might have got him pretty upset.

"Let's take that children's zoo job in Youngstown," said Arnold.

"You want some vitamins for that dog?" Louise asked Kara.

"After I get married," said Kara.

"I got windshield cleaner and Turtle Wax," said Louise. "If you buy in volume you save."

"You full yet?" Grandma Ruzci asked me.

"Yes," I said.

"Have some more."

"Nyaaa," said Grandpa Ruzci.

"He likes you because you eat," said Grandma Ruzci.

"Me and Kara are going to get married," I told her.

"Eat more," said Grandma Ruzci.

"The Youngstown Zoo isn't talking enough money," said Barbie Ruzci.

"We'll take it," Louie told Arnold.

"He's only saying that to be argumentative," Barbie Ruzci said to me.

Grandpa Ruzci poured me some more wine, whiskey, and beer.

"Hey Grandpa Ruzci," I said to him. "Me and Kara are getting *married!*"

"Nyaa-ny-nya-ny-nya-ny-nyaaaa!" said Grandpa Ruzci. I think it made him pretty happy.

"Sit down," Grandma Ruzci told him, "before you hit somebody with your hands. One of these days he's going to die," she said to somebody, it was hard to tell who, not that it mattered, "and what will I have for all these years." She threw her hand out. "Pffft." She said "pffft" a lot like Bush.

Grandpa Ruzci threw his hands and feet out in front of him and followed them out to the stuffy little living room where Arnold and Louise had their kids eating separately at a card table, though I guess he forgot about them or just plain built up too much momentum because there was a crash and some screams and a festbed of nyaa-nyaas. By the time everybody got in there to see it there was just a pile of plates and garbage and a messy tablecloth and the throbbing hands and feet of Grandpa Ruzci.

Polly Doggerel licked him.

"Nyaa," he said.

"Nyaa," said Polly Doggerel.

"There's something wrong with your dog," said Louie Ruzci to Kara. He was sweating under his toupee.

"Vitamins," said Louise.

And that's pretty much the way it went on for the rest of the night and probably the next day and forever for all I know, though me and Kara were back home for two weeks before Barbie Ruzci called Kara on the phone and said, "Your father says Grandma told him Grandpa Ruzci told her you're getting married," and somehow on the phone it got across to those parental Ruzcis that Kara really was getting married and as a matter of fact to me in August on Saturday on the Feast of the Assumption of the Blessed Virgin.

But there was one other thing. When we left New Jersey to drive home, Kara didn't get right on the Turnpike, she started driving that Ford Falcon in another direction and telling me once upon a time she had an older brother, once upon a time because now he was a dead older brother, though I guess now debatably older because he'd been dead for a few years, who got drafted just at the end of the Korean War. Louie Ruzci was just starting to make money then and as much as he believed in the Korean War and stopping Communist aggression everywhere, he preferred that his oldest kid and only son Raymond, that was his name, Ray Ruzci, named after Grandpa Raymond Louis Ruzci, do it somewhere like California or New Jersey and not Korea, so he pulled every string he could to get Ray in the New Jersey National Guard, which he did. Up till then Ray had been an altar boy and the captain of the Hoboken High basketball team and the quarterback of the best Hoboken football team in the history of Hoboken, lost the state title in the finals, and he was pretty smart too, went to Colgate where he disappointedly and unfairly spent four years as a second-string quarterback, though he took it pretty good, didn't quit, and even graduated with two majors, one in English and one in Business, though in those years he picked up kind of a dark side to his personality, he always did have dark searching eyes that looked like they knew everything, and being a quiet, serious guy, sometimes you assumed he did, but in that year after college, before he got drafted and while he was working for Louie, he sometimes wandered off on the weekends, left Friday night and didn't show up again till time for work on Monday morning, and he'd come back brooding and handsome and speechless and looking into the tip of his head like he had something there that nobody else had, some kind of vision of eternity or something, something he didn't get at Hoboken High or Colgate or working for Louie refurbishing zoos, but nonetheless, other than that, he was always good and kind, watched over Kara like a dark guardian angel, and they loved each other in deep speechless ways.

Of course when he got drafted he took it pretty philosophical, actually wanted to go to Korea and was pretty surprised when he ended up in the National Guard. Still he had to go to boot camp somewhere in Texas, just like the regulars, and he wasn't there too long before the family got a pretty shocking notification that he was in the brig. Louie got pretty upset and started calling everywhere to find out what the hell, but by the time he got through to anybody down there he found out Ray wasn't in the brig anymore, he was in the hospital. That's when Louie packed up the family and headed down to Texas. But when they got there, Ray was dead. Died of some mysterious disease. The army couldn't figure it out. And neither could Louie. He cried like a baby for days. He tried getting a lot of answers from the army and didn't get any. Then he tried suing the army and that didn't get far either. Louie was a changed man after that, got real cutthroat, changed his life. "So there," said Kara Ruzci.

"Is this like Igor Kresky's baby?" I said.

"Not Igor Kresky's baby, *my* baby," said Kara Ruzci. "Only not like the baby, like Igor Kresky, only dead."

And that's where we drove, we drove to the cemetery where we parked and walked in a ways, and there, in the center of a giant plot big enough for the graves of Grandma and Grandpa Ruzci, and Louie and Barbie Ruzci, and Louise and Kara and any other Ruzcis who wanted to be there, was a giant stone that said "Ruzci" and a little stone with a flag and fresh flowers that said:

Raymond Louis Ruzci
1930–1953
Korean War

There'd been a little place above his name where a picture used to be, but now it was pretty faded, you could barely see an outline, and it looked like everybody'd decided not to replace it.

"My older brother," said Kara Ruzci.

And I didn't say anything to that.

"My grandmother's name is Kara," she said, "and sometimes I think about when she dies, I'll come here and see my name on a grave."

And I didn't have anything to say about that either.

That's when Kara got a look in her eye that I hadn't seen for quite some time, a dark far-off look as if she'd fallen asleep with her eyes open, as if she saw things that I never saw and never would. I saw the tremor in her throat as she slowly went to her knees in front of that grave and began that low, fluteful welling of sound, like the moan from the center of a dark mirror, Kara Ruzci sang, she wept and sang.

The Marriage of Heaven and Hell, Continued

The End of the World as Jarvis Knows It

I T WAS A warm day in June and I was down in Karl's basement with Karl and Crow and the pig, looking at the pieces of the *Armada* and eating corn curls and drinking Koehler Beer.

"Going to eat that pig for the Fourth," said Karl, "though maybe I should save him for your wedding."

Crow strutted over to the pig, who had pretty much the run of the basement now, even used Kitty Litter in an old bathtub in the corner, and the two of them did a nose to nose. "Polly wants a cigarette," said Crow.

"No more cigarettes," said Karl. "You can't fly a half-a-mile."

Crow pulled a cigarette from under his wing. "Gotta match?" he said to the pig. "Polly wants a match, pig."

But that pig just rolled over. Whatever influence Karl had over those animals it was more or less whatever they could pick up by watching, just like his kids, because sure as dog shit, which there was plenty of on his porch roof, nobody ever listened to him.

Crow went up to the rafters and got a stick match and then

landed on the pig and lit it against his side, then lit his cigarette.

"What's this Polly stuff," I said to Crow.

Crow just exhaled smoke.

"It's good to see Funster back on his roof," I said to Karl. Now that it was summer Funster'd moved all his radio equipment for talking to Funly out onto his porch roof behind the sandbags, didn't even bother to use his telescope to spy on niggers anymore, always had the thing pointed up.

"If you ask me that whole rocket business was bad for the neighborhood," said Karl. "Got half the kids on the block sitting in garbage cans with jock cups over their noses. Besides, we need Funster's eyes on the streets, can't expect the Pioneers to be here all the time, they got their own neighborhoods to protect." He fiddled with some of the boat boards. "When's he landing?"

"Neda says he's got to come down soon," I told him. "Funster says Funly wants to land in the Kremlin and assassinate Khrushchev."

"He'll never do it," said Karl. "They got tracking stations now. You got to sneak in over the North Pole." He scratched his beard and his head. "How you going to support yourself once you're married?"

Well he may as well have said "left bank salami." I opened another beer. "You got whiskey here, Karl?" I asked him.

"You're not an easy person to talk to," said Karl.

"Talk to Polly," said Crow.

"I aint talkin to a goddamn birdbrain," said Karl.

"Suit yourself," said Crow. He got down from the pig and walked over to the corn curl bag. I put a beer out for him. "Thanks for nothin, pig," said Crow, it was all pigs to him.

"That's one ungrateful bird," said Karl. After all those years with him, however many there were, he still didn't know how to take Crow. Karl fingered some planks and looked at me again. "That little girlie of yours aint making much money teaching bayfront welfare niggers," he said. "And if she did, I'd be mad. Further, she aint going to be able to do it while she's having a baby." He stopped and got some Jim Beam from behind a brick in the wall. "Costs money to have a kid," said Karl. "Costs money to keep a kid."

Karl was real big on how other people should live, the more I was with him, the more I noticed it.

"You think I'm dumb," said Karl.

"I don't," I said.

"Well fuck ya," he said. "But I'm going to be out of a job in a month. Bucyrus Erie's layin off and I'm gone. The family can live on my unemployment, but I got a life-style to protect."

So we piled those boards back onto the back of his pickup and headed out Route 5 along the coast of Lake Erie till we got to our cove and started hauling all that stuff down there to rebuild the *Armada*.

In a lot of ways it seemed ridiculous after all I'd been through, but I couldn't quite get an orientation on what should happen in the future based on what had happened in the past. Everything just seemed wide open. I didn't have anything to worry about and I missed having things to worry about. I guess I could have worried about marrying Kara Ruzci and having a baby, and then trying to figure out how we were going to live, but now I didn't have to worry about that because me and Karl were going to pirate Lake Erie again and make a lot of money so we could retire for a couple years. Gave me some logistics to pass the time. Besides, me and Karl weren't common criminals, we were usually pretty smart about it and we had an ontological bias, or at least Karl did, he figured selling cars or owning a grocery store or oil wells was just as criminal as thievery, which I'm sure a lot of criminals thought, only Karl didn't think there was anything wrong with being a grocery or oil or pet store mogul, any more than there was with stealing from them, it was all the same stuff, society just happened to condone one and not the other; that little bit of insight elevated him from the masses, though I, myself, didn't have an opinion on it.

Took us a few days to put that boat together, we hadn't built it the first time and didn't exactly have time to make a blueprint when we took it apart, and I liked puzzles about half as much as I liked everything else I didn't like, but Karl had a real knack for that kind of stuff and he didn't give a shit, if we made a mistake we just jury-rigged or patched up, that boat kind of looked like his truck when we were done, not too pretty but it ran.

We had it set that we were going to get rich in one swell swoop, nothing else made sense; hit that big *North American* luxury passenger liner somewhere in the middle of Lake Erie on the eve of the big combination Fourth of July and "We Love Erie Day" celebration that the Mayor had inaugurated to be held down at the Public Dock with lots of fireworks and food booths, and social dignitaries and economic notables on board the *North American* coming home from London, Canada after a five-day cruise that included stops at leisure capitals like Cleveland, Toledo, Detroit, Sandusky, and Ashtabula. We'd just ambush them and make them drop a lifeboat with an emissary who'd bring us $20,000 in cash plus jewels, once we hightailed it out of there they'd have to have a twenty-mile-wide net or a hundred-story vacuum cleaner to catch us. All we had to do was find out their route, and for a while it looked like we'd have to tail them from London to Erie sometime to do it, which might look a little suspicious.

But one evening after I came back from working on the boat and was getting ready to go out and stand on the corner of Celebration and 24th where Kara Ruzci picked me up if I was there, Neda took me aside and said, "I think you need some counseling." She gathered up her purse and a roll of paper from her room. "For the man who has everything else," she said.

Well I figured I didn't have to listen to her, even if she was a genius, though if there was one thing she was more than smart, it was beautiful, besides having eyes like blue skies and lips that would have shaken Elvis from the pelvis up, her breasts and butt were turning into plump firm cups of um, with a waist like a Hindu goddess, she moved like a cat on vacation, held her head with her brow slightly tilted in a way that made you realize she should have been consulted during the early stages of the universe, besides, as I thought about it, I had to admit she'd sure been right about me buying Kara Ruzci a puppy and learning to drive. So I followed her down to the end of the block to the Old Maids' Field where she broke out the pot and a pint of Jack Daniel's.

"You've been busy," she said, "but all the old maids are dead. They're going to tear this place down."

"Funly going over tonight?" I said to her.

"Who cares," said Neda. We finished the joint and she took out a new pack of Pall Malls, rapped them on her knee, then opened them and lit one. "Pretty soon," she said, "it's the good thin goose for me, the small tree, the shadow ladder, the portable bridge."

"No kidding," I said.

"Dresses, slumber parties, talk about boys, I'm not going to peddle papers, I'm walking on the sidewalk, I'm taking taxis, I'm painting my nails."

Well I was never one to ask Neda what she was talking about, though the last time she got poetic, not that she didn't always have the capability, she'd sure read Shakespeare enough times, she came down with rheumatic fever and almost died of heart stoppage. "You need some aspirin?" I said.

"I need *so* much," said Neda, "I could wash the streets with my blood." She was hitting the whiskey really hard and it was getting hard to keep in mind that it was *my* counseling session. "You think the grave is everything," she said.

"I do not."

"Well it isn't. The womb is an empty grave. Get it?"

"Midol," I said.

"No, transition, misogyny, marriage."

Seemed to me she was talking to a neutron about quantums, meanwhile she was drinking whiskey like an Afghan sailor in Moscow. "You're not going to lighten up," I said.

"No," said Neda. "Spread your legs for the President and die."

"Conformity and alcoholism."

"I knew I could talk to you," said Neda.

She let me finish the bottle and got out another one. Across the street Funster was home from work and having supper behind his sandbags.

"Can we speak English for a minute?" I asked Neda.

"No," said Neda.

"I know you're going to regard this as undue optimism," I told her. "You're going to think I'm saying this just because I'm getting married and having a baby."

"Joining the chain of being."

"You're taking everything personally."

"I've decided from now on I'm taking everything personally."

You had to hand it to Neda, she knew the only way out was in, and that was an illusion.

"Is the world in any way like a game board?" I said to her.

"No, Zooey," said Neda. "Read the *Mulamādhyāmikakarika.*"

"Become a famous scientist."

"Science is for the birds."

"You put Funly in space."

"If I were a scientist I'd say he put himself in space. Science is bad, it kills people, magic is good, people kill magicians."

"That's not true."

"It wasn't intended to be true."

Neda was too smart for truth. Too smart for doom. Too smart. She took the roll of paper from her purse, unrolled it. It was a map of Lake Erie with all the coordinates. "This is my wedding present," she said. "Wait for the *North American* here." She drew an X about midway between London and Erie, I couldn't exactly tell, I figured Karl would know the coordinates. "If you hit them here, everything will turn out all right."

"That's kind of vague," I said.

"I'm not looking for life in outer space anymore," said Neda. "After this it's eye shadow and lipstick."

"That's a cheap dialectic," I told her, because being a Dialectician, even if I wasn't a genius like Neda, I knew a little bit about it.

"The cheaper the better," said Neda.

"So you giving me magic or science?"

"I'm giving you a walk with Bob Barker. I wish I could help you more," she said, "but I've got to make my face."

Well Neda was wrong about me thinking the grave was everything, I didn't, though I had to admit, I thought death and failure were some very important things to think about, kind of why I lived the way I lived, if I had to think of a rationale, nonetheless that whole business about the womb being an empty grave gave me the creeps. I kept thinking about Kara Ruzci walking around with her grave at that moment not so very empty, and what that meant, and what that meant about our baby, and what that meant about Kara Ruzci when there wasn't a baby in there, and what that meant for Helen and Bush and Neda and all the other women walking around like some kind of highly personalized vehicles of disincarnation. You just couldn't deal with a realization like that and not be disconcerted, regardless of its applicability; in fact its inapplicability made it scarier than ever. It was right up there with Stinky Jinx pirouetting above the basket with that scared look of domination, enough, under normal circumstances, to make me go see Willie, except I knew Willie'd have nothing to say.

That's what I had working its way through me when me and Karl set out on the black back of Lake Erie on July 4, 1963 to pirate the ocean liner *North American*. It made me ill humored. Not only that, the day before Kara Ruzci had gone off for one of her excursions to New York and that night I dreamt I was sleeping with our friend Mr. Tony Blanion. I woke up in the middle of the night thinking I was sleeping with Kara in double fetal, though a little surprised to find her breasts had shrunk to zilch, and she looked at me and said, "Shave fuzz, spudnut, you're walking on a glass menagerie," whereupon I realized I wasn't sleeping with Kara Ruzci at all but that rotten corpse Tony Blanion, who even in deaf was striking me at that very moment as the sneakiest guy in the history of Erie, Pennsylvania, if not the world. Apocalyptic as it all might have seemed, I just refused to talk to that son of a bitch.

Not that it ever bothered our friend Mr. Tony Blanion before and it didn't bother him now either, being dead in my bed.

"Listen to me, hubcap," said Tony Blanion, "when I'm through with you, you won't know a funeral from a state fair. You won't know grape jelly from frog shit. You won't know the difference between a pizza and a flashlight. You'll sell your soul to bowl at odd hours."

Well I had to hand it to Tony Blanion, deaf had certainly no dominion over his powers of articulation, though that slight qualification about the "odd hours" was a subtlety he'd clearly picked up only recently, maybe in transition.

"Listen, carp butt," said Tony Blanion, corpselike, "you won't know demeanor from wiener. You're fried spleen."

It went on for quite a while.

"Sounds like a lot of idle threats," I finally said. I thought he might be trying to wear down my powers of discrimination by simple overexposure.

"You won't know a threat from a beret," said Tony Blanion.

That must have been his coup de grace because he sleazed out of there after that. Nonetheless, I couldn't sleep afterwards, in fact don't even remember waking up, and stood on the deck of Karl's boat staring at the blue-black nativity of Lake Erie and, counter to my disposition, ruminated on the womb/grave and that corpse Tony Blanion's enigmatic step into the ambiguous area between French and English rhyme and typography, besides, the whole business bugged me, I'd come too far to become a thoughtful person at such a late stage.

On top of it all, when Kara Ruzci went to New York for her art stuff it always bothered me to think about her with that cosmonaut Igor Kresky; I didn't like the idea of him putting his matzo balls anywhere near her, in fact this whole business of clearing out outside threats was starting to become one of those eternal experiments for which I had yet to discover the proper tool. Though I have to admit it was nice not to have Kara in town and have to explain the particular business enterprise I was at that very moment embarking on with Karl Marxman and Crow, even somebody as socially myopic as Kara Ruzci might think it wasn't exactly the kind of thing her future husband and father of baby, as uteral as it was at present, should risk, as lucrative as it might seem. Still, every time Kara Ruzci went to New York I got terrible visions of plane wrecks and flaming bodies and was convinced I'd seen her for the last time and said the last thing I'd ever say to her, probably something stupid, and I'd never see her again and want to die from sadness, unless of course she'd let that fish Igor Kresky touch her while she was in New York, then she'd have got just what she deserved, all that made me think there was some inapproachable gulf between the male and female psyche, not that I had reason to think it, then I thought about Neda and the womb as an empty grave and started right up again, realizing at that point that all these contradictory and multivariant emotions reminded me of somebody I had a lot of ambivalent feelings about, most often bad. Red. I was becoming a victim of my cerebral cortex.

"You're going to stare a hole in the lake," said Karl.

"I'm thinking about what I'm going to do with all that money," I said.

"Don't think about it," said Karl. "It's bad luck."

Well it was difficult to see what luck had to do with it. We had a sound, simple plan backed by the number-one genius of the world, looked like all we had to do was go out and get it over with, which was a little different feeling for me, usually I was pretty exhilarated about all this robbery stuff, I liked thinking about those rich people, or better seeing those rich people act like something unjust was happening to them, like the world was all lined up for them to be happy; Karl was right about that, justice was an unnecessary concept for justifying the status quo or justifying changing it, on top of that, making that concept disappear made me feel like I was getting back on the right track. I went down below and loaded the M16s, checked the cannon on the bow, where Crow stood, wind in his feathers, lifting his nostrils to the air.

"Yo-ho-ho," said Crow.

"What are you going to do when we're all done with this?" I asked him. "Go back to carrying messages for Andrew?"

Crow stared into the wind. "Saint's okay," he said.

"Some saint," I said to him. All that stuff about Andrew talking to animals and dead people and making cripples walk gave me a lot of sympathy for the Pharisees.

Crow looked me up and down. "Corn curl," he said.

"Karl has the corn curls."

"Deaf," said Crow.

"I don't have any." Which was as true as bad news. I hadn't seen much of Willie since I crossed him during our last experiment, and that whole business was too scary to think about, but along with it I had to cool my experiments with deaf, I was too busy with other experiments, just gave me the feeling again that I couldn't wait to get this *North American* thing over with and be rich and marry Kara Ruzci and have our baby, maybe even have the Dialecticians out for some experiments in the country.

"Suit yourself," said Crow, and went down into the hold.

As we drew closer to Erie it got obvious we weren't the only people interested in boating on the Fourth of July, something I hadn't thought about at all, of course I never thought about boating at all period. I went back to where Karl was steering and said, "There's too many boats."

"There's even an escort party for the *North American* about two miles out," said Karl. "You'd know that if you read the papers, which you don't. They won't be out where we're going, and the Coast Guard'll be in here monitoring all this traffic." He spun the wheel of the *Armada* and headed away from the town again until we didn't see boats for a while, then he headed back toward the center of the lake. Every once in a while, on the way to our waiting place, we spotted a boat off in the distance, but once we got there and dropped anchor we saw nothing, may as well have been in the middle of the Pacific Ocean for what it felt like, a hot late-afternoon sun and the water green and flat like a china plate, not even a lap of water against the side of the boat. It was so quiet you could hear the fish moving around in the water, the sky so still you could see the sun crawling through the blue.

"Pretty calm here," said Karl.

"Too calm," said Crow. "How about a corn curl?"

Karl gave Crow a couple corn curls and sent him out, north, to look for the *North American*. The air was so dead he could hardly beat it hard enough to fly, and it was so quiet we could still hear his wings after he was out of sight. Karl and me didn't say anything to each other, we just waited there like a couple of Cornish game hens, we weren't no common crooks, this was going to be it. After a long wait we heard Crow flapping, then spotted him coming in. When he landed his feathers looked like glass. He was even too pooped for corn curls. He wanted water.

"Well," said Karl.

And Crow said, "Thar she blows."

We looked north, and there, on the horizon, we saw the *North American*.

"All right," said Karl. "Let's get 'em."

Crow went below and me and Karl rechecked the rifles and the cannon, then we pulled up anchor and I manned the cannon as Karl went to the wheel and put the engine on idle. We didn't want anyone to know we were out there, not until the last minute, but if the *North American* spotted us they might radio in, thinking we needed help, or get in a dialogue with us that the Coast Guard might pick up, so before we got in their sights we took our one risk and Karl radioed them, gave them a fake name and license, said we were fine, just fishing, they didn't have to worry, we'd stay out of their way, and congratulations on their wonderful voyage and all that. They seemed to take it flat enough, checked off and kept coming. Karl pulled the boat around so we'd both be going in the same direction.

I'd pretty much thought they'd look more like a giant white mountain in the water next to us, but when they got there they just kind of looked like an extra big yacht. Somebody on the *North American* foghorned us to stay clear but Karl took us abreast and foghorned them back to stay off the radio and park or we'd blow them out of the water. That caused a little bit of commotion before somebody else in a white suit and hat came to the railing and asked who the hell were we and said they weren't stopping and we'd better get the hell out of there. That's when I put one right over the bow, sounded like thunder out there amidst that nothing, then there were a lot of screams and some people ran away from the railing and some more people ran to the railing, but most importantly of all, they really did pull that *North American* to a stop.

We had to wait a little bit for the captain to come out and talk to us, but when he did Karl explained how we'd settle for a bunch of gold and diamonds and $20,000 in cash which he could send to us via one of the lifeboats carrying one person who would be returned to them intact immediately after we counted the money and other miscellanies, all of this, of course, was to be done in the next fifteen minutes or we'd blow a hole in them, also he reminded them to stay off the radio elsewise that too would lead to us having to blow them up. The captain said that was preposterous and then I loaded the cannon and then he said okay.

I don't know what would have happened if he said no, but he didn't say no, people got generally agreeable, even if at times a bit surly, when you held them up with a gun and threatened their lives. In a minute or so we heard him explaining over the loudspeaker how they were being held up but everybody should be calm and stay away from the railing because we were armed and dangerous, then he told them what we wanted and how we'd threatened to blow them up if we didn't get it so he was sending around the stewards and the deckhands to collect their stuff, it was a sad thing but worth their lives, besides we'd soon get caught because what we were doing was ridiculous and heinous and stupid, of which I was willing to give him the ridiculous, and maybe the stupid, but the heinous was a real imposition of conventional values, a habit, I'd started to notice, of people who'd assumed authority for too long, it made me dislike him.

Well waiting out in the middle of that lake wasn't the most fun thing I'd ever done, for one thing it was too hot out there, and of course a lot of those people didn't listen to their captain and came to the railing to look at us, some of them even yelled the most awful names at us, they had some real foul mouths up there amidst those wealthy Erie-ites, kind of made me feel like I was in a zoo, wondered if Louie Ruzci ever thought of this kind of setup for his line of work, more or less an open-air zoo situation, and I kept checking the horizons for boats, thinking maybe I saw something and then realizing I didn't, the only thing in sight was a tiny white line in the blue sky like the smoke that you always presume is following some jet.

But after a while they finally lowered a boat with somebody in it, that made me feel a whole lot better, and back on the other end of the boat I could hear Karl chuckling, all we had to do now was make sure this character wasn't carrying any weapons, then count the loot and get the hell out of there. I sure was feeling a whole lot better.

That lifeboat left the side of the ship, of course it had a motor on it, we should have told them no motor, now we'd have to make him dump it, we didn't want him getting back to the boat too quick, his vulnerability was part of our escape protection. In a minute he was pulling up beside us and that's when I saw the person they sent with the money.

Bobby Hansen.

"Shit," I said.

"Drop the motor," said Karl.

Bobby Hansen pulled out a little gun. "Stick 'em up," said that dumbbell Bobby Hansen.

"Goddammit," said Karl. He raised his M16 to his shoulder and aimed it at Bobby Hansen's head.

"Hmmm," said Bobby Hansen. I guess he wasn't expecting us to be carrying anything smaller than a cannon.

I got my rifle and went to the back of the boat, passing Crow on the inside who I told to stay put, our anonymity was already in jeopardy.

"Win some, lose some," said Crow, made me realize that he had a knack for the appropriate phrase but lacked any real sensitivity.

At the back of the boat, Karl and Bobby Hansen were still having their standoff, except now Bobby Hansen was on board.

"Who thought up this silly trick?" said Karl.

"I did it myself," said Bobby Hansen.

Well you could have figured that, that kid was a terminal hero.

"Get in there and dump that motor," Karl said to me.

"Don't move," said Bobby Hansen, "or I'll blast you." He looked at me pretty good. "Hey," he said. "I know you."

"No, you don't," I said.

"Yes, I do," said Bobby Hansen.

Some people are just too stupid to help, though I had to admit, Bobby Hansen had the capacity to outsmart you with his stupidity by always being stupider than you expected.

"Loop," said Bobby Hansen.

"This some kind of reunion?" said Karl.

"Meet Bobby Hansen," I said to Karl.

"Jesus," said Karl.

"This situation is stacked for justice," said Bobby Hansen, holding on to his gun. "We could all shoot each other, or you could outgun me and get away, but then you'd be up for murder on top of everything else, or you could let me go and then I'll turn you in."

I had to hand it to him, he sure raised my opinion of vegetables.

I could see Karl sweating. "Just give us the money," said Karl.

"No," said Bobby Hansen.

Well I'd been through this before with Bobby Hansen and

there was just a limit to how much you could take. "Look up there," I said to Bobby Hansen, pointing at the jet streak in the sky which had now got pretty big. Of course that dummy looked and I hit him on the head with the butt of my rifle.

Karl just shook his head. "Brave but dumb," he said.

"I think they go together," I told him, which was a rare vocal and opinionated moment for me, I guess I was succumbing to the pressure.

We immediately checked the money sack, looked like there was a bunch in there, we figured counting it was irrelevant now, and the next thing was deciding what to do with Bobby Hansen, though it looked like for now the only thing we could really do was keep him, but our decision got waylaid when out from behind the *North American* came a bunch of Coast Guard cruisers like a half-dozen unordered hamburgers, had to be the most disappointing thing I ever saw, we didn't even have a chance to run for it before we were surrounded, all I could think was that they'd done the best job of hiding since the demise of Tony Blanion, and then all I could think was that maybe that rotten corpse Blanion had finally ratted on me, dead as he was; there's nothing like a crisis to make you try to order your universe.

Somebody on one of those boats suggested we drop everything and put our hands up, which was something we figured they'd suggest, of course I don't know what they figured we'd be figuring, but I, myself, was making some very clear quality of life decisions at that point, and the longer we didn't put our hands up, the longer we were free, besides, we probably had the biggest gun on the lake, if we knocked out a couple of these guys we could be on the run, of course there was always the possibility of getting killed or worse wounded, but it looked like Karl and me had made some simultaneous quiet decision to take it one step at a time, because I took my gun right to the cannon and he ducked down behind the wheel and needless to say, we didn't drop anything or put our hands up.

"Whatever you do," yelled Karl, "don't say nothin to these guys. We got nothin to say to them."

Which was certainly true, all conversation might do was convince us we were nuts to try to get away and we didn't need that kind of reinforcement. Nonetheless, we were certainly surrounded, and if we were going to make a break for it we probably should have done it right off, before they got all set up. Now I could see them lining the sides of their decks with rifles. Somebody out there was advising us to give up, unusually polite for the circumstances, while up on the *North American* you could hear the loudspeaker being a lot less polite in telling everybody up there to clear the deck, which they did, which probably blew one more potential cover, all those innocent wealthy people in the crossfire, more and more it looked like the longer we waited the closer we got to the end of the dock.

Once the *North American* cleared out of there it got so quiet we could hear those Coast Guard boats talking back and forth on their radios. Looked like the only thing we had on them now was our potential to kill a couple of them, which is what they were discussing. At that point it got silly to strain our ears and Karl just tuned them in. Looked like they were going to be willing to hold us there and wait for reinforcements, though who knows how many more boats the Coast Guard had, nonetheless it was going to take another half hour or so for them to reach us.

That gave me and Karl time to talk things over. If we were going to make a run for it, it was probably already too late, but if we were going to do it anyway we'd have to do it before the other boats got there, though that would mean firing first which could put us in even deeper water, the other side being that we were in so deep at this point it might not matter, unless we killed somebody. So we decided we'd try not to kill anybody, just make a lot of racket and charge the line right as the reinforcements were getting there, that's probably when they'd least expect it and it would also centralize them, meaning they'd have to chase us instead of just naming our coordinates and hemming us in again, though they probably had more boats out there anyways, even planes, but maybe we could just run them around till it got dark, sounded like such a lousy plan we decided to go through with it.

So we just sat there, must have looked like a little constellation of boats from above, they looked at us and we looked at them and they looked back at us and we looked back at them, there was a certain peacefulness about it, one of those ineffable stillnesses that occur when one force is just about to overwhelm another, like when you shoot something in the air, just before it comes down. Karl moved inside the cabin where he could cover one side of the boat without giving up a blind side, and they yelled, "Don't move!" over their loudspeaker when he did, and of course he didn't listen. I covered the other side, gun out, head down low. Felt like we'd been out there a year. Every once in a while those Coast Guard characters talked to each other over the radio, threw around a lot of clichés about having us trapped like rats, how it was just a big waiting game, and how they hoped we were smart enough not to take them on, which anybody with any smarts knew was the wrong thing to say to somebody who might want to knock a couple of them off just to prove them wrong. Then we heard the reinforcements were only a few minutes away and they cut off their radios, I guess they figured we couldn't poke our heads up to check things out, they were playing this waiting game stuff pretty good.

It was time to go.

I looked at Karl and saw him swallow, and then I turned chicken. I hadn't been thinking much about the other aspects of my life up to that point, but suddenly I was seeing things, like the night Funster shot me in the leg, and Neda's heart attack, and when Helen had Joseph and then Andrew, and when she almost died, and when Red almost killed her for it, and I thought about Franky Gorky and wondered if anybody was going to bring birthday and Christmas presents to my grave, and about Stinky Jinx hiding behind the big scoreboard in the Harrisburg Farm Show Arena, I thought about how much I'd miss my personality when it was gone, and I thought about Kara Ruzci, I wondered if she'd sing to my deadness at night, or visit me in jail, and I thought about the last time I had a shoot-out with the Coast Guard, I wondered how many times I'd have to kill that man.

"Scared?" said Karl.

"I don't want to do it," I said.

"Afraid to die."

"Yes."

"Well the hard part's already over," he said.

"How do you know?" I said to him. I have to be honest, I barely choked it out.

"Well it may not be true," he said, "but it's comforting." He shifted toward the door of the cabin. "I'm going to count three," he said.

I looked through the cabin and out the cabin door where Bobby Hansen was still dozing on the deck floor, getting a sun tan, and I felt real sorry for myself, because nobody was going to understand our side of this.

"Ready?" said Karl.

"No," I said.

"Ready," said Karl, and moved to the door.

Just then a big commotion started up with those Coast Guard boats. I heard a lot of yelling and screaming and engines starting up. I poked my head out and those Coast Guard boats were backing up and turning around and the guys on deck were jumping around like so many donut holes. In the distance the reinforcement boats were turning away in long curves. That's when I heard the roar in the sky.

Above us that little line of jet stream had turned into a red flare, like the guts of the sky had opened up. The water churned and the sun went dark, and that red wound of sky expanded orange over us. The lake shook, the sky screamed, miles away the earth ripped and groaned, and then the air went yellow, then white.

God.

It was God.

And you couldn't run from The End of the World.

Not even the Coast Guard could protect you from The End of the World.

Something exploded next to us and a waterspout grew like a great quick fungus and collapsed, the boat rolled and we took on a foot of water. Then, out of the rocking lake, I heard Funly Funster.

"Save the capsule!" yelled Funly. "Save the capsule!"

We dragged Funly on board. He looked a little bit like that big blue fish Jimbo Funster brought back from Florida, only silver because of his space suit.

"Don't let the Russians get the capsule!" screamed Funly.

"We'll come back for it," said Karl.

And we got the hell out of there.

Of course Funly sulked the whole night while me and Karl disassembled the *Armada,* but we let him go, didn't even ask him to help, after all, in his own blundering Funly way he'd already helped out. We kept Bobby Hansen in a big sack and he didn't even stir until after we got Funly home and the *Armada* packed away in Karl's basement.

"Any questions?" said Karl to the sack.

"Who am I?" answered that sack, Bobby Hansen.

"That's good," said Karl.

We drove him up to Glenwood Hills and left him off on one of the Hansens' neighbors' doorsteps.

Our only apparent casualty was that Crow was missing, he took off sometime during The End of the World and hadn't come back.

"He'll be back," I told Karl.

"I miss him already," he said. "He's pretty old. Maybe I should go out looking for him."

"Suit yourself," I told him.

I, myself, went looking for Neda, but she wasn't in her room. Helen said she went to a slumber party.

The Marriage of Heaven and Hell

M E AND KARA RUZCI got married on August 15th, on
the Feast of the Assumption of the Blessed Virgin Mary,
1963, in the big lawned backyard of Louie and Barbie Ruzci
somewhere out some extended suburban road outside Hoboken,
New Jersey, on a tiny slope so everybody could see the ceremony,
and above us was the bright yellow sun and below a woods and
a ravine with a stream at the bottom and then a little more woods
before they opened up into a cemetery where right at the edge
of the woods sat the grave, in that way that graves have, of
Raymond Ruzci, and the family plot of all the Ruzcis, while
meanwhile in that temporarily filled grave of Kara Ruzci's
womb was the baby who was going to be Visitor Loop if he was
a boy and Lula Ruzci if she was a girl, and Louie had a Catholic
priest come out there and marry us, had to donate twice the
money it would have cost to have us married in church, not that
I gave a rat's ass, but Kara Ruzci wasn't getting married in
church, that's where she drew the line, you had to hand it to Kara
Ruzci, she wasn't lineless, she was just indiscernible.

And it wasn't a tiny wedding either. Louie and Barbie didn't
get church but they got everything else. You couldn't walk ten

feet without ending up in some tent with a keg of beer and a bar and a buffet of forty-eight kinds of Italian food and some old dago playing the violin or the accordion, except for the biggest tent which of course had a polka band and a guy in a bear suit who juggled bowling pins and told zoo refurbishing jokes that were hard to hear and harder to get. At the back of that big tent, on a table in front of the dance floor, there was a cake that looked like something you'd live in for a few days if you went to Miami Beach.

Before the wedding Kara Ruzci made me go around and give everybody there a daisy while she went around and gave everybody a red rose, except for Red who she gave a white rose; everybody seemed to think that all of that was pretty much nice except it got a little clumsy when I had to give a daisy to a guy, most the women and Stinky Jinx just started crying right away when I gave them their flower, but you could see the men got pretty uncomfortable getting daisies from the groom, so they mostly smirked and patted me on the back and gave me a drink and by the time things got going I was as smashed as an empty cigarette pack.

Stinky and Funly took the bus to Hoboken and Bush and Jon came in the Rainbow with Red and Helen and Neda and Joseph and Andrew, it must have been pretty crowded in there, especially with Jon, all weight and no substance now that he was invisible. The Funster and Jinx families didn't come, but Dean Danger brought Tina Danger and the Dialecticians, and Karl and his family came sans Crow, drove all the way across the Turnpike in that open truck and got a whole tent to themselves when they arrived which pretty much pleased everybody including Karl. Word must have got out as to what kind of major deal Louie Ruzci was throwing because all the relatives from both Red's and Helen's sides of the family showed up too, lined up like opposite sides of the moon, and I learned that Barbie Ruzci's side of the family wasn't Catholic either, though Barbie had converted, and even more though, her side of the family, present in geometrical expansion of great- and grandparents, uncles and aunts, was Pres-

byterian, so they didn't get along with anybody, not that Louie's
dago relatives and Helen's Polack ones got along that great either,
that yard was a melting pot of similar irreconcilables like fried
zucchini and fish sticks.

But that didn't stop anything. After we got those flowers
passed around, which took a good long time, me and Kara Ruzci
got dragged down onto the slope above the woods and the priest
talked about love of God and love of country and love of fellow
humanity, he'd wanted to say "man" but Kara Ruzci made him
say "humanity," then Kara Ruzci quoted a lot of stuff from
George Eliot and Jack Kerouac and Walt Whitman which con-
tradicted everything the priest said, then the priest talked some
more about love of parents and love of siblings and love of
neighbor as oneself and went on to try to qualify what George
Eliot and Jack Kerouac and Walt Whitman said, then Kara Ruzci
talked about what the priest said, trying to put it in the context
of certain conventions, and then the priest talked about the
universality of what he'd said and Kara Ruzci talked about an-
thropomorphism in the concept of the universal, then the priest
quoted Aquinas and talked about deduction and necessity and the
universal application of mathematics to universal law, to which
Kara Ruzci responded concerning the irrational nature of the
moment and the alienation of human consciousness from nature;
just over to the side of us those Dialecticians were sitting under
umbrellas and collecting residue as blue as night, it was a real treat
for them, I'm sure, to see all that old stuff dragged out in a
context of such dramatic ritual, though you could see that the
other twelve thousand people there, deceived as they might have
been into thinking it was part of the ceremony, at least knew for
certain that it was the most boring part of the ceremony, some
old people went belly up on the lawn and Grandpa Ruzci went
down under a pile of his hands and feet with a soft but noticeable
"nyaaa." Other than the Dialecticians, the only person who didn't
look glazed was Helen, who stood right behind me with Red.
She was up on all that Catholic apologetics crapola and had
abandoned Thomism years ago, and I could see she'd immediately

picked up a lot of respect for Kara Ruzci, as naive as her existentialism was, it was still ballpark. Red looked like he needed his bowling ball. And Louie and Barbie looked like they'd eaten about six too many cans of Campbell's Cream of Mushroom Soup.

But as ridiculous as it might seem, that was a moment of pure bliss for me, I felt like smoked herring in sour cream, like I'd been born in sour cream, I looked over at Kara Ruzci debating with that priest in her pale blue silk gown with tiny unrecognizable flowers on it that reached to the lawn, and was suddenly so filled with her beauty and femininity, which startled me, because being a Dialectician I clearly knew the difference between the female and the feminine and always believed myself to be in love with the female of Kara Ruzci, but suddenly I was embarrassingly and shamelessly in love with her femininity, not just her shape, but the shape of her gown on her shape, like a shadow in the moonlight, not simply the higher pitch of her voice, but its frailty and confidence, not just her arguments, but the simplicity of her qualifications, her assertions becoming questions and her questions assertions; there I was in the middle of that ridiculous act of getting married and suddenly I was more in love with my bride than I had ever been, all I wanted to do was hold her and take her somewhere and be alone, I had so much love in me I couldn't stand it. Kara Ruzci was the most beautiful woman in the world.

Not that it stopped anything. Kara Ruzci and that old priest obviously underestimated each other, he must have gone through the seminary years ago before the Church got desperate for vocations and let anybody in who could sign their name because he had his Aristotelian six-guns out, he was probably against saying the mass in English, though I guess I was too, as I thought about it, even though I didn't go; Louie must have paid a fortune to get that old rascal out there and now he was getting a lot more than he bargained for, and so was Kara Ruzci. Those two went on longer than the equator, until that old rascal somehow drew a beeline from Thomas Aquinas to St. Paul and sleazed right into the Epistle to the Corinthians, next thing you know he was saying the wedding vows, pronounced us husband and wife, Kara Ruzci made him agree to say "husband" instead of "man," and before Kara Ruzci could slip in another word we were married. Everybody woke up like they'd been taking a nap next to the refrigerator.

"Hooo-hooo!" said Stinky Jinx. He had on a shiny silver jumpsuit with a pastel blue leather belt, thin as a mint, and matching silk scarf and eye shadow, though his mascara was a bit smeared from all the crying he'd been doing. He must have jumped over eight rows of newly awakened generations of old relatives to be the first one down there to give me a hug. I hadn't seen him so happy since the day he got his picture in *Vogue*.

Funly was slower getting down there and less ecstatic. "When are we going back for the capsule," said Funly Funster.

"You'd think he'd be glad he was back, even if he can't be civil," said Stinky.

Funly tried to open his trench coat so his gun would show and Stinky buttoned him back up.

"Six months in space hasn't taught him a *thing!*" said Stinky.

"Did you see *Sputnik?*" said Kara Ruzci.

"It looks like a little moose," said Funly. "It's nothin."

"He means a mouse," said Stinky.

"Don't tell me," said Funly. "I been up there."

"Do you think you could teach me baseball, Jarvis?" said Stinky. "Dad had me watch a match on TV. It really did seem pleasant."

"I can't play baseball," I told Stinky. "I'm afraid of the ball."

"They do throw it at each other," said Stinky.

Funly grunted.

"I'll teach you baseball," said Kara Ruzci.

"Do you play baseball?" said Stinky.

"We'll learn together," said Kara.

"You know," Stinky told her. "I don't think I'll ever get married after seeing this. I'd always be comparing!"

Stinky and Kara got along really great. They really admired

each other's outfits. Though they didn't get long to talk because soon me and Kara were getting pushed everywhere in every which way by photographers and other people we'd never seen before to do every wedding thing that any of them had ever thought of or seen before in some other wedding and that this wedding could not be a wedding without; I barely got to see Kara Ruzci amidst all the shuffling, though when I did, at some point when we accidentally got shoved together during some pictures with obscure relatives on Barbie Ruzci's side, Kara Ruzci said, "Let's get divorced."

Then we got whisked away to jump through brooms and walk under chapels of hands and drink stuff from cups and share symbolic blood and dance on the priest and hug every other person of the other sex for money and dance being held upside down by our ankles while drinking champagne and get chained to bowling balls and have our pictures taken while eating flowers and trading clothes and get juggled by the man in the bear suit while singing songs about menstrual blood that none of those people would ever have tolerated in a different context.

Finally we got dragged over to cut that Miami hotel with a silver gilded fat knife and shove cake in each other's faces, which everybody was to witness, but that's where I drew the line. Unfortunately there were about a million people packed into the main tent for the main event with Red and Helen off to the side and Louie Ruzci standing behind us with his chest out, it was just then I noticed all the miniature cages and animal environments on the cake, and Barbie Ruzci and every female from her side of the family hovering around that cake like bumblebees.

"I'm not cutting the cake," I told Kara Ruzci.

"Fine," said Kara Ruzci. "We're not cutting the cake," she told Barbie Ruzci.

"Just do it like this," said Barbie, and she made a little sawing motion with the big silver gilded fat knife.

"I'm not afraid of the cake," I told Barbie Ruzci, "I just don't want to cut it."

"You can't keep it in one piece," said Barbie Ruzci.

"Don't be an asshole," said Louie Ruzci.

"You've done everything else," said Barbie Ruzci.

"That's why I'm not cutting the cake," I told her.

"Tell that asshole husband of yours to stop being an asshole and cut the cake," Louie Ruzci told Kara Ruzci.

"I don't think he can stop being an asshole," said Kara Ruzci.

"If you don't cut the cake," said one of the female Barbie Ruzci relatives, "you'll regret it all your life."

Barbie Ruzci gave Helen an imploring look.

"I don't think he's going to cut the cake," said Helen. She'd been eating her lunches outside up at Marycrest and she had dark tan skin and a short pink dress that she made Red buy for her even though she had the money.

"Tell him to cut it," said Barbie Ruzci.

"Cut the cake, Jarvis," said Helen.

"No," I said.

"I got to pee," said Red and left the tent; I wondered how he felt when he had to get married in the rectory instead of the church and sign all his kids away to Catholicism and then cut the cake, he probably never thought of it till right then, but just then he probably figured he regretted cutting that cake all his life, felt guilty for regretting it, hated me for doing what he should have done, and glad I wasn't getting married in a Catholic church and not cutting the cake, and ready to kill me for embarrassing him in front of everybody by being an asshole; taking that pee was probably the most subtle, sophisticated thing he'd ever done in his life.

Nonetheless, that socially adroit exit on Red's part allowed me and Louie Ruzci to have a not so subtle fatherly moment that we might not have had if Red were there. Louie grabbed my lapel, which kind of took me off balance because it was my first lapel I'd ever had, and rented at that, though it felt like Louie had a lot of experience grabbing them.

"Cut the cake," said Louie Ruzci. Connotatively speaking, it was hard to decipher the intonation.

"I would prefer not to," I told him.

"Be a little reasonable," said Louie. "Why do you think I went through all this."

At present, I preferred not to be even a little bit reasonable. Up to then I hadn't thought at all about why Louie Ruzci did all this, I was sure there were myriad complex as well as simple motivations, some conscious and some unconscious, some good and some bad, depending on one's ethical predilections, it just seemed to me that he *did* do all this, and that's what he did, and up to that point I'd gone along with it and now I'd stopped.

"Everybody expects you to cut the cake," said Louie Ruzci.

Needless to say, that wasn't a motivator. But it did seem like things had reached a sort of climax, I either cut the cake or I didn't cut the cake. Kara Ruzci didn't give a shit whether we cut the cake or not, probably made her a better person, you certainly did seem to inflict a lot less consequence on the world when you kept your opinions out of it, or better yet kept yourself out of opinions, I guess Neda was right about me after all, once I started thinking about something, though I did my best to avoid starting, I eventually just reduced it all to some absurdity whereupon I did what I pleased; it got me real depressed, there was nothing like self-realization for making you feel bad about yourself.

I walked over to the cake and punched it.

If you're going to be bad you may as well be all bad, if you're half bad nobody remembers that you were also half good, you can be good all your life and go to prison or hell for one bad act and that's all most everybody's going to remember. There's just no half bad. You're good or you're bad and I was bad. Every good reason in the world for punching that wedding cake was bad, but I didn't have to do any more things or take any more pictures. Barbie Ruzci and her female relatives just hustled that punched cake onto plates without even looking up, Louie Ruzci disappeared, and Grandpa Ruzci came out of a cloud of his hands and feet and threw one big red swollen old hand at me and said, "nyaaa!" We shook hands and then he licked the cake off his fingers. All around people lined up for cake and Helen gave me two pieces and said, "Take some to Jon and Bush."

"You don't think I'm bad?" I said to Helen.

"I'm your mother," said Helen, which was certainly true though it lacked a certain degree of valuation.

I looked over to Kara Ruzci who was at the end of the cake table fielding cake commentary from her relatives who said stuff like, "Your new husband can sure punch a cake," and she said, "Yes, he certainly can," and they said, "I'd keep him away from soufflés," and she said, "He's never seen a cake before," and they said, "He certainly is aggressive around food," and she said, "He learned it from my dog," and one said, "I like that better than smashing cake in each other's faces," and Kara said, "He was supposed to pick it up and drop it on me but he got too excited," and a man said, "Just the opposite of the girl jumping out of the cake," and Kara said, "No, it's the obverse," which made me feel kind of good because I'd taught her about obversity, and somebody else said, "Is this some kind of new thing?" and Kara Ruzci said, "I don't think it's an old thing," you had to hand it to Kara Ruzci, her etiquettal oblivion was a comfort to her relatives.

Bush and Jon, though you could only see Bush, were down in a small tent by the garage next to the house with the rest of Helen's side of the family, they didn't have any food down there but they had an accordion player and a keg of beer and a bunch of whiskey and a tent to themselves, sending out platoons of young shovel-faces and pinheads for ham sandwiches and sausage.

"Is there anything on those plates?" said Bush. "It's hard to see those tiny pieces."

"I don't cut cake, I just punch it."

"You get old," said Bush, "and everything disappears."

"You think it's easy being disappeared," said Jon. "It's not."

"What do you know," said Bush. "You're just hiding and throwing your voice."

"Not true," said Jon. "I'm simply very, very tiny, tinier than those pieces of cake."

"He's eating like a horse," said Bush. "Next time I see him he'll be fat."

"Have some cake, Uncle Jon," I said.

"Not just now," said Jon. "I'm not hungry."

"He's hiding," said Bush. "It would blow his cover." She poured me some whiskey. "You can't play pinochle with an invisible man," Bush said.

"I'm simply incorporeal as well as invisible," said Jon.

"He eats real good when I'm not around," said Bush. "My icebox is empty. Maybe he's hiding in the icebox."

I told Bush about Christmas at Kara Ruzci's grandparents' and how they left dinner out for the dead people.

"For their own dead they leave good food," said Bush. "This ham is smoked like an old cigar."

"The scotch is pretty good," said Uncle Jon.

"What scotch?" said Uncle Stanley from behind his sandwich.

"It's hidden under the bar downstairs," said Jon, probably pointing towards the house.

"I knew I should have brought my own chocolate," said Bush.

"There's some in the pantry," said Jon, "but you have to look for it."

"Not everyone is invisible," said Stanley.

"Actually," said Jon, "if you could count them up, you might find there were more invisible people, like the men, for starters."

"They're also inaudible," said Bush.

"Not to me," said Jon.

"Can you see them?" I asked him.

"Don't be ridiculous," said Jon.

"That's right," said Uncle Stanley, "don't be ridiculous."

"Have some more whiskey," said Bush.

"Besides, they're in Vietnam now," said Jon. "We're not going to let happen there what happened in Eastern Europe, even if I have to reenlist."

"Except for Poland, they can have Eastern Europe," said Bush.

"How I cried the day we gave them Eastern Europe," said Jon.

"He can cry with the best of them," said Bush.

Uncle David got up and came over and shook my hand. "At an opportune time," he said to me, "tell your mother I won't be able to pay her back right away, it seems I made some bad investments."

"Like a color television," said Bush.

"And a couch and hi-fi," said Stanley.

"He bought me a blender," said Aunt Eleanor.

"Not a cent on his mother," said Bush.

"Any cows?" I asked.

Uncle David shrugged. "A couple."

"He forgot to get a bull," said Bush.

"Just tell your mother it could be a while," said David.

"But sometime this millennium," said Stanley.

"A grown, married man, can't tell a bull," said Bush.

"Half that money was Red's," I told David.

"Not to speak ill of Red," said Jon, "but he's a killer and a nut."

Aunt Frances came over and kissed me on the cheek. "Move to California, David," she said. "Red won't follow you to California."

But just then Red came out of the garage. I guess he couldn't find a place to pee in the house, I could tell because he had pee stains on his pants and he was looking real defensive, besides, if he peed in the back of the garage then he probably heard everything that was said.

"Have a drink, Red," said Bush.

"Move to California, David," said Jon. "Who knows who he'll try to kill now that I'm invisible."

Red lifted his right hand and tweaked the air.

"Ouch," said Jon.

"Have a drink, Red," said Bush. "It's your oldest son's wedding."

Red sat down like a pile of muscle and looked around at the table.

"You're a good man, Red," said Bush.

"Yeah," said Red. "Good for nothin and good for shit."

"It could be worse," said Jon.

Red looked up, like he was the only person there who could see him. Then he smiled, which was unusual, he was usually mulling over whatever little there was to mull. He and me and Bush drank.

Bush filled the glasses with whiskey again.

"You can see him?" said Bush.

"I can smell him," said Red. Nobody else in our family could smell a damn thing anymore, but Red's nose compensated for everybody's. He reached into his suit pocket and pulled out a small box of chocolate. Bush filled the shot glasses again.

"You shouldn't have punched that cake," Red said to me, and we all laughed and toasted.

Just then Edju and Aunt Elizabeth came into the tent.

"Oooh-oooh-oooh, so very sorry much," said Edju.

"Are we too late?" said Aunt Elizabeth.

"Not for pinochle," said Bush.

"Mmmm, hmmm, so," said Edju.

"We hope Neda likes the gold-plated chess set," said Aunt Elizabeth.

"Now all she needs is a wedding," said Bush.

Edju dipped his hat. "So, Jarvis, no, so very no."

"It's all right, I don't play chess," I said.

"I thought she was rather young," said Aunt Elizabeth, "but Edju so loves to give Neda things."

Edju took me aside. "Hmmm, Jarvis," he said, "hmmm so very big much so so here, hmmm?"

Well you had to give it to Edju, he spoke enough languages badly but he could see with his eyes. He had me over there quite some time and gave me a lot of advice of which I never understood a word, and good thing, because I just don't enjoy advice that much.

Not too far from the main tent Dean and Tina Danger and the Dialecticians set up a bunch of umbrellas and started barbecuing ribs and deep-frying chicken and they had quite a lot of people gathered around there to get a break from all that pasta and ham, Dean Danger standing behind his barbecue pit and deep-frier like a used tire sculpture and Tina Danger giving him advice on what to do even though he'd done it all a million times before and she'd given him the advice at least that many times, you couldn't really see it as dialogue, it was more organic, you could see why someday Dean Danger would become such an effective ambassador, he was so charming and threatening and large, and of course he invited everybody to come on in to his bar and grill if ever they were in Erie, Pennsylvania, where they'd probably get killed, kind of black humor on his part, and meanwhile the Dialecticians sat under their umbrellas and drank Thunderbird and Tiger Rose on ice, they were certainly a self-conscious bunch.

"If you think this ends your experiments," said Revis.

"Then it's time for us to make some dents," said Revco.

"In your consciousness," said Raymon, "in your state of mind."

"Just a metaphor," said Revis, "to save us time."

"So if you're thinking about changing the might to is," said Revco.

"Then you better be thinking," said Raymon, "where Aristotle is."

"Dead. Uh-huh," said Willie. "That's deaf to you."

"Speaking of which," I said, and we formed a tight circle and had a quick experiment with deaf up our noses which made the day feel nicely warmer and faster and cooler and slower, not necessarily in that disorder but not necessarily not.

"We can't be in the future," said Revis.

"We can't be in the past," said Revco.

"We can't be in the present," said Raymon, "because it don't last."

"We try to reconstruct," said Revis, "a reality."

"That never was," said Revco.

"And will never be," said Raymon.

"Truf," said Willie, "is the next best fing to being there."

Well you had to hand it to us Dialecticians, we certainly had a sophisticated sense of humor. We spent quite some time there drinking wine and sitting in the sun, and after a while Kara Ruzci came by with Polly Doggerel who'd been kept in the basement till then and who was behaving very well with her feet on the ground and not taking food out of anyone's hands, though once she tried to mesmerize Raymon for a piece of chicken and got a bop on the head, she might have been smart for a dog but she couldn't go head-on with a Dialectician.

Kara Ruzci got along fine with those Dialecticians, having some deaf and making light talk about Proust and Merlieu Ponty.

After a while I left them and visited Karl and his family up in their tent at the far end of the yard; they hadn't brought any of their cats or dogs, just a couple of caged birds and the pig who was kind of serving in that instance as a self-portable couch. Sophie sat in the middle of the tent and said, "arp, ruble, rubble," and Karl said she had a stomachache, which probably covered most any ache she could have other than a headache.

"She going to be all right?" I asked Karl.

"She's had a stomachache for months," said Karl, "almost a year."

"Blbl remf," said Sophie. I think that was the first time I ever heard her use a short "e."

"Tell Red we're eating the pig for Christmas," said Karl. "You might recall we were busy on the Fourth, and now he's depressed, you kill something that's depressed and the meat isn't any good."

Karl Jr. came over with his mop of red hair that made him look something like a paintbrush with too many handles, you would have said he had a stupid look in his eyes but they were the smartest thing about him. "I'll kill that pig," said Karl Jr. "I'll kill him."

"I'll kill you," said Karl.

"I'll kill you," said Karl Jr.

"Kid's going to be all right," said Karl.

"Seen Crow?" I said.

"No," said Karl. "That birdbrain."

"He'll be okay," I said. "He's smart."

"Never said a thing somebody else hadn't already said. But now I got nobody to keep the pig company, which means he'll stay depressed."

"I'll kill him," said Karl Jr.

Maggie and Beema came up and pushed out their hands and kicked their legs. "Shoot the pig," they said. "Shoot the pig."

That pig never moved an inch, he'd been on deaf row so long he was on the installment plan.

Just then Sophie started arfing and rubbling a lot louder than usual, her cheeks shook and her eyes made wake, then her belly, which was most of her, shook a little bit. She reached under her tent dress and pulled out a baby.

"Oh-oh," said Karl. "Looks like another kid."

Looked like they were going to be busy for a little bit so I went on down to visit Red's side of the family who had a tent just off the main tent where Uncle Lefty Limburg was telling the story about the time Babe Ruth came to Erie, Pennsylvania and hit three straight home runs over Roosevelt Jr. High School, just stood at home pl— am — Field and pointed the top of the

p, you

ty.

ty.

, or Hitler, ha!" said Bif.

a Emma Loop.

e eye

ve the tent, though I got

reaty

k her opportunity to give

heir

h she got nostalgic about

eral

edroom and all our plans

ing first cousins, and look

mebody else pregnant and

cry and burp, reminding

in

with a dress on.

a

"Well he could sure hit," said Lefty Limburg. "The only other person who could hit like him in Erie, and maybe the world, was Red."

"Red, heh, heh," said Grandpa Whitey.

Grandma Emma Loop just sat in the corner of the tent like many pounds of something with a pie for a head, impersonating a garage door that didn't open often, though you knew there were many important and valuable treasures in there that no one was ever going to get at.

"Hey," Bif said to me. "You sure can punch a cake, ha!"

"Punch cake, heh, heh," said Grandpa Whitey.

"I think Red was the best puncher I ever saw," said Lefty.

"So you two going to be Catholics?" my Aunt Tilly said to me, her eyes moving like four-dimensional uncoordinates.

"Moslem Existentialists," I told her.

"Muscle tensionitis, heh, heh," said Grandpa Whitey.

"I used to get that," said Lefty, "when me and Red played ball. I remember the time a guy kept stealing second and the second baseman kept blowing the tag from Red, the next time that guy stole, Red just threw that ball right at him, stuck right in the side of his butt. Boy that other team was mad, but that ended the stealing."

"Red's a hothead," said Jelly.

"He's a redhead," said Aunt Tilly.

"Jesus, he could play ball," said Le

"No talking about Jesus, Shakespeare

"Get me some cake," said Grandm

And I took that opportunity to lea

followed by my cousin Nancy who too

me about a dozen wedding kisses, the

all the great times we had up in her b

to run away and get married, despite b

what she got for saving herself, I got s

had to get married, then she started t

me very much of a large motorcycle

"It was just an experiment," I told her, handing her many paper plates of cake.

That's pretty much how my wedding to Kara Ruzci went, every once in a while we ran into each other, she pressing against me with the soft belly of our future, whispering to me in the nothing of her dream talk.

"Forever," said Kara Ruzci.

"Yes," I said.

"I love you forever."

And I lost myself in that sad long notion, kissing her ears and eyes and lips, and then we would be gone from each other again. The day passed, and the night, and the day again, and in the twilight Red took out his guitar and sang his songs, and I remember Helen sitting next to Red, her eyes like dark deep places, and Red, as happy as I'd ever seen him, singing to all around, looking Kara in the eye, and Bush in the eye, and even Barbie Ruzci, Red sang his songs in the twilight and Helen put her arm around him, barely reaching around him, and he turned to her and sang, and then he sang more, for a moment Red looked so happy his eyes glistened, and Helen placed her head on his shoulder, and laying her hand on her stomach briefly, so briefly that if you did not know her you wouldn't have guessed, wouldn't have known, she turned her hand and opened her fist, exposing an empty cupped palm, and it wasn't till then, not till then, that I saw her cry.

～～～～～～～～～～～～～～～～～～～～～～～～

M E AND KARA RUZCI didn't have much of a honeymoon, Louie Ruzci kept threatening to send us to San
Diego to see the zoo, or even send us on a zoo tour of the United
States, it was clear he didn't want to make any permanent invest-
ment in our relationship, he was worried enough about me being
legally tied into his zoo mogulship and that zoo tour just smacked
of too much ambivalence. Of course one of the things I hadn't
planned on about that wedding was presents, and we got about
approximately three billion presents which we opened the next
day under the main tent with a number of people who stayed the
night by sleeping in it, along with me and Kara Ruzci, ourselves,
Stinky and Funly, Joseph and Andrew, the Dialecticians, and a
bunch of Kara Ruzci's beatnik friends from the Culture House,
though they weren't beatniks anymore, they were calling themselves Vietniks because they thought Ho Chi Minh should take
over Vietnam and fill up all the hotels with refugees like in *Doctor
Zhivago*, and Neda was there too, only she didn't sleep outside,
she had to have a bathroom so she could get dressed up and look
like Brigitte Bardot.

First thing we had to do was pass around all the salad bowls so everyone had one they could wear, then we took the big salad serving forks and spoons and hit ourselves on the head for a while, we all said, "bungle, bungle, bungle, I don't want to leave the jungle." The Vietniks wanted all the grinders and blenders for cleaning their marijuana, and we burned out most the toasters that afternoon during the toaster contest, we had to test them for endurance and speed and capacity to pop the toast out of the toaster and onto a nearby plate, but it was clear none of them were built for the long haul. Funly took the electric can openers and knife sharpeners for the bomb shelter and Stinky took the vases so he wouldn't have to use his trophies for flowers, which had been a long-standing disagreement between him and Big Dick. There was some kind of tiny tape recorder which we gave to Andrew so he could take calls from the dead while he was out or sleeping, and Joseph got a radio with an earphone, which he put in his bad ear because he was just into the ambiance of music anyways, though he could stick it in his good ear when he wanted to phase out; he was pleased it didn't come with a battery. Neda took all the linen and sheets and ashtrays, Amy Vanderbilt said you could never have too many ashtrays. Those Dialecticians took all the Corning Ware.

We kept the money.

Must have been several thousands of bucks, which along with all the money I made during The End of the World, and the money Kara Ruzci made at the Culture House, left us with a good stash, enough so Kara Ruzci could take off the last month of her pregnancy, and a few months afterwards of course, and when she went back to the Culture House I stayed home with the baby and sometimes Polly Doggerel, depending on whether Polly Doggerel wanted to go to work with Kara Ruzci or not.

Naturally Kara Ruzci had that baby on Christmas Day and it was a boy so he got to be a Loop instead of a Ruzci and as planned we named him Visitor, sometimes the Viz for short, which didn't go over too big with Red once he figured out that Visitor began with what Jarvis ended with, v-i-s, made him a Viz III, which was a little too Freudian for words, good thing Red only read novels and not any psychoanalysis during The Year of Two Hundred Books. Nonetheless, Visitor Loop's getting born on Christmas made me miss Bush's Last Christmas that year, and seeing as Bush was eighty-three and getting older every second, we all knew it might be her very last Last Christmas. That kind of birth-death stuff brought the worst out in Helen, especially since that little cute fat Pope John XXIII who made all those ecumenical changes in the One True Church which made it a lot easier to live with Red, canonologically speaking, and who was always wandering around the Vatican without his Swiss body-guards, that little rascal, died, and John Kennedy got assassinated before that; Helen could see it was a big year for beginnings and endings and she took it all pretty personal; Neda hated to admit it but she and Helen had a lot in common.

So Helen got a little weird, you couldn't talk to her without her going cerebral on you, Red would say, "Let's get a ham," and Helen answered, "Just don't plan on anything," which I'll admit was a good philosophy in general but wasn't necessarily applicable to ham-buying, besides, Red did all the shopping anyways and never once did he decide to get a ham and come back without it. Red could buy a ham as good as anybody.

I always had a particular knack for avoidance so I enjoyed staying at home and sticking bottles of liquid in the Visitor's face or cleaning the shit off his butt or holding him for a while if he just felt like being a shithead and making a racket, and I kept the windows clean and the plants watered, and the floor, what little there was of it amidst Kara Ruzci's piles of artifacts and photo albums, clean, though more often than not I started looking at some of the photos, Kara Ruzci collected photos, all photos, any photos, even other people's photo albums and family photographs and vacation photographs, and all kinds of ancient old photo-graphs of people dressed up like the turn of the century, some of them weren't even on paper, they were on tin or something, and Kara Ruzci had got me hooked on looking at those photos and seeing histories and generations and connections and chronologies, like walking through a graveyard, most of which you just made up anyways; I could lose myself for hours in those photos, and I found if I kept the Viz upside down, much as I loved him, he shit and pissed a lot less, probably some law governing stuff like that, so I got him a harness, spent some time upside down myself, just so he wouldn't feel unusual; I have to admit, I think it did me some good, and once I got adjusted to looking at the photographs upside down there wasn't much else that could please me till Kara Ruzci came home, whereupon the Viz forgot I existed, I had to let them put in their time before I could hardly get near Kara Ruzci, but then we'd make dinner together, outside if it was summer, and if it was summer me and Kara Ruzci and Visitor and Polly Doggerel went up and sat on the top of a shack in the backyard and watched the sunset over the lake. Then we put the Viz to bed and me and Kara Ruzci drank wine and looked at photos or just held each other and said, "love, love, love," which pretty much summed it up.

Through the nights we dreamed, making love under caves of fire near a frozen lake, in red moist canyons of red, on the crests of waves of snake-filled seas, in dark nameless empty places under the earth; my glands poured with the purest waters with which I bathed her, and Kara Ruzci song-whispered to me, "you will never die, you will never die, I love you and you will never die," and in the morning we awoke before dawn and held each other until the light came over us like a wing.

Sometimes, still, Kara went to New York, where some small galleries showed her photographs and she visited old friends like that Soviet weasel Igor Kresky who Kara still had some unmistakable love for, and though she would have let me come with her I always decided not to, I just wasn't ready to see the ocean on a daily basis, I always told her I was afraid of the World's Fair, besides I'd recently gained a certain hesitancy about her private life, there was a part of Kara Ruzci I preferred to leave unreachable. Then Kara would return with all her New York rolls of negatives and bury herself in that tomb of a darkroom for days before she became articulate again, days without speaking to each other while we re-formed into a family, all of which gave me the strangest peaceful feeling, and I saw myself in those speechless generations of family after family of accumulated photograph albums, frozen and ephemeral.

Some days I drove her to work and spent the days taking the Viz to the zoo and watching the flies buzz around the faces of the lions, or visited the Dialecticians who had long upside-down dialogues with Visitor Loop, he and I really seemed to infect those Dialecticians with the pleasures of hanging upside down, and the Viz, of course, hadn't yet formed many dualisms; sometimes all us Dialecticians packed into the Falcon and bought ice cream cones and Thunderbird wine and went out to the country to sit under shade trees, or later, when the weather got cold, watch snowdrifts, and sometimes I left the Viz with the other Dialecticians while me and Willie went for walks during which one of those times he said to me, "The Dialecticians are contemplating the adulthood."

Well I guess it was inevitable.

Other times I picked Helen up from work and drove her home to her holy room where we had Mogen David and talked about whether or not that little fat nice Pope John XXIII knew what was in that letter that the Blessed Virgin gave to the children at Fatima, and what language it was in, and we changed our minds every time. Helen didn't really get along with Visitor that much, she'd pretty much had her fill of kids, but when Red came home he threw him around and read him storybooks and acted like the most wonderful father he never was.

Then, no matter whatever, I'd leave there or take everybody home or end whatever I was doing and go get Kara Ruzci and Polly Doggerel and have the lives we had that always were and would never end and never existed.

Because one winter day, returning from New York, in a bus, or a plane, or a train, Kara Ruzci was in an accident, and many people died, and Kara Ruzci died, impaled by a rod that went through her back and passed through her pelvis, Kara Ruzci died. I took her car, and with her dog and her child, drove to New Jersey where we buried her, across from the woods, at the foot of a hill near her parents' land, next to her brother, we buried her, and then I returned home, home to Red and Helen, with only my life and a dog and a child, and the knowledge that there are no dreams, and no one has ever talked to the dead, and beyond that I have learned nothing, nothing.

ABOUT THE AUTHOR

Chuck Rosenthal's first novel, *Loop's Progress,* was published in 1986. He has a Ph.D. in English and American Literature. He lives in Venice, California, with poet/playwright Gail Wronsky and their daughter, Marlena, and teaches at Loyola Marymount University in Los Angeles. He is at work on book three of the Loop trilogy.

27 million Americans can't read a bedtime story to a child.

It's because 27 million adults in this country simply can't read.

Functional illiteracy has reached one out of five Americans. It robs them of even the simplest of human pleasures, like reading a fairy tale to a child.

You can change all this by joining the fight against illiteracy.

Call the Coalition for Literacy at toll-free **1-800-228-8813** and volunteer.

**Volunteer
Against Illiteracy.
The only degree you need
is a degree of caring.**

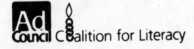

Ad Council   Coalition for Literacy